Just Fall

BALLANTINE BOOKS

NEW YORK

Just
Fall

A NOVEL

Nina
Sadowsky

Just Fall is a work of fiction. Names, characters, places, and incidents either are the product of the author's imagination or are used fictitiously. Any resemblance to actual persons, living or dead, events, or locales is entirely coincidental.

Published in the United States by Ballantine Books, an imprint of Random House, a division of Penguin Random House LLC, New York.

BALLANTINE and the HOUSE colophon are registered trademarks of Penguin Random House LLC.

LIBRARY OF CONGRESS CATALOGING-IN-PUBLICATION DATA
Names: Sadowsky, Nina, author.
Title: Just fall : a novel / Nina Sadowsky.
Description: New York : Ballantine Books, [2016]
Identifiers: LCCN 2015037179 | ISBN 9780553394856 (hardback : acid-free paper) | ISBN 9780553394863 (ebook)
Subjects: LCSH: Marriage—Fiction. | Secrets—Fiction. | Psychological fiction. | BISAC: FICTION / Psychological. | FICTION / Romance / Suspense. | FICTION / Suspense.
Classification: LCC PS3619.A353 J87 2016 | DDC 813/.6—dc23 LC record available at http://lccn.loc.gov/2015037179.

Printed in the United States of America on acid-free paper

randomhousebooks.com

2 4 6 8 9 7 5 3 1

FIRST EDITION

Book design by Dana Leigh Blanchette
Title-page image: © iStockphoto.com

DEDICATED TO G. H.

My darling Ellie,

 I am so, so sorry.

 Please follow the instructions enclosed with this letter exactly and it is my fervent hope all will be fine.

 You are my love, and always will be, believe that.

 You are everything.

Rob

Just Fall

Now

Salt tang and the slight, sickly sweet scent of alcohol, sugar, and fruit too long in the sun. Orange-tipped sun, baby-blue skies, sand fine as powder, azure waves lapping dreamily against the shore.

The room in question is on the third, the top, floor of the hotel. The building runs long and lean, a jagged spine along the pristine shoreline, rooms staggered for optimal views.

The rooms are broad and deep. Each opens out to a private terrace or patio. Sliding glass doors pair with plantation shutters in the event of a desperately necessary lazy afternoon nap. Or fuck.

Juxtaposed against the beauty of the beach, a juicy array of the human species: pale, bronzed, brown, sunburned, leathery, crispy; thin, fat, plump, beefy, curvy, lanky; reading, sleeping, drooling, floating, swimming, sailing. Kissing, snoring, drinking, flirting.

Hotel staff circulates, offering menus, bringing cocktails and towels and sunscreen, planting thatched umbrellas, jerking open extra chairs. You are lucky indeed to be a guest at this hotel.

Directly in front of the room in question, hard-muscled young men toss a football in the surf. They shout and laugh and grunt, their sounds wafting up on balmy air caresses.

At the window of the room in question, a woman watches the men play.

The woman, blond, graceful, is poised just on the lip of the balcony, half in the room and half out. A shadow slices her lovely face in half, leaving her eyes recessed in darkness.

She leans out to better watch the game below. Her skin is pale, but for two spots of flush, high on her cheekbones. A slight, sudden inhale through her plummy mouth as one man dives for a catch, his taut body arcing into the air and slicing down hard into sand. He grunts on impact and then groans theatrically before springing up with a laugh.

The blonde backs away from the window.

Behind her, in the room, in the soft white bed, a man is sprawled. A drunken arm crooked across his forehead, a swath of cool sheet twisted over his naked torso, he is completely still.

He looks healthy. That would be anyone's first impression. His legs are strong limbs, and deeply tanned, fading paler toward his thighs. A man who lives outdoors, wears shorts, uses his body. His shoulders are thick, his arms powerful. His hands are palms up, open, relaxed.

What do these two mean to each other? Let's hazard a guess. Or two.

A holiday hookup, the pure anonymity of it, the thrill? Possible. They don't seem quite a pair, somehow.

Newlyweds, finally alone together after the pageantry of their wedding? Or more telling, after a tearful and regretted fight, the very first bitter sticks of marital kindling upon which the funeral pyre of their relationship would be built? Don't think this cynical. Open-eyed pragmatism is actually romantic.

Or could they be longtime best friends, passion unleashed by mojitos—only to face uneasy regret? Adulterous lovers, mixing their urgent guilt and needy thrill-seeking into a heady cocktail? John and hooker, sex as transaction, the body quite separate from the mind or heart?

Let's look closer.

The blonde gives us little at first. Her lovely face is composed, her beautiful body at ease. There is that high flush on her cheeks. Could be sunburn. Or fever? But note this: Her eyes look everywhere but at the man in the bed.

Two wineglasses on the dresser. One empty, one full. A bottle of wine lolls on the floor. A joint smolders on the nightstand, burning a small char into the finish, right next to the placard declaring this a No Smoking Room. There was some kind of party here. Maybe it's still going on.

The blonde crosses to the smoldering joint and considers it. Then crosses to the bathroom and flushes it down the toilet. Returns to rub her thumb over the burn mark it has left on the nightstand.

She lifts the bottle of wine from the floor and empties its contents down the sink, rinses it thoroughly. Rinses both glasses.

The blonde crosses to the man on the bed. It's time to at least check. She can't put it off any longer. She looks at his face.

A shock of sun-streaked hair drapes onto his forehead. He looks peaceful. She darts a glance down toward his abdomen.

Is that blood? Yes, it is. No other signs of violence. Just a sticky carnation of blooming blood in the twisted sheets. And the knife that caused it to grow.

Well, that changes things.

Accident? Misadventure? Attack or defense? What happened here? We still have more questions than answers.

Has she done this to the man?

She's delicate, but she has confidence in her young, strong body. She's athletic, at home in her skin. Still. She's half the size of the man on the bed.

No blood sours her lime-green bikini or the white gauze cover-up, with its angelic float around her body. That seems in her favor.

But then what is she doing here? What does she feel about this dead man?

She pulls the wisp of white cover-up over her head, wraps it around her hand, and wipes down the room. The phone, the desk, the sink and shower and bathroom counter, the book of guest services. The wineglasses and bottle and bed frame and mirrors. Thoroughly. Methodically. Even the handle of the knife in the man's belly, careful to avoid the well of blood. Meticulously.

There's no anger here. Or fear. No sorrow or loss.

Resignation maybe? Calculation? Shock?

Or all three?

A shudder of revulsion courses through her like an electric shock as she notices a strand of her long blond hair on the pillow next to the man's graying face. She plucks it up. Walks to the balcony and releases the hair into the wind.

A pair of joyful, leaping dolphins appears on the horizon, their freedom and exuberant beauty a reproach. She is not free. Her face twists. As she turns to exit the balcony and reenter the room, the raucous hoots of the young men on the beach float up as if to mock her.

Carefully, she spreads a beach towel over the room's sole armchair, a large, cushy bucket of crisp navy cotton. She settles in, pulling her knees up to her chest and wrapping her arms around them.

A square of sky and sea and pearl-hued sands can be seen through the window. But she closes her eyes. The sea is spectacular, brilliant turquoise, and she knows the fish and flora below its surface are also marvelously colored. She's not snorkeled or swum; she doesn't know this from personal experience, but rather from the Internet crash course on the island she gave herself before she arrived.

She could at least look at all that beauty if she opened her eyes. But that would mean looking past the dead man with the knife in his belly, his thickening puddle of blood.

She has to wait now. Be still and calm and purposeful. Every cell in her body is screaming at her to run. But she will wait.

Then

Long blond hair was twisted into an elegant chignon. Ellie sat stoic and still, a well-mannered girl who usually doesn't fuss this much, simultaneously a little disdainful and more than a little thrilled by her transformation into a princess for a day. Her hairdresser, Franco, worked his magic. And babbled. "They're totally lovely people. Been clients of mine for years. After the wedding, you and Rob must come out with me on their boat. A yacht really. Super chic."

Ellie made some noncommittal sound. She contemplated herself in the dressing table mirror. Her face was flawlessly made-up. Her creamy shoulders were bare, emerging from the beaded lace bodice of a pouf of a wedding dress. She was gorgeous, if a little chilly. What they used to call a Hitchcock blonde.

Mrs. Robert Beauman, she thought but didn't say aloud. A smile crossed her face, and suddenly she was warm, and therefore even more beautiful. Franco noticed, stopped his rambling. "There you are, sweetheart! I was a little worried. No one should be so somber on her wedding day."

The door burst open and Ellie's bridesmaids, Tara and Collette, spilled into the room fizzing with energy, a bottle of champagne and glasses in hand. "We got it! Ellie! You look gorgeous!" said Tara.

Ellie looked at her friends, elegant visions in lavender silk charmeuse. "You too," she told them. "You both look wonderful."

"I took a peek," said Collette. "The place is filling up fast. This wedding is a hot ticket."

"Are you nervous?" asked Tara.

"Why would she be nervous?" Franco interjected. "They're perfect for each other."

"I'm not nervous," said Ellie. "But isn't 'perfect for each other' just one of those awful clichés? I'm sure we'll have to wade through our share of shit just like any other couple on the planet."

"Please!" Collette laughed, a bubble of merriment. "Hang on to a little romance at least for the duration of your wedding day, will you?"

"Collette is right," said Tara. "Lay down the cynicism. Just until the reception is over, okay? Now have some champagne."

"All right, all right." Ellie laughed. "A toast to my groom, Prince Charming, Superman, and the Dark Knight, combined. Let's all believe in fairy tales."

"You ever notice how Prince Charming has no backstory?" Tara asked as she poured four glasses.

"And Superman and Batman have tragic pasts. No wonder everyone has daddy issues," observed Collette.

Ellie laughed again. "And you're accusing me of not being romantic?"

They clinked and sipped and chatted, and Ellie set down her glass to let Franco put the finishing touches on her hair.

Slippery little doubts leapt like fish in the pit of her stomach.

Shouldn't she be glowing with romantic idealism? Or were the nervous tugs of doubt that she felt the norm? The enormity of the commitment of marriage, even in these days of easy divorce; the sense of finality. And they hadn't known each other that long after all, she and Rob, and given her history . . .

But then her dad was knocking on the door and saying it was time. Ellie took a good long last look at herself in the mirror and let Tara and Collette fluff out her skirts. Her mother plucked an invisible thread from Ellie's shoulder and dabbed at her eyes. It was showtime. Ellie pushed her anxieties aside and smiled her radiant smile.

Later, Ellie remembered her near trip as her spike heel caught in her dress going down the aisle, how her dad steadied her and gave her arm a reassuring squeeze; Rob's warm, loving eyes as he slipped the ring on her finger, the two of them turning to see the laughing, happy faces of her friends and family after the judge pronounced them husband and wife; the triumphant walk back up the aisle arm in arm with her man.

She had expected to feel as if the night flew by; everyone had warned her: It was the way of weddings.

She was wholly unprepared for the single sentence that tipped her into surrealism, clouding as it did all subsequent events and making every moment of her prior life irrelevant.

They were alone. The two of them. Bride and groom, brand-new husband and wife. The wedding planner had given them fifteen minutes, had promised them they would welcome the chance after the ceremony, before the duties of hosting their wedding pulled them in well-meaning opposite directions. It was a moment that should have been all kisses and sweet nuzzles, clasped hands and murmured endearments. A private little celebration of the two of them, the nucleus of this whole lavish event.

Rob's admission was sudden, downright bizarre, and, if true, terrifying. Insane words coming matter-of-factly from his familiar, dear lips. The way he gripped her forearms so she had to look into his eyes. The intensity of his voice. The clench of his jaw.

And then before she could process, or determine if this was some kind of sick joke (but why would he joke about something like this?

Why?), it was time to enter the party. Their guests were waiting; they heard the drumroll that was their cue.

Tara and Collette swung open the doors. Rob took Ellie's hand, kissed her lightly on the lips. He raised their linked hands in triumph and led Ellie into their reception.

And so they had made their grand entrance: "For the very first time, Mr. and Mrs. Robert Beauman!"

"What were you talking about?" Ellie asked Rob urgently, sotto voce, as everyone cheered. "I don't understand. That can't be—"

Rob put his fingers to his lips and shushed her. Kissed his fingers and tapped her lightly on the forehead. "Later," he said. He smiled, she smiled back, uncertain, and they were swept in and away.

Their wedding party had begun.

Ellie shook hands, kissed cheeks, brought arch effusiveness to a greeting when she couldn't, for the life of her, remember the name of that coworker of Rob's she had met at least half a dozen times. She accepted good wishes and compliments. The photographer's camera flashed. Food was served.

Ellie spun through her wedding party, propelled by love, happiness, obligation, ritual, friendship, champagne, and kisses. She pushed aside the confusing and repugnant nature of what Rob had just told her. It couldn't be true.

They had planned this wedding together, she and Rob, they didn't fight once, they never fought at all really, she knew him, he was her best friend, she loved him, he loved her.

They danced their first dance together. Kissed when it was over. She was pulled away by her cousin Andrea and drank more champagne. Did one shot of tequila for old times' sake.

But then, later, talking to her tedious aunt Sonia (or rather listening to Sonia talk, which left Ellie completely free to roam her own thoughts), the phrase "He's too good to be true" popped into her head. Everyone said so. It's what people said all the time about Rob. What if they were right? But she loved him. She was being ridiculous. He was kidding. What a nervous bride she turned out to be! Ellie made her excuses to Aunt Sonia as she saw her friend Marcy Clark out of the corner of her eye.

"Excuse me, I have to thank—"

Sonia waved her off and Ellie caught up to her friend. "It means so much that you came."

They hugged, sharp contrast between Ellie's snow-white fairy princess dress and Marcy's tailored black sheath, young widow chic. Ellie's veil fell forward and shielded both their fresh faces. Cocooned.

"I hope you'll understand if I just slip out when I feel I need to leave, okay?" said Marcy.

"Of course, sweetheart." Ellie's eyes had filled with tears then. "I know Ethan is here with us in spirit."

Marcy's eyes had filled too. But she brushed away Ellie's tears, smiling, and then her own. "He is. Now be happy, darling. It's your wedding day."

Then the wedding planner was there and it was time to cut the cake. Ritual enacted for endless photographs. Rob and Ellie fed each other tidy morsels. A quick sugary kiss. The cake was whisked away for service.

Her mother got in a jab. Of course she did; Ellie wasn't surprised, even though she was hurt. Thank God, soon she and Rob would be alone. Ellie needed a breath of air, craved her husband's reassurance. She went looking for him in the hotel's back garden. And found her world indeed destroyed.

Now

The blonde, and, yes, the blonde is Ellie, is just where we left her, huddled into the large, cushy chair, folded into herself. The light has a different slant, a deeper blue cast; the ocean sounds rougher. Ellie sighs deeply. Stretches and stands. She takes a long, steady look around the hotel room. Finally her eyes settle on the dead man in the bed. He's not her husband, Rob; that much is evident.

Ellie pads softly into the bathroom. She opens a flower-patterned toiletry kit. Digging past the sunscreen, lip balm, and toothpaste, she pulls a powder compact into her palm. She clicks open the compact. Clicks it again. Another layer opens. A second compartment holds a powder puff. From underneath it, Ellie extracts a razor blade.

Ellie crosses back to the man on the bed. Peers over to examine the pool of coagulating blood near his belly. She's waited long enough. She squares her shoulders. Steels herself. Then deftly slices off the dead man's bottom lip. There's remarkably little blood, which is what she's planned, why she waited.

Ellie places the severed lip neatly into a handful of folded tissues and then winds it into a swath of plastic wrap retrieved from her brightly striped raffia beach bag. She plucks a padded mailer from the beach bag. Tucks the lip inside. Stuffs the package back into the bag. She's trembling. She feels faint.

She sways, drops the beach bag, reaches a hand to the wall to steady herself. Stands there for a moment, taking deep, steadying breaths. She looks down at the beach bag. It's done. There's no turning back. She looks at her hand flat against the wall. Pulls it away as if it scalded her.

She grabs the towel from the armchair and scrubs at the spot on the wall where her hand had been. Then she wipes down the entire room again. It's as much wanting to be thorough as it is being afraid to take the next step.

She picks up her beach bag and checks that all is secure inside, popping in her toiletry kit, tucking the padded mailer deeper, toward the bottom. She stuffs the towel on top. Pulls her white cover-up back over her golden hair. She uses the hem of the cover-up for a last polish of the doorknob. She exits the room, taking a quick look down each side of the hallway to be sure it is all clear. She loops the *"Ne Pas Déranger"* sign over the door handle. Wipes that too. She walks down the hallway toward the elevator bank. She doesn't look back.

The lobby of the Hotel Grande Sucre is vast and light and airy, with a clear line of sight from the massive open doors facing the hotel driveway to a view of sand, sea, and distant cliffs. It's designed to be breathtaking and it is. The vaulted skylight at the center of the lobby filters sparkling light onto its central feature, a rocky pond replete with a waterfall and a selection of lazy tortoises.

At the front desk, a line of weary travelers checks in. The concierge is busy assisting a family organizing a snorkeling trip, showing on a map the precise location of the beach with the best coral reefs and most colorful fish. The bellmen are concerned, as bellmen should be, with luggage. Overexcited children shriek and race about, delirious with sun and sea and a sense of incipient adventure.

Ellie crosses through confidently, a beautiful woman with a purpose, emerging with a blink into the afternoon sunlight. No one pays her much attention. She spots a convertible with the motor running, the keys still in, and is in the driver's seat and pulling away before the valet has even registered her presence. Only when she is cruising along the coast road does she relax.

Her shoulders slump. And then the tears start to fall. But she has no time for tears. She swipes them impatiently off her cheeks. Distracted, coming around a curve a little too fast, she doesn't see the rickety open truck in front of her, stuffed full with green bananas. A stand of bananas bounces off the truck, directly into her path! She swerves to avoid it, scraping the driver's side of the convertible against the cliff side with a horrible ragged shriek of metal against rock. She hits the brakes. The car skids across the median. She wrenches it back to her side of the road before finally slamming to a stop.

Breathing heavily, she casts her eyes about wildly for a moment as she realizes the danger is past. The bananas missed, the truck gone, the road empty. She drops her head into her hands and slumps over the wheel. Irony. To have come this far and done this much. And she could have been killed. Just like that.

Then

Air. *Yes,* she thought, *I need air.* And a moment away from the madness of the wedding, away from toasts and tears and air kisses and music, and her mother, especially her mother.

Where was Rob? Ellie scanned the dance floor. No sign of him. Clearly they needed to talk. Surely he had been kidding? A twisted but humorous way of saying "We're married, now you're stuck with me, good and bad"? A parade of memories, odd phone calls and missed appointments, all blamed on "work," began their march through Ellie's mind.

Determined to distract herself from this disturbing line of thought, she moved through well-wishers, accepting kisses and compliments, her eyes darting in search. *I bet he snuck out for a smoke,* she decided. *I knew he hadn't quit. Bastard.* The thought floated through her head before she could stop it: *I wonder what else he's lying about?* She frowned. She pushed the thought away. He was her Rob, the man she loved, her husband.

"Husband." She said it aloud, smiling. She would trust and she would have faith, just as she had promised in her vows a few short hours before. It had been a joke. That must be it. Ellie pushed at the door opening into the hotel's small garden. Gulped in some cool air.

The laughter and music of her wedding faded as the door swung closed behind her. It was lovely out here, the air scented with flowers, the softly bubbling fountain. The *thud,* when Ellie heard it, popped the fragile membrane of quiet. Another *thud,* followed by a groan. Something prickled the back of Ellie's neck, her reptile brain warning her to fight or flee. She moved forward cautiously, lifting the voluminous skirts of her wedding gown, holding her breath as she edged toward the sounds. She peeked around a hydrangea, its bluish flowers a darkening purple in the night air. She stifled a gasp. Pulled herself out of sight. Peeked again.

There was Rob. On the ground, his nose bloody, his jacket torn. And the two men standing over him, yes, those were weapons in their hands. One held a gun, the other a knife, light glinting off its curving blade. Ellie froze. Stared immobilized for a second.

The taller, thinner man spoke to Rob: "I don't know why you ever thought this would work out any differently."

The other man, the shorter, stockier one, hauled Rob to his feet.

Then just as she was about to do something, anything, move, scream for help—Rob saw her, made eye contact. With the slightest of gestures he signaled that she must be quiet. Then mouthed a single word: "*Go.*"

The stocky guy walloped Rob hard in his stomach. *Thud.* Rob ricocheted back, stumbling, and then willed himself into a twisted run toward the garden's back wall. Ellie sensed he was trying to pull the men away from her, trying to protect her. She whirled and ran back toward the hotel. Her hands scrabbled at the door and missed, once, twice, before she finally hauled it open. Her breath was ragged, her heart beat wildly, the noise in her head was a dizzying roar, she felt like she was drowning . . . until she finally broke through to the surface and screamed, "Help me! Help us! Please God, someone, help!"

Now

Ellie is dry-eyed. Determined. She pulls the scraped and dented convertible into the crowded parking lot of a Dollar General store. Parks and slips on her sunglasses, slides from the car, darts inside. She picks up a bright orange plastic basket and moves through the aisles at a leisurely pace, sandals slapping on the floor. A shiny red lipstick, a box of brown hair dye, a gauzy scarf, a set of crystal-encrusted fake nails (*bling!*), a cheap rayon sarong, a pair of oversized sunglasses, white zinc sunblock.

She moves over to the small hardware section. A memory douses her like a bucket of icy water. She and Rob, the first week they lived together, breathless with thrill but also threaded with anxiety about this next step. They had laughed a lot, fucked a lot, but also endured two awkward bathroom encounters, broken a prized antique perfume bottle of hers, and washed, instead of dry-cleaned, his favorite cashmere sweater.

It was a Sunday. Rob unveiled his tool chest: a sturdy green, with a well-organized and well-maintained selection of implements. Hammers and screwdrivers. Pliers and wrenches. Saws and sandpaper, nails and screws and bolts. They spent the afternoon hanging pictures, installing hooks, building a shoe rack. Rob in charge. Ellie his eager assistant. They worked well together and as they did, settled into each other. Stopped feeling like strangers. Anxiety faded. Thrill remained.

Now, in the Dollar General store, Ellie hesitates in front of a selection of screwdrivers. They seem handy, utile. And also a reminder of a time when she felt secure. She lifts a screwdriver from the rack and taps the flat tip lightly against her palm. She replaces it and selects a Phillips head with a clear red plastic handle. Presses the point into the soft flesh of her wrist. The pain is sweetly exquisite. She adds the Phillips head to her basket.

She pays in cash, carefully counting out the candy-colored East Caribbean dollars. She slips back into the car and out of the lot, her survival tools in shiny green plastic bags piled reassuringly on the seat next to her. She feels exposed in the convertible and closes the top. Cranks up the air-conditioning to create a protective bubble, the thrum of the car, the whoosh of the air.

A little while later, Ellie pulls up near the Soufrière post office. The gauzy scarf is wrapped in a turban around her head, completely hiding her blond hair. The oversized sunglasses, owl-like, obscure her face. Her lips are painted white with zinc sunblock. The bling-studded nails are affixed to her fingertips; the crystals send shivers of dancing light with every move she makes. She exits the car. Adjusts her breathing to the hot afternoon air, which is moist and startling after the icy air-conditioning of the convertible. She reaches in to extract the padded envelope. It's addressed with nondescript block letters.

The town of Soufrière is a colorful jumble. Royal blue, tangerine, hot pink, lavender, the small buildings are as cheerful in their paint colors as they are decrepit in their repair. The post office is an exception. Gray and severe, but well maintained. As Ellie crosses the street to enter it, a pack of stray dogs blocks her path, tails and noses raised, sniffing, jaunty, tongues lolling in the heat, on the hunt for scraps of food. They seem good-natured, but still she pauses, there are just so many of them. She counts as they go by. Eleven. A ragtag canine family. They make her feel lonely.

The words she's written run through her mind: *You don't know me, and I don't know you. But Rob has told me that in this situation you are our only friend.*

Help me, Obi-wan Kenobi. Ellie thinks it and nearly giggles. She reminds herself to keep it together. Hysteria is not her ally.

She enters the post office. It's dark and cool. A ceiling fan spins lazily overhead. The sole clerk, inky dark skin, a thousand braids, some dyed a virulent orange, long curving nails painted in a zebra print, looks up, and does a quick second look, her eyes skidding past the obscured face and weird white lips, alighting on Ellie's nails. Ellie's long, gaudy fake fingernails adorned with crystals. Perfectly tacky. And a perfect distraction.

The kind of screaming detail that draws the eye, so that it is the only thing remembered by someone giving a description, a distraction easily added, then easily discarded when necessary. A lesson Rob had taught her in wholly different circumstances, in a place and time that now seem eons away. As Ellie's eyes adapt to the dim light, she reflects on that day briefly, wondering if even then he was trying to prepare her in some way for this incredible, horrible unknown. She shivers. Shakes it off and gets to business.

The transaction is swift. First, Ellie pays cash in advance for a month's rental of a post office box. She neatly writes the box number on the padded envelope as the return address. Then she opens the box, places another envelope inside, locks the box, and puts the mailbox key into the padded envelope. She seals the envelope. As her parcel is weighed, the postage for overnight delivery purchased, the talk is of nail care strategies. Instant bonding, the razor-focus commonality of strangers. The check, so to speak—or should we say it plain—the lip, is in the mail.

Then

He aimed and pulled the trigger.

Nothing.

Annoyed, he shook out his wrist. Adjusted his stance. Tried again.

Zap! A flash of red light.

One dozen Waterford crystal wineglasses, added to the registry. Rob was aiming a scanner. The locale: the bridal registry of an upscale department store.

"I told you it would be kind of fun. Like playing house." Ellie smiled at him. His heart still caught every time she did.

"Since we're getting married, doesn't it mean we're not playing house? Aren't we doing it for real?" he teased.

"Well, this part anyway. Oooh, look, a candelabra. Is it mermaids? Perfect! I've always wanted a mermaid candelabra."

She darted away, drawn like a magpie to shiny objects. As he watched her aim her own "gun" at the candelabra, a tall, thin man in a dark suit crossed Rob's line of vision. Rob froze. It was something about the hitch in the thin man's gait, the easy menace in the set of his shoulders . . . Rob turned, coughed as bile rose into his throat, hurried away. He stepped easily onto the down escalator, texting as he glided away: *Stewart calling. Back in 10.*

Rob hadn't seen Quinn since he had been in New York. While not wholly unexpected, given that Rob was pretty sure he had been followed the last few weeks, seeing Quinn still came as a shock. Rob's first instinct was to lead Quinn away from Ellie, even as a panic-stricken counterpoint in his mind thundered the futility of the attempt. How much did Quinn know? What angles would Rob have to play in order to protect Ellie? Rob knew that if ever there was a time he needed to be strategic, this was it.

Later. Rob and Ellie lingered over the last of their lunch. His back to the far wall of the department store café, his eyes scanning back and forth across the room.

"Anyway, I'm glad the call went well, but now you're just going to have to not only accept the cuckoo-clock-shaped napkin rings, but learn to love them. Not to mention the flowered teapot cozy, the Scandinavian cheese set, and the Soda Stream."

"Did you really?"

She looked at him with amused affection. "No. I told the registry associate that I couldn't possibly commit to anything without my fiancé and put the whole thing on hold."

"Do you want to change your mind?"

"What, and actually register?"

He nodded.

"God, no, sweetheart. Like I said, playing house. We'll still ask for donations to the foundation."

Rob's eyes skimmed the room again and he wondered if his mind had been playing tricks on him earlier. And even if it hadn't been, if it had been Quinn, couldn't it be pure coincidence? He frowned. He knew better than that.

"Rob? Are you okay?"

He shook it off. "Sorry. Just thinking about candelabras." He smiled at her.

She smiled back. "Well, we certainly won't get one if they make you look so worried. Let's go home."

Still later. Ellie was astride him. He thrust powerfully up into her and she rocked back, gasping. They were slick with sweat. Her nipples were rose pink and tight. He gripped her slim hips and pulled himself into her deeper, then flipped her, so she was suddenly underneath him. He withdrew slowly, teasing, then plowed into her welcoming body with a grunt of pleasure. Her hands raked across his back. Again he thrust. And again. She came with a deep cry, and he let himself explode into her. She held him tight as his prick pulsed inside her, quivering, then turned her head, burrowing the side of her face into the pillow.

"I love you." She uttered it low and hoarse.

"I love you more." He breathed it into her ear with tender care. Softly kissed the hollow of her throat.

Now

Ellie sits at a beachside hotel bar, far away from the Grande Sucre. A tropical cocktail sits before her, not her first. The cheap sarong, she's rocking as a dress. Somehow she's made it look expensive. The gauzy scarf, she's loosened, no longer a tight turban. Tendrils of her soft, shiny blond hair escape, effortless, calculated. The weird white zinc lips are gone. Her lips are now painted red; her eyes are bright, lashed with mascara. She's made an effort.

She looks the part of a beautiful young woman on vacation sipping drinks and just maybe, idly, looking for a little trouble. Only if it's "worth-it" trouble, not a sure thing; whoever "he" is, he's going to have to work for it. Ellie's learned that a little studied indifference can inspire a surprising amount of interest.

And she knows just what she needs. For tonight at least. A place where she can sleep without having to use her passport or credit card. Anonymity. And rest. She needs time to think and sleep, and re-fucking-group because people, *police,* are going to be looking for the blonde who left a dead man in her room and stole a convertible from the valet of the Grande Sucre Hotel. Fleetingly, she thinks about the car, abandoned with the keys in and the motor running on a Soufrière side street. She hopes it's been picked to pieces by now.

Ellie eyes a man at the end of the bar. He wears his deep tan well; his blue eyes are a little watery from sun and sea salt and dirty bananas (rum, coconut cream, crème de cacao). No wedding ring; better, no wedding ring tan line. Ellie has come to truly value simplicity. She catches his glance at her. She makes an elaborate show of unknotting her scarf, shaking loose her silky blond hair.

The smile on her face is genuine, if born not of her interest in him (as he so readily believes) but in the delight of how easy it is to snare his attention. This is a new skill for Ellie, honed in recent days out of pure survival. The woman who always prided herself on being direct, intellectual, a whole person, not a *girl,* has discovered the technique of seduction. It is just a *faster* line from A to B. She was shocked at the deep simplicity of its mechanics. Also relieved, amused, and a little annoyed for having waited so long to put this particular technique in her arsenal. Memories flash through Ellie's brain: smiling at the man at the airline desk as she negotiated successfully for her standby seat to the island; the gentle graze of her fingertips across the knuckles of the St. Lucia customs official; her slow saunter through the lobby of the Grande Sucre, Carter Williamson, her soon-to-be victim, trailing behind her.

The man at the end of the bar rises. Makes eye contact. Ellie drains her glass, tilting back her neck to swallow the dregs.

"Buy you another?"

Several cocktails later, Ellie laughs at something the tanned man has said. Truth is, she's hardly paying attention. The cues of seduction are absurdly easy to read and she's on autopilot.

She thinks of Rob, of the safety and comfort and protection inherent in their private little bubble (now so rudely popped). She wonders if she will ever see him again. She wonders if he's dead.

Ellie drains her drink. She senses the tanned man needs the en-
couragement and so gifts him with a smile and a giggle. He signals
for another round.

"My name is Harry."

She offers him her hand in a demure way. A slight dip of the head.
Then a lift of the eyes. Direct into his. She takes note of the one large
black fleck in his gray eyes. Before dipping her lashes flirtatiously.

"I'm Lauren."

Then

Ellie carried the last of the boxes labeled "kitchen" and set it down on Rob's granite countertop. *Our* countertop, she corrected with a smile. She was thrilled. Rob had suggested they move in together soon after he proposed. He saw no reason to wait, he had told her, and every reason to start their lives together. So she had negotiated an early termination of her lease. Rob had taken care of the rest: hired movers, insisted on paying for them, consulted her on which sofa they should keep, which television, which coffee table. He had arranged the sale of the superfluous items and started a joint checking account with the proceeds. The first thing they had purchased together was a new bed crafted from sturdy dark maple, along with all new sheets and a luxurious plum-colored silk comforter. The bed's delivery had been scheduled to coincide with Ellie's move-in date, which she took as practical, but also a romantic gesture marking their new life together.

So what if Rob had seemed a little distracted lately? A little distant, as if he had drifted away to a place she couldn't quite reach. Not always, but there were definitely moments. When she tried to peg exactly when the shift had occurred, his remove seemed to coincide with the day he had met her parents before the two of them larked off to pretend to register for wedding presents.

Did he not like her parents? Plenty of people didn't like their in-laws. So what? Lord knows she had enough of her own issues with them (her mother so controlling, her dad far too passive). Was Rob afraid to tell her he didn't like them? She tried speaking disparagingly about them a couple of times (quelling the small nibble of traitorous guilt this engendered) in an effort to get him to come clean, but he hadn't risen to the bait.

Or had pretending to register made their impending marriage more real for him? Was he getting cold feet? Ellie couldn't help it. She fretted she would be left again. People always seemed to leave.

But every other aspect of their planned wedding and moving in together had proceeded without a hiccup. She had racked her brain to see if it was something she had done or said, she even asked him outright one night, gathering her courage and steeling herself for a painful answer, but he assured her it was work, nothing to do with her.

She comforted herself that at least she was asking the questions. There was no way she was turning a blind eye this time. She was vigilant and alert.

Now she watched as Rob methodically turned over every coffee mug in the cabinet, making sure the open sides faced down onto the shelf. Amused, she asked, "Is that really necessary?"

"It is," he replied. "If you leave the cups facing up, they collect dust, and then you're just including dirt in your morning wake-me-up."

"How much dust could possibly collect?" she teased. "We don't have that many cups, so it's not like any of them are sitting on the shelf for that long—they're in constant rotation."

"How much dust do you want to drink?" Without waiting for a reply, he continued, "'None' is the correct answer."

"You're kind of a nut, aren't you?" She asked it with affection.

"Yes, but I'm your nut," he replied, grinning.

He began chasing her around the apartment. In and around the half-unpacked moving boxes, the furniture that was still in temporary positions, the garbage bags that held the last few items Ellie had packed up from her apartment—a haphazard tangle of her flatiron and cosmetics, the pile of rarely worn winter sweaters she had almost forgotten to pull from the deep recesses of the closet, the now half-empty jumbo pack of paper towels that had been purchased to help her efforts to leave the old place clean enough that her landlord wouldn't ding her on the security deposit.

Round and round they went, Ellie shrieking with glee, until finally she slowed long enough to allow Rob to catch her and throw her onto the sofa, both of them breathing heavily and laughing. Rob asked, "You let me catch you, didn't you?"

"You're so smart," she said. "It must be why I love you."

"And here I was thinking it was my fine ass and big guns."

"Well, actually, you're right. It's the guns. And the ass."

"What? I'm just a piece of meat to you?"

"Exactly right. I only praise your mind so your fragile male ego doesn't collapse."

"Oh, is that right?" And with that, he began to tickle her relentlessly, despite the pleas for mercy that rose and fell over her giggles. Only when she was gasping for breath and her eyes streaming tears did he stop, kissing her lightly on the tip of her nose.

Rob shifted himself to a seated position and pulled her onto his lap. She leaned her head into his shoulder and sighed deeply, a sigh born of contentment and the all-abiding release a spectacular laughing fit can provide.

"How did we get so lucky?" she asked, her voice soft, as she lifted a hand to stroke his cheek.

"We must have been very worthy souls in our last life," he replied.

"People like Mother Teresa or Gandhi, who sacrificed so much personally to help fellow members of humanity."

"Are you comparing yourself to Gandhi?" Her nose crinkled to hold back her laughter.

"Not me. Past-life me. And I could compare you to Mother Teresa except that you have a way more developed sense of style. And I don't think she reached quite the level of perfection you have with a blow job."

"Oh, is that all I am to you? A good BJ?"

"Exactly right. I only praise any of your other qualities so your fragile female ego doesn't collapse, but at the end of the day, it's all about the BJ."

"Maybe I better give you one, then. You know—just to keep our equilibrium."

She smiled slyly at him as her fingers worked the zipper of his fly open.

"Who am I to argue with maintaining equilibrium?" he asked as her head descended.

His eyes closed and his head dropped back as her mouth found his cock.

Now

Detective Lucien Broussard of the Royal St. Lucia Police Force begins his day with the dream. The dream is always the same. In the dream, he is asleep. In his sleep, he hears the sound of a child crying. Lucien tries to wake up, but his body feels heavy, immobile. He can't open his eyes; his eyelids are weighted. He finally wrests his leaden hands up to his eyes and pries his eyelids open. When he does, he realizes he is blind. His eyes are open but he still can't see.

He wakes for real, gasping and sweating.

Detective Broussard has been having the dream ever since the first child disappeared. Seven months ago, 219 days. Three more boys have been reported missing since then, a total of four small children, their families first frantic, then as time went on, sodden with grief, guilt, and the loss of hope. The latest report had been filed just four days ago, another boy, aged five, who had been with his mother in an outdoor market, drawn to the sounds of the steel drum band playing nearby, and then simply gone. Little Olivier Cassiel, last seen in jean shorts and a red T-shirt. A little boy lured by the carefree, spirited music of the island to an unknown fate. Lucien rubs his eyes hard as if trying to erase the image of the photo of the boy the child's mother had given him: impish smile, frizzy curls, scrawny arms braced in a classic muscleman pose.

Lucien's wife, Agathe, is already up; he can hear her softly humming along to the radio playing in the kitchen. He is relieved; he does not want her to see him like this, unnerved and distressed. He showers and dresses. As he does, he desperately catalogues what he knows about the missing children, raking through the facts as if doing so will somehow provide the answers that have so far proved elusive. Four boys, taken respectively from an outdoor market (Olivier, five), a playground (Jacob, six), a harborside diner (Pierre, four), and most eerie, the boy's own trundle bed in the dead of night (Sebastien, three). Little boys, there one minute and gone the next. The dark shadow spiriting away these children stalked the island with no apparent fear of getting caught. No one had been spotted and no clues left.

Then there were the places the St. Lucia police had searched for the kids: the docks; the warehouse district; Constitution Park (known for its homeless population despite a recent renovation); Maison Marianne (a now-abandoned mansion that had been the scene of an infamous triple homicide); a banana plantation that also housed one of the island's tawdriest brothels; an under-construction resort hotel. Anywhere and everywhere children could be hidden. But the four boys had simply vanished.

Lucien contemplates himself in the bedroom mirror. His coal-black skin looks rough, his large eyes deeply weary. He puts on his game face and emerges composed into the cozy kitchen.

Their cottage is cheerful. Bright yellow café curtains, sewn by Agathe, lend warmth to the kitchen, which is the heart of their home, as do the madras plaid tablecloth and the array of carved masks by St. Lucian artists gracing the walls. Lucien and Agathe have lived in the city of Castries, the capital of St. Lucia, their entire lives, and the masks are the works of their friends. Each one has a story.

Agathe, her green eyes (as ever) glowing against her café-au-lait-colored skin, thick curls caught up in a glossy ponytail, hands him a cup of strong coffee.

"Didn't you sleep?" she asks.

"Not too well. But I'll be fine. Baby still asleep?"

"Yes. I just checked on him. We get to have breakfast alone for a change."

He grins at her, pleased. Agathe serves him: French toast, fresh fruit. He grasps her hand and kisses it after she lays his plate down, and is rewarded with a honeyed smile. They eat in silence, Lucien grateful for the sweet taste of the food and Agathe's understanding that he needs quiet.

But then his wife, his lovely, trigger-tempered wife, informs him she is pregnant again. With a baby only thirteen months of age, and the notion of uninterrupted sleep only a recent rediscovery, Lucien does not react to this news with the adoring jubilation Agathe has clearly anticipated. When he asks if she is sure, she flings a china plate at his head. The shattering plate wakes the baby, Bertrand, who begins to wail. Lucien begs off; he has to get to work. This only infuriates Agathe more. There he goes again, hiding behind work and avoiding his family! It is like he is always trying to avoid them as of late! His mind is absent even when his body is present! She could have predicted this reaction! Agathe rants on.

Lucien retreats into the baby's room and picks up the crying Bertrand. He strokes his son's small, fragile back, calming him. Then he hands the baby over to Agathe, kisses her on the forehead, and makes for the door. He can't tell Agathe how heavily the four missing boys are weighing on him. Can't bring any of this case home to her warm embrace. Not with their baby boy, and now another child on the way.

Then

"Where are we going?"

Ellie was practically skipping, leading Rob down the Chelsea street.

She smiled at him. "I told you, it's a surprise."

She brushed a wisp of blond hair from her forehead. Light fractured in Ellie's brand-new diamond engagement ring. The day was fine and clear, and even if Ellie wasn't trying to move her hand just so to catch the light (which of course she was, just a little bit), the sun would have worked its magic. The diamond refracted spectacular prisms with every move.

They turned the corner.

"Here we are."

Now Rob knew. Before him was a little pocket park. But the playground at its center was like nothing he had ever seen.

Four topsy-turvy miniature skyscrapers, paired off like two sets of lovers, rose from a padded, softly molded magic garden, a riot of fantastic shapes in brilliant hues. The skyscrapers resembled the buildings around them in appearance (except for their scale, of course); they looked like they were constructed of glass and steel. They were in fact the latest in environmentally sound "green" technology, and also crafted to reflect the latest concepts in the "science of play."

The four play structures were spirited little imps with attitude: windows placed strategically to suggest faces, rope bridges suspended between each pair suggesting dance partners who might burst into movement at any moment. Sturdy ladders twisted around and led inside each building up to a porthole, out of which a child could gleefully slide shrieking to the padded ground below. A protective, slightly raised circle of bleachers enclosed the playground like a hug.

The project had been Ellie's baby. Rob had been hearing about it as long as he had known her. He had seen her sketches, had heard her talk about the project, but she had wanted him to wait to see it until the playground was officially open and put toward its intended use. Kids now jumped and swung, clambered and climbed on the structures that had sprung from Ellie's research and imagination, while their mothers, fathers, nannies, and siblings reclined on ergonomically designed benches that offered comfortable views of the entire park.

"Wow. Baby, it's amazing." Rob's admiration was genuine. She showed him around, delighted with his reaction, reminding him excitedly of things he had seen in the design phase and showing him how, now, they were manifest.

Rob was suffused with love for her. She had put her mind and heart, time and energy, into creating this safe harbor. They found themselves kissing deeply, oblivious for a moment to the world around them. Then they parted lips, foreheads still touching, bodies close.

"Let's go."

They held hands tightly as they exited the park. Rob steered Ellie away from the three men walking none too steadily toward them. Well fed and sleek, with two-hundred-dollar haircuts and Brooks Brothers attire, the trio emitted an air of entitlement and a waft of lunchtime gin martinis. They were like a herd of fat cows, in the wholesale complacency of their own luxurious, cud-chewing existence. They pivoted to give Ellie a pathetically unsubtle and lascivious once-over twice.

Then one of them, prematurely thinning hair and a jaunty polka-dotted silk pocket square, locked his gaze on Rob.

"Kevin?" the man asked, incredulous.

Rob looked directly at the man for the first time. For an instant Rob froze, his body stilled to a single heartbeat.

"You've mistaken me for someone else," Rob answered, trying to move past them. But the man was insistent. Blocked his path. His two companions stopped, waiting, looking, listening.

"It's me—Spencer. I never thought I'd see you again!"

Spencer wavered on his feet, then lurched forward and tightly gripped Rob's elbow, his fingers pinching.

Spencer addressed his companions. "This is the guy!" His friends looked mystified. "You know. My best friend from back in the day. The one that I was just telling you about last week?"

Rob pulled away from Spencer's grasp. "Like I said, you're making a mistake." He draped his arm around Ellie's shoulder, moving away.

Spencer said in a stage whisper: "Hey, I get it! You don't want me to say anything out loud, still on the run!" Then a happy drunken bellow, "But I know it's you. What are the odds?" he asked his companions. "Isn't that just the craziest thing?"

Rob kept his arm around Ellie's shoulder. They turned the corner.

"What was that about?" Ellie asked.

"I have no idea."

Rob's mouth was tight, his face white.

"Are you sure you didn't know him?"

"Of course." Dismissively, he continued, "He was drunk. I just didn't like his aggression." Then, tenderly, "It worries me sometimes, when I think about how vulnerable you are . . . walking around the city by yourself. After all, it is my job to keep you safe, right?" He pulled her closer to him, and she snuggled in.

Ellie accepted this explanation. Why shouldn't she? She was loved, wholly loved, by a man who wanted to take care of her and who had put a ring on her finger to tell the whole world just that.

They went home and fell on each other in mutual, silent agreement, hungry for the other's body as they had often been, but today there was a new intensity.

Clothes dropped and peeled, shoes were kicked off, breath quickened, buttons popped. Ellie felt slick and liquid. Rob was urgent, rigid. He laid her back on the bed. Climbed atop her with delicious deliberateness and mounted her slowly. Teasing and tormenting. She pulled her legs up high. He held her face still between his hands. He looked directly into her eyes. It was almost too much for her. When her eyes closed, he brushed them open with the pads of his thumbs.

The rhythm of their bodies, now that they were more familiar with each other, the way he cradled her head like it was a priceless objet d'art, the intensity of the silent communication of staring into each other's eyes. The intimacy of it was like nothing she had ever known.

When she came with a heaving cry, his grip on her face tightened almost painfully. He kissed her deeply, then finally loosed his hands and closed his eyes as he too was swept into orgasm, his body shuddering on top of hers. He burrowed his head into the soft curve of her neck. *I've never been so happy,* she thought. Then she said it out loud.

Now

Ellie lifts Harry's arm, which is draped over her midsection, and gets out of the bed they share. They are in a sweet little beach bungalow, nicely furnished: carved wood furniture and batik cushions, sisal mats on the hardwood floor, a private little patio, a luxurious and well-appointed bathroom. Ellie peeks through the window. The hot noon sun bakes the soft sand. Seagulls circle and cry. She's stayed as long as she can in the relative safety she's wrangled. She hasn't slept, really; every time her eyes drifted, she jolted awake, breathless, chest squeezing. She's exhausted. Her brain feels fuzzy, her thinking blurred by the endless convoluted permutations of "what next" she's been running all night.

She turns and looks at Harry, his position an eerie mirror of the dead man she left in the hotel room twenty hours ago.

Look closer. Is there a knife? Is there blood? Has Harry met the same fate?

No. He groans heavily and rolls to his side, twisting himself up in sheets.

Ellie moves swiftly and quietly, gathering her things. She steps into the bathroom and closes the door, locking it behind her. She takes a good long look at herself in the mirror. Not too bad, considering. Dark patches beneath her eyes, her skin is a little dry, but beyond that her face does not reveal the ordeal that has become her life.

She checks that the door is locked and pulls out the box of hair dye. "They" are looking for a blonde, so she can be blond no more.

She slips the plastic gloves from the dye kit over her hands. Mixes the dye with its activator and shakes the bottle. She takes one last look in the mirror. Contemplates her pale skin and shiny blond hair, the girl she has always been. A look of pure melancholy crosses her face. Her entire body slumps; she places her palms down on either side of the sink, stands there, curled over, staring at the drain. Can she do this? Who is she? Who is she becoming? Should she have walked away when she had the chance?

She lifts her head and stares at herself in the mirror once again. Suddenly, her fingers are clawing through the beach bag, searching until she finds the gold wedding band that is twisted into a handkerchief inside. She stares at the ring Rob had slipped on her finger as he recited vows about loving and protecting her that now seem ludicrous. He is a complete mystery, snarled henceforth and forever with her utter debasement. She has committed grotesque and venal acts for this man. How much further will she degrade herself? His remembered assurances fade, empty echoing memories. She feels her anger flare. She just wanted to have some fun, was all. Break a dating losing streak! How did it ever come to this? The things she now knows about him are inconceivable. He's her husband. She shudders.

Then her thoughts drift to that day in the hospital. Waking up, no recollection of how she got there, Rob so kind, so grateful and relieved she was all right. Isn't that the man she married? He loves her. Doesn't he? Is that enough?

These thoughts are useless. Paralyzing. She's come this far.

She twists the ring back into the handkerchief and puts it away. Then, resolutely, methodically, she applies brown dye to her hair, careful also to coat her eyebrows.

Already she doesn't look like herself; the dark dye makes her blue eyes pop. The heavy eyebrows change the shape of her face. She waits the required twenty minutes on edge. She wants to get out of there.

Finally. Into the shower. Ellie rinses her body of Harry's smell and feel. She soaps her hair and the dark rinse circles down the shower's drain. Her hands run over her breasts, down her hips, along her thighs. She thinks of Rob, fearing him, questioning him, hating him, wanting him. She wishes this were all a bad dream. There's a rap on the door. Ellie jumps, clutching at the shower rail.

"Uh, honey . . ." She hears Harry through the door. "Uh, sugar . . ."

A sour smile twists her lips as she realizes he doesn't remember her name. Even though she had given him a fake one, it's just as well. She turns the water off and answers him.

"Just taking a shower. I'll be out in a sec."

"Uh, okay, but I gotta piss like a racehorse."

"Like I said, one sec."

Ellie exits the shower and dries herself briskly. She ties on the sarong, then wraps the scarf around her head once again, careful to completely cover her dark tresses. She shoves all of her belongings into her bag, including the box of dye and the tubes and bottle and gloves. Puts on the oversized sunglasses. She takes a last hasty look in the mirror. Then flings open the door.

"There you go."

"Thanks."

Harry hurries past her into the bathroom, only half shutting the door behind him. There is a loud sigh as the spatter of his piss hits the toilet.

"Uh . . . honey," he calls. "Last night was fun—do you maybe want to spend some time together today? Rent a catamaran, do some exploring?"

His only answer is the sound of the front door closing. Harry flushes the toilet and steps out of the bathroom, his eyes searching, but she is gone.

Then

Ellie readied herself for the blind date with a practiced measure of high hopes tempered by low expectations. After all, she had been single and dating in New York for six years now, which meant she had had her share of encounters and flings, and one or two small romances, not to mention one solid heartbreak.

The prevailing wisdom of her dating-jaded girlfriends seemed to be true: The good ones were either gay, taken, or looking over your shoulder for the next hotter thing. Still, despite the wealth of unsolicited opinions from others and her own experiences, Ellie reasoned that if you didn't put yourself out there, you would never know. Despite the fact that the last seven dates she had gone on had all turned out to be first *and* only dates, a small drumbeat of hope still tapped inside her. Ellie was trying to keep an open mind, even as it all felt stupid and a little tired.

As she brushed her hair, she amused herself by cataloguing the last seven. Number one, Sean, had been perfectly nice, a federal prosecutor with a real passion for his work, but it was too soon after Hugh (who had moved to London just the week before, leaving her heart a bit battered). She just couldn't follow the saga of Sean's latest case, too distracted in mourning his predecessor to really listen. That one was definitely on her. Oh well.

Number two, Marcus, talked incessantly about his ex-wife, "the model," leaving Ellie feeling inadequate, even though Marcus himself had a belly that strained against his shirt buttons and a nose like a squash blossom. Number three, David, took her to a Ukrainian dive bar, touting how cool it was, and it was kind of cool, until the rat scuttled directly in front of them and David leapt onto the pool table shrieking like a girl. Number four, Wilhelm, an international bond trader, was just too German. Number five, Gregg, was charming and polite and thoughtful . . . until after a couple of drinks his conversation slid into a racist rant. Number six, Frank, was two inches shorter than Ellie, and his wrist bones more slender than hers, no chemistry there. Number seven, Vic, was a brawny and hunky fireman, who slung her over his shoulder and carried her up the stairs to her third-floor walk-up after escorting her home from a concert in the park. They had made out passionately in the stairwell, but she hadn't let him in and he hadn't called again. Even so, she thought the make-out session had been a good sign. It had made her feel desirable, and had helped to squelch the perpetually gnawing little mouse of insecurity that nestled deep within her.

Acknowledging the little mouse, even momentarily, put Ellie on edge. She spent a lot of energy keeping these feelings deeply buried, enveloped as they were in a toxic black cloud of self-loathing that too often threatened to overwhelm her. Sure, she had hashed it out in therapy, week upon week of it after her sister had died, but the foundation had already been laid and life had only built upon it.

Ellie's sister, Mary Ann, had been diagnosed with leukemia when Ellie was twelve and Mary Ann fifteen. The next five years were absorbed by Mary Ann's illness, like a sponge soaking up a rancid spill.

Ellie's parents were always at the hospital or seeking out some experimental cure. Ellie's failures, her triumphs, her strivings and dilemmas, went unnoticed because Mary Ann took everything. One day, home alone while her parents were at the hospital, Ellie impulsively thrust a soft white pussy willow nub into her ear. After one week, her hearing was fuzzy. Within a couple of weeks, her hearing was noticeably compromised and her teacher sent home a letter requesting a hearing test. By this time, Ellie's ear was inflamed and throbbing. Her mother finally took her to the doctor and the nub, now virtually unrecognizable, black and oozing, was extracted. Ellie denied any knowledge of how the nub had gotten into her ear, and the doctor prescribed an antibiotic.

In the car going home, her mother turned to Ellie at a stoplight and said coldly, "Don't I have enough on my plate?"

Ellie protested convincingly. "Why am I in trouble for needing a doctor? For fuck's sake, Mom."

"Watch your language" was the only response.

After Mary Ann died, Ellie thought she might get her parents back, but they were lost and misguided in their grief. They never let Ellie see Mary Ann's body, believing it might be too difficult for her. They got her a shrink to talk to but didn't talk to her themselves. They devoted themselves to raising money for leukemia research, and once again Ellie's triumphs and failures continued to be her own, not shared with her family. She won design competitions and learned to salsa, mastered the perfect popover and built a car engine one piece at a time; she graduated at the top of her high school class and got into an Ivy League college. Through all of it she felt invisible to her parents and as if she was seen by everyone else as "the girl whose sister died."

It was in college that she began to feel visible. Her first best memory of college was Freshman Orientation week. The school had organized an outdoor, nighttime glow-in-the-dark capture-the-flag game. Ellie had gone along to it reluctantly, herded with the other freshmen on her floor by their RA. She was lying low, in the game but not really playing, when suddenly she saw a wide-open pathway. Without even thinking about it, she kicked into gear, sprinted downfield, and secured the flag in one easy sweep. Her success excited the cute guy on her team who up to that point had seemed equally reluctant to be there. "Yo! Stealth!" he had yelled, before sprinting over to give her a high five. Stealth had stuck as a nickname. Ellie liked being called Stealth. It completely suited who she wanted to be in college, a departure from the inherited notoriety that had surrounded her when she was "the girl whose sister died." She was seen in her own right, and had a cool nickname, one that also spoke to being unseen, which felt like a private little irony. She and Jason became friends that night. Over a year later, he initiated a tentative and surprising kiss after a late-night study session for a shared class (Ethical Thought in Contemporary Politics). The kisses grew more confident in the wake of her pleasurable response and sent them tumbling back to her dorm room. In the morning they emerged, satiated, nervously exhilarated, and coupled up. Jason was her first real boyfriend, her first love.

Ellie had been determined never to go back to her hometown after college and she hadn't. She had moved to New York City. Now, as she readied herself for date number eight, she reminded herself that she was solid. Tangible. Visible. Worthy.

So, Ellie thought as she always did, *it'll be a good date or a good story.* At least this one, Rob Beauman, was a setup through someone who actually knew Ellie, not a random Internet dating hit, or a friend of a friend of a friend. No, this time, the connection was her colleague Marcy Clark.

Ellie and Marcy had been working together for a year in the design department, had shared a number of lunches and the occasional drink. Marcy was married to her college sweetheart, Ethan, blissfully content in her relationship, trying to get pregnant. She wanted all of her single friends to "be as happy as I am," although up until this point, she had never suggested a fix-up for Ellie. When she had done so on Monday, it had been with a high degree of excitement.

Marcy and her husband had been out with a group of friends on Saturday night, a boozy pub crawl of an evening (although Marcy was careful to stress that she drank only water and one spritzer in pursuit of the deeply wanted first Clark baby).

This guy Rob came along, she told Ellie. He'd been working with Ethan at the investment firm for just a couple of weeks. Single. Gorgeous. Moved to Manhattan from Chicago for the job, still basically unpacking, so no attachments. But that was all just surface. Why did Marcy think of Ellie for this charmer? Why not any of her other single girlfriends? Marcy just "knew." And her husband, Ethan, whom Ellie had only recently met—an evening of cocktails and laughter for the three of them that had moved Ellie and Marcy's friendship to a whole new level—completely agreed. Marcy and Ethan both had a hunch, a big one. Couldn't even say why. Marcy had grinned at her. "It just feels like magic."

Ellie had googled him, of course, it would be foolish not to in this day and age. (She had, for example, been asked out by an attractive guy who had found her on a dating website, and while he had seemed perfect on paper, once they had exchanged names and she had run a check on his, she had discovered he was twice married with five children.) But when she googled Rob Beauman there were no red flags. Four Rob Beaumans came up: a dentist in Rutherford, N.J., a high school student in New Hampshire, a retired ophthalmologist in Florida (locally notorious for having crashed his two-seater prop jet into a golf course but walking away without a scratch), and the one she was about to meet, Rob Beauman, investment strategist. There wasn't a lot, his profile on the firm's website and not much more, but Ellie kind of respected a guy who wasn't living his life in the public arena of social media.

Ellie took a final check in the mirror. Blond hair sleek. A hint of cat's-eye eyeliner. Naturally pink cheeks and a coat of plum lipstick. Her favorite, deep navy body-con dress. If she liked him, she'd take off her coat slowly and let him see how the dress clung to her body. A rush of desire for sex flooded her unexpectedly. Hugh was old news now, and while at first she couldn't imagine being with anyone else, that session with the fireman had stoked her fires. Maybe she'd take off the coat even if she just liked him a little. Ellie smiled at her reflection. She was ready for some fun. The hell with it, she didn't even want a relationship. She wanted a good time. It looked like Ethan's friend could get lucky.

Later. Rob opened the door to the restaurant for her after dinner and they emerged into the brisk, sweet first wisp of New York autumn. Ellie took her time slinging her coat on, making the most of the moment. She caught Rob looking at her, surreptitiously, adjusting his collar. She could tell he liked her. Dinner had been fun, easy.

She gave him a little half smile. "Well, then—" she began.

"Can I walk you home?" He blurted it out. Ellie got the sense that he was surprised he had asked the question. Still, she wasn't going to say no. She was reckless. Ready for adventure.

Ellie's half smile slid wider. Her pink tongue darted out and licked her lips. "Sure."

Now

Detective Lucien Broussard knows he is offering useless platitudes even as the words leave his mouth. He hates himself for it, but Yvette, mother of poor missing five-year-old Olivier Cassiel, desperately needs some kind of comfort. Her eyes are red and raw; her crumpled face has aged decades in just a few days. She sits hunched in Lucien's office guest chair, coiled in on herself as if cowering from blows.

Yvette's boyfriend, Rudy, with impotent, frustrated rage seething just below the surface of his perspiring skin, stands next to her, awkwardly dandling their squirming two-year-old daughter.

Then it erupts. Rudy drops the toddler into Yvette's lap. And his hands curl into fists.

"This is your fault!" he yells at her. "Olivier was with you! You are the mother!"

Rudy smashes his fist into the wall, shattering the plaster. Yvette flinches. The baby girl howls, agitation morphing into panic.

Lucien understands Yvette's defensive posture with a fresh, sad clarity. He rises and forcefully grabs Rudy by one arm.

"Cut that shit out, or I'll arrest you for destruction of public property. This kind of outburst helps nobody. Yvette and your daughter need you, Rudy."

Rudy raises his free arm high and rears back to crash his fist down into Lucien's skull. Yvette gasps.

Lucien catches Rudy's forearm on its downward swing. "That's enough!"

Rudy darts a glance at Lucien, then slumps and nods, the fight gone from his body. Lucien releases him. Rudy brings his hands together and brushes the plaster dust from his sore knuckles.

Lucien does his best. He does well. He counsels patience and mutual support, the power of maintaining faith and grace, and, more important, he demonstrates those qualities as he outlines the steps he and his men are taking to locate Olivier. He offers the little girl a shortbread cookie from the secret stash in his desk drawer.

At last, the couple leaves, holding hands, the toddler cradled on her mother's shoulder and contentedly sucking the last damp, crumbled bits of cookie from her sticky fingers.

That's when the call comes in about a dead man at the Grande Sucre Hotel.

Fifteen minutes later, Lucien walks into the chaos that has overtaken the resort, never mind its prime "sell" was tropical peace. The hysterical hotel maid who had found the body, the anxious hotel manager freaked about the bottom line, the curious hotel guests who hover and whisper and gossip, all shred this image of serenity. Not to mention a very dead man with a knife in his belly and a mutilated mouth.

Lucien's captain, Pierre Bonnaire, has made it clear this is the force's top priority. Given the importance of the tourist trade to St. Lucia, a murder at a resort hotel is the island's worst nightmare. Agathe has also called seven times (and Lucien has not yet answered her calls).

Lucien rubs his temples wearily as he reads the hotel manager's name tag: *Desmond Hippolyte*. Lucien knows that how things begin is often how they go. He speaks diplomatically but forcefully. "Desmond, you will have to ask all guests to gather in the ballroom. Employees too."

The hotel manager is apoplectic. "You know we are talking about hundreds of people! We are at ninety-two percent of capacity . . . I can't detain . . . Some of the guests aren't even in the hotel! They could be anywhere on the island!"

"Those not here will go to the ballroom upon their return to the hotel. I also need a complete list of guests, as well as employees, as soon as possible."

The hotel manager begs Lucien to speak to his fearful guests, many of whom are frantically trying to find other accommodations on the island. Rumors are rampant! Detective Broussard must tell the guests they are safe! This request Lucien denies. He can't assure any of the guests of their safety; he has no idea what he is dealing with yet.

Desmond Hippolyte's arms flap in the air. He blinks rapidly. Doesn't budge.

Lucien's tone turns sharp. "Surely you can see that an efficient investigation and a speedy arrest will be the most beneficial to the hotel in the long run, yes? Your first priority is getting me any information you have about the woman the room was registered to."

Hippolyte blinks again. Finally he chokes out, "What shall I tell the guests?"

"As little as possible. Tell them there has been a death in the hotel; you don't need to specify a murder. Certainly don't tell them about the mutilation. And if they ask about it, if they've heard rumors, deny them. Is that clear?"

Hippolyte nods.

"Tell them that the hotel has pledged its cooperation with the police and that you hope to be able to release them soon. Then I suggest you provide food and lots of it, gratis."

A small glimmer of an idea forms in the manager's eyes. "And cocktails!" he says decisively.

Lucien sighs. "No. Not cocktails. We will need any potential witnesses clearheaded. Look, I understand what is at stake here; believe me, I do. It will be best for everyone if we handle this properly. Now get to it."

Hippolyte scurries off.

Lucien dispatches a team of officers to the ballroom to take initial statements. He himself will interview the maid who discovered the corpse, but first he needs to examine the crime scene.

In the doorway of the room in question, Lucien affixes booties to his feet and snaps on latex gloves. The dead man looks like he is asleep, except for the congealed blood circling the knife wound and the grotesque absence of his lower lip. Nothing in the man's clothes (a pair of loose-fitting linen pants, a thick cotton T-shirt, sandals, and a hat, found heaped on the floor) contains a clue about who he was.

Lucien takes note of the empty bottle of wine. The small scorch mark on the night table also catches his attention, although there is no way of knowing when it had been made. Hippolyte has told him the room had been registered to an American woman. The woman had checked in two days prior. She had paid cash, in advance, for her room, but had put a credit card down for incidentals. Hippolyte is pulling the imprint of the card for Lucien.

The body had been discovered shortly after noon. The maid, having been informed that the woman was supposed to check out that morning, had waited to clean the room. But when checkout time had come and gone and the *"Ne Pas Déranger"* sign still hung on the door, she had knocked and entered.

Lucien looks closer at the murdered man's face. The lower lip has been cleanly sliced away; it gives the corpse an oddly ribald grimace. The man is deeply tanned; Lucien's guess is that he was not a casual tourist. Maybe an expat living on the island, maybe a member of the international community of yacht owners who frequent St. Lucia's ports.

He consults with the techs. No good fingerprints as of yet. A few smudges, but that's it. Given the amount of traffic a hotel room has as a matter of course, this means someone has been careful to eradicate them.

Lucien's phone buzzes. He glances at it. Agathe again. He sighs, knowing that if he doesn't answer, he is only going to create more trouble for himself. He steps through the billowing curtains and out onto the room's balcony to take the call. For a moment before hitting the "talk" button he contemplates the beautiful natural vista of sand and ocean and sky.

"Hello?"

She is in full throttle the instant she hears his voice. An invective-laced assault pours out at him. He is insensitive, he is cold, he doesn't love her—he pulls the phone away from his ear. He does love her, of course he does, but some days he can understand why people have the urge to kill.

Then

The first time Rob killed someone, he was sixteen years old. Of course his name wasn't Rob then, but the name of that sixteen-year-old boy is as deeply buried as the man he killed.

But let's start earlier. Rob was raised by a single mother until she remarried; Rob was eight then and accustomed to the rhythm of their lives together as a pair. The big house in Devon, Pennsylvania, with the apple trees; the Sunday visits to his formal and stiff grandparents; the school uniforms and rigorously scheduled activities. Horseback riding, of course (his mother rode), tennis lessons, piano.

Rob never knew his "real" father, his "birth" father, the sperm donor—call him what you please. The man wasn't spoken about much either, at least in Rob's presence. There were the occasional weepy mutterings he overheard when his mother's best friend came over and the two women poured multiple vodka tonics. The muted but angry conversations between his mother and grandfather. And that endless three weeks the summer he was six, when he was left at his grandparents' estate, feeling like an ungainly interloper: too loud, too fast, too messy, too much. His mother came back red-eyed but resolute. His grandfather seemed pleased, somehow, as if he had "won." Won what, Rob wasn't sure.

But then there was a new man in his mother's life. A big, jovial presence, full of bonhomie and gin. The newcomer was talked about constantly and openly. Welcomed into the extended circle of family and friends. A lavish wedding was planned and executed. Rob was the ring bearer and included in the vows. Rob and his mother moved from the big house with the apple trees to an even larger house closer to the city. Rob didn't mind his stepfather, really, at least not at first.

Rob was nine when he saw his stepfather hit his mother for the first time. He froze, unable to process what he was seeing, even as her head slammed into the kitchen wall and blood erupted from her nose and mouth.

It was the sound even more than the blood. The *whomp* of her soft skin, hard bone, and pliable cartilage smacking into the tiled wall, a sickening tearing crack that he would never forget. She had been running, his mom. Running to get away from the man she believed loved her, but who revealed himself as a monster. She was nearly out of the room too, had a good long lead, but the bastard caught up with her in three furious strides, seized her hair, and shoved her face into the tile. Rob, drawn from his bedroom by the commotion, stopped in his tracks and his sleepy eyes popped wide with terror. His mom saw him, and laid a gentle hand on her husband's arm, turning him slightly so he could also see Rob was observing them.

"Go back to bed, baby."

Rob stared at the smear of blood on the rectangular tiles, garish against their cool mint green. Rob's fingers worried the edge of his penguin T-shirt.

"That's right, kid. Go back to bed. This is just about your mom and me. Just a little fight. All grown-ups fight."

Still Rob hesitated, but his mother shot him a weak smile, and pressed the sleeve of her silken shirt into her face to absorb the blood. Then she gave a little laugh.

"It looks worse than it is. Don't worry, baby." She gave her husband an imploring look and upon his nod, walked over to Rob, laid a hand on his shoulder, and guided him back toward his bedroom. She tucked him into bed, grabbed a handful of tissues from his night table, and replaced her sleeve with the wad of paper. She turned on his solar system projector, dusting the room with whirling stars and planets, then sat down on the edge of his bed and stroked the hair away from his forehead.

"It's okay, honey. He's right. All grown-ups fight. We just got a little carried away."

He tried to protest, tried to ask questions. This made no sense to him and he was frightened. But she just hushed him, tucked his down comforter up around his neck, told him to go to sleep, and promised that this was the first time this had happened, it was all a terrible mistake, and it would never happen again.

But of course it did. Over and over again.

The violence was a constant, lurking specter in their otherwise privileged lives. But she didn't leave him. She didn't even fight back. There were tears and apologies and ice packs. Emergency room trips cosseted by improbable lies about falls and accidents. And then vacations and jewelry and new cars.

After each brutal storm passed, the routine was the same. His stepfather buried his face in his mother's lap and pleaded for forgiveness. She stroked his hair and crooned, "It's all right, baby, it's all right," the same sweet song she had murmured to Rob when he was little and had had a nightmare or a hard fall in the playground. And then the bastard would carry her off to their bedroom, shooting a wink and smirk at the cowering boy. Then the sounds, the grunts and moans that clawed their way into the otherwise silent mansion as Rob struggled to make sense of it all.

Rob never did make sense of it. It went on for years, that same grotesque cycle. The prick would drink then lose it, he would beat the crap out of her, there would be tears and murmurs and then the animal sounds that Rob learned were the noises of make-up sex. He hated it. Hated how passive his mother was, hated even more the fact that the bastard hit her and then she kissed him, consoled him, fucked him. Hated how the bastard would inflate afterward, proud of himself, that motherfucking cock of the walk, delighted with his dominance and her submission. It twisted Rob's guts into knots every time.

When he was fourteen, he tried to talk to her about it. His stepfather was at work. Rob came into the master bedroom as his mother was putting the final touches on her outfit for a lunch at their country club. He watched as she pulled a baby-blue cashmere cardigan over her elegant, sleeveless sheath dress, carefully hiding the latest set of bruises that marred her narrow shoulders and soft upper arms. She gasped when she realized he was standing in the doorway watching her.

"Do you need something, baby? Some cash?"

"No. Not cash."

And then he launched in; he at least had to try. Surely there were options; surely this merry-go-round of rage, abuse, tears, and reconciliation could be abandoned, along with the creep who perpetuated it. But his mother didn't see it that way. She sighed. She twisted her fingers. She explained that he was too young to understand, that despite it all, she knew her husband was a good man, a man who worked hard and provided for them both, and if he didn't always handle his stress so well? She was willing to live with that. She loved him. She knew he didn't mean it. As she explained that he always, *always* apologized after, Rob felt disembodied, as though his spirit had risen out of his body and was watching this whole sordid scene from miles away. He tried to get her to see, but her face shut down and she changed the subject.

After that he stopped trying. He spent more and more time away from the house, avoided his stepfather when they crossed paths, tried for dinner alone with his mom at least once a week, even when she didn't seem that interested. His stepfather seemed amused by his self-imposed exile, which only made it easier to stay away. And so it went. Rob kept his distance and his mom and stepfather danced their ugly little dance.

So began Rob's campaign of subversive disruption. A near fire in the school science lab, a result of fucking around with the Bunsen burner. A spray-painted caricature of his headmaster, both accurate and cruel, on the school's tennis court. Missed classes and a bad attitude. After a while, Rob needed to up the stakes. He got more aggressive. A fight in the boys' bathroom left a kid with a broken jaw, and Rob was expelled. He was lectured and grounded and then his stepfather paved the way (paid the way) for Rob to attend another elite private school.

There he met Spencer. The two of them together were a conflagration just waiting for a spark. Spencer was the son of a local career politician. He had spent his childhood "smiling for the camera" and now turned that smile into a snarl. The two teens drank, smoked pot and cigarettes. They abused Spencer's Adderall and raided Rob's mother's supply of Vicodin; her prescriptions were plentiful and she never noticed.

They pretended they were thugs, listening to rap music and letting their pants slink low on their hips; everything was "yo" this and "bitch" that, as they shaped their hands into gang signs and rolled fat blunts. They had no idea how pathetic they really were: two rich, privileged white boys pretending to be street.

They had big dreams. They were going to New York together and they were going to own that town. Supermodels and Cristal and Ferraris and yachts.

When they were driving wasted one icy night, toasting their future with a case of beer and a couple of bumps of Adderall, Spencer's brand-new BMW, his sixteenth-birthday present from his parents, spun out on the ice as Spencer took a sharp curve way too fast.

The BMW drifted across the median in a lazy 360-degree spin, once, twice—before broadsiding a 1996 Chevy Impala. The driver, a retired electrician, was in the hospital for three weeks. Broken leg. Punctured lung. A lot of talk about what a miracle it was he wasn't killed.

Rob's stepfather and Spencer's dad settled with the electrician, who was persuaded to take the more-than-generous sum offered. And sign an NDA.

The criminal charges were also dropped, a relatively simple call to a friend. A favor owed. Or paid. Currency was fluid in these circles.

His stepfather now acted as if he owned Rob; he had cleaned up the boys' shit and Rob had to pay the price. The violence inflicted on Rob's mother became even more casual. Sometimes the bastard just liked making her flinch. A raised hand, the sudden bark of an order, a slammed door. Then he would laugh as she cringed, and try his hardest to goad Rob into doing something about it. Call him a pussy when Rob fled the room, jaw frozen, fists balled.

Rob, seething with rage and impotence, became more reckless. He was caught dealing drugs at school, suspended again. When he was caught a second time, he was threatened with another expulsion. His stepfather came into the headmaster's office, slid a check across the desk.

The headmaster's eyes widened. The next thing Rob knew, his stepfather seized Rob by the scruff of his neck, hoisted him to his feet. The powerful man in the two-thousand-dollar suit locked eyes with the headmaster, who nodded meekly once before looking away—and then did not raise his eyes as Rob was hauled out of there, his kicking, protesting feet flailing against the marble floors, his one cry of "Stop" silenced by the sharp crack of a backhand that split Rob's lip.

Rob's mother was waiting in the car. Silent. Angry. Worried. They drove home. Rob slouched, surly, in the back, his mother twisting the handkerchief she had offered him (and he had refused) into tighter and tighter knots, his stepfather a thundercloud with two hands on the wheel and a heavy foot on the gas. Rob spat a globule of blood down the front of his impeccable white school uniform shirt. It was even bloodier that night when his stepfather was done with him.

The beating only made Rob more defiant.

Rob's mother and stepfather rode a carousel of fundraisers. A steady rotation of cancer research, animal rights, and historical preservation initiatives, with a sprinkling of election season Republicans. One Saturday night, eighteen days into Rob's house arrest (as he called it), Rob took advantage of "Save the Duck or Whatever the Fuck" (as he later named it to Spencer, feeling clever).

Rob snuck out of the house and bicycled over to Spencer's, where the two played pool and drank vodka (keeping track of the bottle level and filling it with water before replacing it in the liquor cabinet). For both, who had been bitch-slapped and unjustly imprisoned for varied offenses, it was the best night they had had in weeks.

Later. Rob glided up to his house silently, dismounting his bike in one fluid motion and walking it through the side yard, toward the shed. The enormous garden was peaceful and pretty in the darkness, the bright blooms muted violet and indigo. Rob left the bike leaning and walked softly toward the back door. He slipped in through the kitchen. He glanced at the alarm pad. Disarmed.

He noticed his stepfather's keys and his mother's sparkly little handbag on the kitchen counter. He glanced at the clock. It was early, not even midnight; they had said they would be home around two. His heart quickened. Had they come early to check on him? Or had they lied about coming home by two in order to set him up? Rob slipped off his shoes and crept across the kitchen. If he could just get into bed . . . maybe they hadn't checked his room yet . . .

Rob crept into the central hallway. An ominous murk filled the big house, a thick fugue of feeling. It felt like dread. Naming it sent a tingle down Rob's spine, a voodoo doll stab.

Rob switched on the hall light. He shook off his nerves. Fuck it if he was caught. So what? He needed light in this fucking house.

The cut crystal teardrops of the elegant chandelier shimmered. Rob crossed under it to the great room. Flicked the switch. A series of recessed ceiling lights illuminated the expensively framed art but revealed the room was empty. A pair of martini glasses sat on the coffee table. Rob crossed to them. One was empty. Rob slugged back the dregs of the other.

The dining room was silent, sixteen empty chairs around the handsome antique table. His stepfather's office, empty. The media room, the pantry, the laundry room, the guest bath. He hurried through them all, leaving all the lights on, increasingly frantic, an unknown fear poisoning his belly, snaking up around his heart. Rob ran up the stairs to the second floor.

The thick spray of blood on the apricot-colored wall was the first tangible piece of evidence. Then the hank of his mother's glossy hair, curled on the hardwood with a scrap of bloody scalp still attached. Terror flooded his body; he sprinted down the hall to his mother's bedroom and flung open the door. The room was dark, the blinds drawn, the lights off. His eyes refused to adjust, and while he was still struggling to make out the shapes before him, his mother's low keening hit him like a blow. He snapped on the light.

The first thing he saw was the shattered dresser mirror, scattered about the opulent room and refracting the light in a crazy quilt of directions. Then the kaleidoscope of bloody images it reflected. He stepped in the room and saw the lump of blood and bone and pain that had been his mother. Her eyes were dull; one of her front teeth had been knocked out and she showed it to him in her outstretched hand.

In a few panicked steps he was by her side, kneeling, pulling his T-shirt over his head to staunch the blood flowing from her mouth, her nose, the gaping wound on her head.

"Is he still here?" he asked in whisper.

She didn't answer, just looked up at him with those dead, dazed eyes and continued the low animal moans that had first greeted him.

"Mom. Listen to me. Is he still in the house?"

She reluctantly made eye contact with him. Mumbled a reply distorted by her broken, bloody mouth. He didn't understand, made her repeat it.

"Do you think they can fix my tooth?"

Panic gripped Rob, bile flooding his mouth, as he heard a flush from the bathroom and then a stumble and a curse. He cast his eyes about wildly, looking for something he could use as a weapon, finally seizing on a razor-sharp shard of mirror glass with its violent, jagged edge. He wrapped his now bloody T-shirt around his hand to protect it from the glass. He gestured to his mother that she should be quiet, not sure she comprehended. He flicked the light back off and crouched down low behind the side of the dresser, where he knew he could not be seen from the doorway to the bathroom. He realized he was panting loudly, his heart thudding in his chest, and he breathed in and out, in and out, in and out, long and slow, willing his body to settle, his brain to cool.

There he was. A looming shadow. He stumbled again and grabbed the doorframe to steady himself, cursing, leaving a bloody handprint. Then he strode over to where Rob's mother crouched and kicked her in her stomach. It was the casual nature of the brutality that made Rob react. That and his mother's passivity. She didn't cry or beg him to stop, she didn't even try to protect her soft belly. She just took it. Like she deserved it. Like she expected it. Like she wanted it.

Rob sprang to his feet with a grunt and flung himself at the bastard, slashing wildly with the shard of mirror. He caught him right above the eye and the blood flowed, blinding him. Rob took full advantage, slashing at the arms his stepfather had wrapped protectively over his face, and then as they came down, at his throat, leaving a welter of nicks and cuts. His stepfather bellowed with fury and launched himself at Rob, tumbling them both to the floor. Rob's head smacked hard; the bloody shard dropped from his fingers. For a moment, he felt dizzy and winded. But as his stepfather scrambled to his knees, swearing, rearing back to give leverage to the fist he had aimed at Rob's face, Rob grasped at the piece of mirror and shoved it, as hard as he could, into the man's throat. Blood spurted; the hand that had been clenched in a fist opened and clutched at the wound. Shock swamped the eyes that moments ago had only known drunken fury. And as he tumbled off Rob and onto the thick carpet beside him, Rob could hear his mother's anguished cry.

"Please! Don't hurt him! Please! Stop it!"

Rob turned to look at her, knowing that she was trying to protect him, that finally she had had enough. Instead, he saw that she was crawling toward her husband, weeping. And that her imploring had not been for him, her only son, but for the man who had nearly killed them both.

Now

Ellie stares at the ocean, digging her toes into the warm sand. This strip of beach is nearly empty, a couple of hard-core, leathery tanners prostrate in sun worship, a young mother and her toddler digging with yellow plastic shovels and a bright red pail. A translucent pink crab scuttles by Ellie's feet. Her newly brown hair is wind-blown dry and pulled into a ponytail, her blue eyes startling against the rich mahogany tones. Her crystal-adorned fake nails glint madly in the sun. She tries to pick them off, but they are firmly affixed. She needs another run to the Dollar General store; she wants to change up her appearance even more.

Ellie shakes her head. When did she learn to think like this? This kind of attention to the details of distraction and deception is another new tool in her belt, necessity being, as they say, the mother of invention.

She half laughs to herself as she realizes that changing her appearance is as far as she has gotten in terms of formulating a plan. And a plan is what she needs.

She thinks a little more, idly twisting her ridiculous nails so the crystals explode the sun into sparkles on her bare thigh. *Okay,* she thinks, *the first thing, what's the first thing I should do? If I can just figure that out, then I will know the next.*

Her thoughts drift to Rob, back to the beginning. It was on their third date that she began to hope this could be something serious. Something more than what she had thought he was: a body between, the bridge between getting over Hugh and moving on to something "real." Rob had arranged for dinner at Per Se because she had casually mentioned it was on her bucket list of restaurants. He ordered wine with assurance, was charming and witty and solicitous throughout their meal, asked her questions, was just so *interested* in everything she had to say. He had a car waiting to take them home, this time to his place. His apartment was masculine in a standard way, dark wood, leather chairs, but an attention to detail was revealed by the bouquet of yellow tulips on the coffee table and a lovely large-scale photograph of a woman floating suspended over a bridge. He made love to Ellie tenderly that night, a contrast to the fierce animalistic passion that had marked their first coupling. When she woke in the morning, he was up, sitting next to her on the bed, sipping coffee, freshly showered. As relaxed and casual as if she lived there. Soon she did.

Ellie sighs. Then she sees him, Harry, last night's conquest, jogging down the beach. *Shit.* Images flood into her brain. The cocktails they knocked back at the bar. How she carefully slipped Seconal into his last two drinks. Stumbling to his room. The sloppy kisses. Harry's laugh as he stumbled and fell onto the bed, pulling her down on top of him. Her revulsion as his chapped, greedy hands cupped her naked breasts. The relief she felt when he abruptly passed out, snoring, drooling. The way she startled awake from her wary, shallow doze when he woke several hours later. How she whispered in his ear, *"What a fantastic lover you are, baby."* His confusion. Her reassurance that they had done it, that she was satisfied, too sore to go again. How she shuddered with relief when he fell asleep once more.

Swiftly, she rises and makes her way across the beach toward the first open-air café she sees, one that spills out onto a wooden deck adjacent to the sweet little hotel it services. She passes through the deck and into the café and realizes she is starving, can't even remember the last time she ate. The first thing is to eat. She asks the nut-brown hostess for a table.

Seated, she catches a waiter's eye and orders: eggs, bacon, toast, home fries, mango, coffee with cream. The order placed, she drums her fingers on the table, suddenly unable to think of anything but food. She can't remember ever feeling so hungry.

With a smile, the waiter deposits Ellie's food in front of her. The scent of the food makes her dizzy. She starts with toast and coffee. *Just eat.* Forks up some egg. *Just eat.* Home fries. A bite of bacon. A sip of coffee. A luscious chunk of mango. More eggs. *Just eat. Then I'll know what to do next.*

But as the couple seated next to her pays their check and leaves, she notices the local paper they have left behind. MAN FOUND DEAD AT LUXURY HOTEL, the headline screams. Ellie grabs for the newspaper.

Trembling, she scans the article. Phrases swim in and out of her view: "*. . . an unidentified man . . . not registered at the hotel . . .*" "*Detective Lucien Broussard . . .*" "*. . . room registered to a woman . . .*" "*. . . police not releasing her name at present . . .*"

But the detail, the crucial detail, is not in the article. Ellie exhales. So far, so good. They know he is dead. That was part of the plan. The crucial detail's omission? That was a calculated risk that paid off.

But then her stomach sours. She pushes her plate away. Something about seeing the cold details of the murder she has committed in solid black and white.

Ellie's thoughts turn to Rob. How could she have seen none of it?

Or did she just blithely commit to willful ignorance? Hide the truth from herself when it was staring her in the fucking face? It wouldn't be the first time in her life. Sometimes a smart woman can be so stupid. The food she just gobbled rises in her gullet. Her hand covers her mouth. Who is this person she has become? Devious and deft. Predatory when necessary. Murderous. The word thunders through her brain. Murderous. *Murderess.*

A tendril of her newly dark hair flops in front of her eyes, startling her. She feels foreign in her own skin. Itchy and burning, skittish and scared. What has she done?

She signals for the check. Fuck this. She is going right to the airport. She is flying home to New York on the first plane she can catch. She doesn't even know if Rob is still alive! If he is, she has no assurances he will remain so. And what has she become for this man, this stranger? A killer. She hates herself. And she hates him, this man who lies as easily as he breathes. How could she have believed a word he said? Done the things she has done? She is frantic. She throws cash down to pay for her breakfast. Stumbles to her feet. She is flushed, shivering in a clammy sweat. She runs from the café, oblivious to the startled looks of staff and patrons.

Then

Ellie stared down at her sleeping sister. Cancer had wasted her body; treatment had cost her her glossy blond hair. Dark circles wreathed her eyes. An oxygen feed tubed her nose. A broken doll.

For five years they had spiraled down this dark tunnel, the first faint lights of hope swallowed by an all-encompassing darkness.

Mary Ann stirred. One clawlike hand batted limply at nothing and then dropped onto the pink thermal blanket. They were in their childhood bedroom. Mary Ann had come home from the hospital to die.

Ellie looked around. Their twin beds on opposite sides of the room, Mary Ann's all rosy pinks, Ellie's dark purple. The shelves that housed their books and a few childhood relics, a favorite doll, a Monopoly set. Ellie's desk, a jumble of textbooks and makeup, her iPod and keys; Mary Ann's neatly laden with tissues, pill bottles, a water bottle, and a bedpan.

Ellie had been sleeping on the sofa in the family room. She was grateful college orientation was only three months away. She would never be able to sleep in this room again.

Ellie stroked the star-shaped pink plush pillow nestled next to Mary Ann's emaciated body. Picked it up. Pushed it down into Mary Ann's fragile face, covering her nose and mouth.

The bookshelves began to rattle, their shaking mimicking the trembling in Ellie's arms as she pressed the pillow harder onto Mary Ann's face. Ellie twisted her head to look at the shelves, never relaxing her pressure. She saw the china plate emblazoned with "My love will stop when this rooster crows" tip from the top shelf and arc through the air in slow motion. Weird. That plate was always kept in the kitchen.

The plate hit the hardwood floor and shattered into a hundred pieces.

A rooster crowed, its raucous call echoing hollowly. What the hell?

Ellie startled awake to midnight shadows. She was in her bed. She looked over at Mary Ann's. It was empty, neatly made. Stuffed animals ringed the edges in lumpy silhouette. There was a rap at the door. Her mother opened it without waiting for a response. The light from the hall spilled in, a harsh yellow. Her father stepped into the room.

"She's dead," her father choked out. "The hospital just called."

Now

The routine of investigation clicks into place with all of its satisfying familiarity. Lucien is oddly grateful. Here is a body that has to go to the coroner, fingerprints taken first in the hope they would identify the victim, witnesses that have to be interviewed, a crime scene to be photographed, evidence to be analyzed. There are things he can *do*. After months of chasing the elusive vapor trails of children gone missing, swept from the streets of the island only to vanish without a trace, a solid, corporeal dead body feels like a gift, albeit a macabre one.

Lucien assembles his team, assigns tasks, puts what they know so far on the murder board in the squad room. He calls the coroner, Alphonse Dafoe, and after the expected exchange of gallows humor, asks that Dafoe put a rush on the examination of the corpse.

He reports to his captain, who approves of the team and the delegation of tasks, but who can't hide his agitation. Already, Bonnaire is fielding calls from reporters, as well as from the governor general and the prime minister. Not to mention the wealthy and influential CEO of the chain that owns the Grande Sucre and is in the process of building another multimillion-dollar resort on the island.

"This has to be our absolute priority, Lucien," insists Captain Bonnaire. His right eye twitches, a tic Lucien has seen before when the captain was under pressure.

"Of course, sir. As for the missing kids, I suggest Detective Gagnon run point. She's been working very closely with me and—"

"No, no, no. There is nothing more to be done about the kids at this time. All eyes must be focused on this hotel murder."

"But—"

"Don't argue with me! We have no leads on any of the children and you know as well as I do that given how long they've been missing, they are probably dead."

Ire floods Lucien, along with a sick, sinking feeling. He knows Bonnaire is probably right about the kids being dead. It's a likelihood he hasn't allowed himself to name.

Bonnaire continues. "But without bodies, we can't even declare them homicides!" His eye twitches faster.

Bonnaire takes note of the distress on Lucien's face and his tone softens. "I'm as sick about those kids as you are, don't think I'm not. But we're stalled there, you know it too. Now go catch me a murderer."

Lucien nods once and leaves Bonnaire's office.

Lucien knows Bonnaire to be a good man (although more ruthlessly political and ambitious than Lucien could ever be), and the captain's seeming callousness more a function of the external pressures he is now enduring than disregard for the fate of the missing children. But Lucien also knows that if these four unfortunate children had been the offspring of white tourists instead of island kids, it would be quite different. This thought he shoves from his mind. It is pointless; its truth makes it no less frustrating.

Back at his desk, Lucien takes a moment. Surreptitiously he

reaches into his bottom drawer and pulls out a sealed plastic bag. Inside is a blue-and-green chiffon scarf. He slides open the bag's seal and takes a quick whiff of the aroma imbued in the delicate fabric. It smells of perfume and powder, hard work and church Sundays. It carries the scent and the memory of his mother. Hastily he closes the bag and shoves it back into its hiding place under cold case files and the half-eaten packet of shortbread.

Lucien had been an only child, raised by a single mother, a hard-working woman who spent most of her life toiling in one of the island's high-end resort hotels. His mother had started in the kitchen doing prep work, rising after many years to become an assistant banquet manager. She had applied to work in the kitchen initially (after Lucien's father left one season to work on a cruise ship and never returned), rather than as a maid (which would have been an easier path), because she figured if she were a kitchen worker her son would never go hungry. And Lucien never had. She had made certain he was fed and schooled and loved. She had encouraged his intellect and made him go to Sunday school. She was both mother and father to him, took him fishing, played catch, made him lunches, checked his homework.

She finally retired at the age of fifty-nine, just after Bertrand had been born, anticipating a new chapter of relative leisure and the joy of helping to raise her grandson. She died abruptly of a heart attack just three weeks later.

Missing her is still an acute ache in Lucien's heart. Yet he is grateful his mother had met Bertrand before she died, also grateful that she had loved Agathe, and that she was proud he had become a cop.

After his mother's death, Agathe's family had become his own. Her parents, Therese and Moses, her sister, Gabrielle, and Gabrielle's husband, Peter, all of them had embraced him even back when they were still just dating, but after his mother's sudden death it was even more so. He remembers the pride that swelled in him the day Moses had asked Lucien to call him Dad. He has done so ever since.

Agathe. He had been understandably distracted while talking to her at the scene of the murder; had held the phone away from his ear and just let her rant, until a subordinate asked him a question and he had unceremoniously ended the call. But he loves his wife dearly, loves their son, and knows he will love this new baby about to grace their lives. Agathe was his high school sweetheart; he has loved her every day of his adult life. She is also the person who grounds him, soothes him, is his respite from the brutal debasement he faces daily. When the creeping shadows of man's seemingly infinite capacity for ugliness and evil threaten to overwhelm, Agathe provides light and grace.

Now, as Agathe answers her phone, it is clear her bad temper has dissipated. That is the way it is with Agathe. Her temper flares, bright and hot, floods out of her in a torrent, and then fades away, leaving cheerful good humor.

Lucien apologizes about his reaction to the news of their second baby. He assures her he loves her and is happy to expand their family. He can hear their Bertrand gurgling softly in the background and his heart expands. Maybe they will have a girl this time, a little sister he can raise his boy to protect. He shares that thought with Agathe, who is pleased. Her sister, Gabrielle, has one child, Thomas; it is time they welcomed a girl into the family. Agathe asks what he wants for dinner, and when he hesitates, unsure if he will make it home in time, she offers to make a curry with dumplings, his favorite, and so he knows all is forgiven.

Then

The first time Ellie saw a dead body she was twenty-one. It was the night before college graduation. She and her crowd of friends were partying hard, a noisy, carefree last hurrah. The obligatory stodgy dinners with families in town for the ceremony had been endured, then one by one they had peeled away to the house on Rose Avenue where the music was pumping and the alcohol flowing. The house, which had been the central gathering place for this group all of senior year, was a gracious old Victorian, a somewhat battered Painted Lady graced with faded multicolored hues, remnants of her heyday. Given the house's disreputable history (it was rumored to be a former whorehouse), and current standing as the best party house going, it had been christened the House of Pleasure by its residents.

The actual residents of the house were four: Jason Briggs (Ellie's boyfriend, an ambitious business student with a work hard/play hard ethic), Doug Holland (Jason's best friend, a feckless history major with no fucking idea about what he wanted to do with his life), Shyam Hemarajani (a hard-striving first-generation son of immigrant Indian parents, who possessed a surprisingly scalding sense of humor), and Collette Guichard (a once and forever tomboy, always more comfortable tossing around a football or playing beer pong than any traditionally "feminine" activity).

Ellie loved Jason, tolerated Doug because she loved Jason, had formed a surprisingly solid friendship with Shyam, and maintained a polite rapport with Collette, with whom she could never quite get into a conversational groove. Ellie was at the house a lot, practically the fifth roommate, and a vibrant part of its never-ending-party policy. This night was no different. She, like everyone else, had ditched her parents as soon as was decently possible and sped over to the house. Beer? Check. Vodka? Check. Tequila, lime, salt? Check, check, check.

Knowing this was the last night of senior year, of college, of this honeyed window of time before "real life" began, gave the evening a surreal quality. There was an electric current in the air, a sense of wildness, a frisson of infinite possibility.

People who had never before spoken fell into deep philosophical discussions and emerged hours later bemoaning the fact that they had only just now discovered each other and vowing to stay in touch. Shyam finally made a move on Rachel Marcus, the dark-haired beauty he had been crushing on for two years but had been too shy to approach. To his utter astonishment (and perhaps hers) he persuaded her to disappear with him into his bedroom. Collette ruled the foosball table, taking on one challenger after the next, winning each match with a whooping war cry of victory. Doug drank. And drank.

Although none of his friends knew this, Doug's dinner with his parents that night had not been a gathering of proud affirmation of their only son's accomplishments. Doug's parents had arrived on campus for a meeting with the dean to learn that Doug was not going to graduate with his class. His last exam, a series of essays for a history of religion class, had been an invective-blurred rant against the professor, a rigid bureaucrat with whom he had butted heads from the onset of the semester. The dean had given Doug every chance—to take the test again, to apologize to the professor—but Doug, for reasons not even he could fathom, had refused. Consequently, dinner with his parents had been a battleground. His father's more measured and confused questioning had been punctured by his mother's shrill and desperate anger. "How could you do this to us, Douglas?" And as their narcissism raged, Doug retreated further and further into himself. Until he got to the Rose Avenue house.

There, Doug was the life of the party. He started drinking the minute he got in the door, played the impeccable host, pouring endless shots and tapping countless kegs. He circulated, greeting one and all; he danced; he took Collette on at foosball and lost. But while everyone else was feeling the sharp tang of incipient release and celebration like sea salt in the spring breeze, Doug was spiraling deeper and deeper into a dark, lonely place of oppression and despair.

Ellie and Jason had played host and hostess until about two A.M. Then Ellie had grabbed Jason's hand and led him upstairs. They hadn't spoken much about what was going to happen after graduation. Jason had been accepted to Wharton, so was Pennsylvania-bound. Ellie was planning a move to New York City, just a few short hours away. Both had adopted a somewhat wary, somewhat hopeful "wait and see" attitude. But tonight, Ellie felt profoundly sad. It was the end of all of this—school, with its defined schedules and expectations, falling in love with Jason and then being in love with him, the first time in her life she could really say that she was in love. Suddenly, the mature restraint with which they both had approached their imminent separation seemed ludicrous to her. She wanted to lick every inch of him. She wanted to eat him up.

As they walked into his bedroom, she was the aggressor, pushing him down on the mattress, tugging breathlessly at his clothes. Jason was receptive, a little amused, but also turned on by her urgency. The room was dark, except for the slice of yellow light that cut in from the hallway through the partially open bedroom door. Ellie paused in the light, smiling seductively down at Jason, who was lying on the bed propped up on his elbows, as she slowly, seductively unbuttoned her shirt. Just as she tugged it off and tossed it to him, they heard Doug bellowing from downstairs.

"Jason! Jason! Where are you, man?"

Ellie saw Jason's torn look. She unhooked her bra and with one swift move of her hip butted the door closed. As she turned the lock with one hand, she twirled the bra over to the bed with the other.

"You're mine tonight, baby," she said as she joined him on the bed, her long blond hair swinging, her body ripe with desire and need.

The next morning, Jason was still asleep when Ellie woke, parched with thirst and needing to pee. She hit the bathroom, grateful it was littered only with red plastic cups partially filled with stale beer. Some of their parties had seen it left awash with puke, and, on one memorable occasion, three naked, intertwined people asleep in the bathtub. She picked up the best she could, pouring beer down the sink and piling the cups. She drank from the tap, but the smell of old beer made her gag. She decided to go to the kitchen in search of juice. She made her way downstairs, picking gingerly over the debris of the party. More red plastic cups, empty liquor bottles, an overflowing ashtray, a stray shoe. When she saw Doug slumped against the wall, she thought he was asleep. Her first thought was that the weird angle of his neck was bound to be painful when he woke up. It was only upon taking a closer look that she saw the congealing blood that ran from the ragged vertical slices in his forearms, the sticky red serrated kitchen knife that lay by his limp hand. It was then that she began to scream.

It was nobody's fault, Ellie and Jason assured each other. Doug had been troubled, mentally ill. But Jason alone among all of their friends had known the trouble Doug was in, the depth of his angst. And so, the echo of Doug's anguished cries for Jason, the cries that they had heard even as Ellie had swung the door to Jason's bedroom closed, reverberated through their relationship and eventually killed it.

Now

Ellie hurries through the lobby of the little tropical hotel and out onto the sunbaked circular driveway planted with riotously colored flowers—a grandiose flourish to the otherwise simple establishment. She takes note of the idling taxi, a battered blue Volvo with one red door. She climbs in.

"Where to?" asks the driver.

"Hewanorra Airport. Please."

He flips on the meter and pulls out of the driveway. Ellie's wired, on edge. She watches palm trees flash by as well as tropical blossoms: ginger lilies, anthuriums, birds of paradise. Two grazing goats, bells around their necks, lift their heads when the taxi rattles past them. Ellie shifts uncomfortably on the hot seat of the cab. The backs of her thighs are sticky and pull away from the vinyl with a snap.

She wills herself to think, to plan. She will fly home. And then say what? She racks her brain and comes up empty. Should she go to the police? Or say nothing at all? Let the gossip mill turn? Whatever the gossips can invent would be better than the truth about Rob. But what if he *was* still alive? What if he found her after she abandoned him? What would he do then? What would his captor do when he learned she had fled? A trickle of sweat runs down between her breasts and she fans herself uselessly.

"Nice nails."

She's so lost in thought she's not even sure the driver is really talking to her.

"What?"

"I said I like your nails."

His accent is peculiar, not the lilt of the island; she can't place it.

"Oh. Thanks."

"So, he's dead."

Ellie's head jerks up. Did she actually hear that? Or was it that shape-shifting accent of his?

"What did you say?"

"He's dead, yes? Unless you left some other poor sucker in your room."

For a second the landscape blurs before her eyes. A roaring sound swirls through her brain. Breathe, she reminds herself. *Breathe.*

"Yes. He's dead."

She says it firmly but she's wary, prickling with apprehension.

"But you didn't follow directions, did you? What happened to doing it on the boat?"

"He showed up wasted. He was causing a scene. I had to make a judgment call."

"Quinn is not happy. He likes people who know how to listen. How to obey."

"I killed the guy, didn't I? I did what I was told to do."

The driver gives a dissatisfied grunt.

"So, I take it you're not driving me to the airport?" She keeps her voice steady only with effort.

"No."

"But how did you know where to find me? How did you recognize me?" She can't help herself. She blurts her confusion; her voice cracks.

He laughs, and she gets a flash of a gold tooth reflected in the rearview mirror. "Oh, little girl." His voice is full of pity.

They turn onto the main drag of the little town of Vieux Fort. It is dazzling with color and noise. Candy-colored buildings, dabbed with exuberant graffiti. Women selling fruit and vegetables, bracelets and beads, pungent spices and black lava soap, men hawking live chickens and throwing dice. Tourists threading through, sniffing, bargaining, flashing cash.

At least he took me to a town, she thinks. *He could have driven me anywhere. Done anything to me . . .*

She stops herself. If he wanted to he would have. He still could. She tries to get another glimpse of him in the rearview mirror but, sensing her scrutiny, the driver pulls his dark blue cap lower on his forehead.

His cellphone bleats and he answers, immediately switching into the particularly flavored Creole of the island.

Ellie doesn't speak Creole, but she strains to pick up words or phrases she can identify, relying on her mostly forgotten high school French. Her ears prick at the phrase "Maison Mary Ann." She knows "maison" means house and Mary Ann of course was the name of her long-dead sister. The house of Mary Ann? What could that be? What could it mean?

Gold Tooth clicks off the phone.

"What am I to do now?" she asks.

"I'm going to drop you at a hotel. The woman who runs it has a soft spot for a woman in trouble. Check in. Lay low. Stay away from cops. We'll be in touch. We'll find you when it's time."

"Time for what?"

"For whatever Quinn decides. Since you went off script, he's coming down here to deal with you himself."

He pulls over and stops the taxi. Gestures that she should get out of the cab. Points to a small hotel across the street, gaudy paint fading, with a hot-pink neon turtle above the door fizzling and half lit. The sign reads "Lou's Royal Retreat," a grandiose name for the rundown establishment. She hesitates.

"Now go. And don't get stupid and think about getting to the airport again. We have eyes everywhere."

It is only after she has stumbled from the taxi and is gasping for air on the hot, crowded street that she realizes she is trembling. From exhaustion. From fear. From a sense of helplessness so powerful, she is terrified she will never again in her life feel in control. She is stunned to discover she aches with longing for Rob. She has never been so confused. She stares down at her ridiculous nails, feeling foolish as well as unbearably afraid.

Then

Ellie had run screaming back into the hotel, imprisoned by and stumbling in the full skirts of her wedding gown, but before she encountered someone, anyone, who could help, a sinewy arm looped around her lacy waist and yanked her back outside. She felt the cold steel pressed to her throat and her voice deserted her. She stood frozen, except for the involuntary tremble that ricocheted through her body. She looked and listened intently for any sign of Rob, but it was as if the world had shrunk down to a tiny sphere consisting only of her and this wiry, powerful man with a knife.

She chanced a look at her captor. It was the tall, thin stranger she had seen in the garden with Rob. She strained away from him, forcing the cuff to slide up his arm. She made note of the tattoo peeking from the sleeve of the arm gripping her waist. The tattoo was a skeleton, grotesque limbs akimbo as if it were dancing, an arrow gripped in one bony hand.

His breath tickled her ear. "Do exactly as I tell you. Understand?"

Ellie choked out a soft "Yes."

"You are going to go back into your party. You will tell everyone that Rob has planned a surprise for you. You have come to say good night on both of your behalf, and then you are meeting him."

"Where?"

"What?"

"Where am I meeting him?"

"You two were to spend your wedding night at the St. Regis, am I right?"

Ellie nodded.

"I see no reason to change that plan. Make your goodbyes and get there as soon as you can. Or your wedding night will be the night you become a widow."

He released her then, striding swiftly toward the garden. In an instant he was swallowed by the shadows.

Ellie did as she was told. She managed to keep the smile on her face as she hugged and kissed and said "Goodbye" and "Thank you." When her father, concerned by the unexpected disappearance of the groom, asked if everything was all right, she nearly broke. Her kind dad, who had fixed so many little-girl problems, could not fix this one. For fuck's sake, she didn't even know what this one was. So she told him she loved him, and thanked him again for the wedding, hugging him tightly.

"Take care, Eleanor," he said gruffly as she released him. "All happiness to you and Rob." As her father escorted her to the waiting limousine, Ellie wondered if those were the last words she would ever hear him say.

The driver, neat and natty but for his nicotine-stained fingertips, swung open the car door and offered Ellie his arm. He settled her in, deftly arranging the billowing cloud of silk and tulle around her. His dirty fingertips on her pristine white dress should have bothered her, she noted idly. But she felt numb.

"The groom?" the driver asked, his expression carefully professional.

"Meeting us there."

They drove. The driver had the partition up. A split of champagne rested in a silver ice bucket next to a pair of long-stemmed flutes. Etta James's ode to love, "At Last," crooned through the speakers. The thrilling pulse of millions of lives vibrated outside the tinted windows. Ellie had never felt so alone.

They arrived at the St. Regis. The limo driver opened the door for her, and offered an arm to help her out. Light-headed, as if she were moving through a sticky dream, Ellie glided into the lobby, was welcomed by hotel staff and escorted to the elevator, assured by a beaming manager that "Your husband has already checked in and may I offer my congratulations! Please let us know if there is anything you need."

The elevator doors slid shut. She noticed a loose seed pearl on the bodice of her gown and plucked at it, unleashing a string of beads and sequins that bounced down the frothy waves of her dress. What was stopping her from asking for help? Surely she could have slipped the manager a note? She could still tell someone, couldn't she? A rising scream caught in her throat and stayed there as the image of Rob's bloodied face flashed through her mind. She was his lover, his bride. She would do anything to spare him pain.

She exited the elevator and slipped off her white kid-leather high heels. Her toes pinched and she wanted to feel grounded. The carpet in the hallway was plush. The walls were painted a rich orchid color; the glittering light from crystal wall sconces added romance. Antique chests displayed blooming plants. There was a hush, the quiet of money and discretion.

Ellie neared the Imperial Suite. Its blood-red doors were wide open. She paused at the lip of the doorway. Rob's confession, the one she had dismissed as a joke, echoed through her thoughts. She couldn't make sense of any of this, but at least she owed it to Rob, and to herself, to hear him out, get an explanation. She stepped into the suite.

The entryway to the suite was luxurious, ornate. A gilded table with a black marble top sat in front of a mirrored wall. Her reflection shocked her. She looked deformed. She gasped. Then she realized the huge bouquet of white roses atop the table was merging with the reflection of her wedding dress, distorting her image. She wasn't hunchbacked after all.

Panels of gold raw silk, also hung with crystal sconces, flanked the mirrored wall. The floor was highly polished marble, so much so it shimmered like ice. Ellie tentatively stepped in. The marble felt cool and slippery under her stockinged feet. There was a soft *thunk* as she dropped her wedding shoes onto the marble table.

Ellie padded into the suite's living room, every nerve on high alert. The walls were the same blood-red as the doors. The gleaming parquet floor was covered with a black-and-white geometrically patterned rug. Two large round windows had cozy window seats beneath them, heaped with pillows. A cream-colored sofa, also awash in pillows, was flanked by a cushy cream armchair with an ottoman and a pair of side chairs upholstered in soft gray velvet. An ebony coffee table was at the center of this grouping, a crystal vase overflowing with more white roses at its center.

She froze. The wiry man who had grabbed her uncoiled himself from one of the window seats. He gestured toward the bedroom. Through the open door, Ellie could see Rob, slumped on the edge of the four-poster bed, his head in his hands, red silk moiré walls shimmering behind him.

Ellie walked into the bedroom and half turned to close the door, but the wiry man shook his head.

"I would prefer we kept that open, if it's all the same to you," he reproved in a mild tone. Ellie did.

She walked to Rob and stood before him. He lifted his eyes to meet hers. The unfathomable sorrow she saw there made her heart break.

Now

The Royal St. Lucia Police are puzzled. Dead bodies show up in hotels on occasion. It is almost inevitable in a relatively poor country whose prime business is tourism. Armed robberies, drug deals gone sour, these things happen. What is puzzling the police, Detective Lucien Broussard in particular, is the peculiar detail of the missing bottom lip of this specific victim.

It isn't the "message" of any of the known local drug cartels. It was done after death, so that rules out torture. The victim in the hotel room has been identified as Carter Williamson, a local businessman. He may have, regrettably, dealt in counterfeit handbags and sunglasses, but that line of work is not often one that results in death and post-death mutilation. He was thirty-six, an American, born in Atlanta, Georgia. Williamson had been residing in St. Lucia for five years. His home, when Lucien pays a visit, proves to be a modest place, except for the expensive toys (a huge flat-screen, state-of-the-art stereo system, Jet Skis, three motorcycles; his Porsche had been recovered from the hotel's valet). Poking around the garage, Lucien spots life jackets, nautical rope, and a container of Bombardier Grease, and makes a mental note to check if Williamson owned a boat. Thinking about boats makes Lucien dwell painfully on the missing children. He's almost certain the four kids have been spirited off the island by boat (they've found no bodies on the island and airplane manifests have been checked). He prays the boys are alive, repeating their names—Pierre, Jacob, Sebastien, and now also Olivier—in an expanding litany he has offered up daily to an unhearing God since the first boy disappeared.

Williamson's girlfriend, when he tracks her down, is also surprisingly modest. An attractive but all-natural girl who works at a local dive shop, she goes by the nickname of "Cookie." Cookie seems appropriately distraught about Carter's death, has no idea why her lover had been at the Grande Sucre Hotel. She had been at a friend's birthday party the day of the murder (a boat cruise around the island where she was surrounded by eleven other women virtually every minute) and proves useless to Lucien's investigation.

A visit to Williamson's place of business is no more illuminating. His business partner—another American by the name of Pascal Jarett, a stoner type with white-boy dreads and a pierced eyebrow—opens up expansively when Lucien explains he is not interested in their counterfeit goods and will look the other way (for now) if Pascal is forthcoming with respect to the murder investigation.

While the offer certainly gets Pascal's attention, he is of little use. He and Carter had been in business together for three years. They had met in a bar six months before that. Became drinking buddies and later business partners. He confirms they have a rich business importing counterfeits (handbags, sunglasses, and the like) from China and peddling them to the gullible tourists who pour in off cruise ships daily. According to Pascal, Carter had been more or less faithful to Cookie (mostly less), but in any event the murdered man had favored the brown-skinned island girls; the idea that Carter had been found in the room of a blond American woman seems to Pascal a head-shaking mystery.

Lucien does not mention the lip; it has been Captain Bonnaire's decision not to release this salacious tidbit to the media, or anyone else for that matter. The mutilation of the dead man is strictly on a need-to-know basis. The reasoning is simple: They are hoping the culprit will reveal him- or herself, either by (and Lucien prays this will not be the case) leaving another victim, or—when they have the murderer in custody—by his or her knowledge of this private little detail.

Despite the fact that the room had been paid for by an American woman, and despite the fact that Williamson had been seen in the company of a beautiful blonde in the hotel bar before his death, Lucien does not leap to any conclusions. He's been on the force long enough not to get caught on the obvious or misled by the crumbs someone else wants him to follow.

This particular murder showed remarkable care and forethought. The bedroom and bath were wiped down, devoid of prints. The lip had been removed some time after death, which would seem to negate a crime of passion. It also created less mess. Had the murderer known the blood would cease to pump, so that the mouth, normally an area prone to heavy bleeding, would create less blood flow? But why would a killer care if the victim bled less *after* death?

The woman to whom the hotel room had been registered was one Eleanor Larrabee, of New York City, described by the hotel staff as a blonde. Unfortunately Miss Larrabee has not surfaced elsewhere on the island since Carter Williamson's body was found. By the time they were looking for her, hours had passed since the time of death. She could have flown out, or been a passenger on one of the many cruise ships that dock here each day. Eleanor Larrabee *could* be the person who stabbed Williamson to death, but nothing Lucien has been able to find out about her adds much strength to this theory. He has run her information through a contact in New York and learned that Eleanor Larrabee is a playground designer from New York, quite recently married, supposedly honeymooning in Bali. Lucien suspects identity theft, even as he flags the name with customs and immigration—if indeed the blonde is the killer at all. One has to keep an open mind. After all, a man and a blonde could end up in a hotel room for any number of reasons. More often than not, the reason isn't premeditated murder.

Then

It was night. Ellie slept peacefully, her hair spread across the pillow, her body curled into a fetal position, her breathing even and slow. Rob watched her sleep. Gently stroked a wisp of hair from her cheek. God, she was beautiful. And God, was he fucked.

He was in love with her. The thing he knew he should never have allowed had happened—he had let someone in.

Ellie sighed and turned, burrowing deeper into the bed. Rob got up and walked out of the bedroom, letting her sleep. He was resigned to sleeplessness. Try as he might, he struggled to sleep with Ellie in the bed. Years of building walls, paranoia, and necessary loneliness kept him in a state of perpetual monitoring. He was exhausted, but also used to operating on fumes.

As he poured himself a cognac, carrying it onto the small terrace of his apartment, he asked himself how he had let it all go so far.

There had been that first date. The banter that had come so easily, the sense of connection he had felt instantly with her and that had rocked him to the core. He had been so careful up until this point. He had moved frequently, blindly following Quinn's instructions about where he was supposed to go and who he was supposed to be once he got there. He never allowed any relationship to go too far, taking care of his needs, both animal and emotional, on a surface level only.

Ironically, he well knew his very distance served as catnip to some women. His refusal to allow intimacy was a siren call that only drew them deeper toward him, which more often than not resulted in anger and tears. He stoically withstood any and all such onslaughts—there was nothing he could say. These women were right—he was aloof, emotionally unavailable, unwilling or unable to let them in.

But then Ellie came along. He walked her home after that first date. Their conversation had rippled and spun, they found humor in the same things, discovered they agreed on all the important basics: Indian food, yes, indies over mainstream movies, coffee as an essential food group. Of course, even as he engaged in the data mining that is part and parcel of early dating, he was aware that he was presenting a fiction, that even to this girl with whom he connected so easily, he must never reveal who he really was. But still. There was something that linked them. By the time they had gotten back to her apartment building, he knew he didn't want to say good night.

Outside the building, she paused. "This is me."

"Really? You're an apartment building? How's that working out for you?"

Her lips quirked. "Not too bad. The tenant in 4G has an unfortunate tap dance addiction that has wreaked havoc on my parquet flooring, but other than that, my life as a building has been pretty chill."

He looked up at the rows of windows, wondered which set was

hers. Wanted more than anything to take her up to her apartment even though he knew he was fast spiraling into dangerous ground. He realized she was watching him, that delicious pink tongue once again darting out to skim her lips. *Walk away,* his brain screeched, right before he reached for her and kissed her.

The kiss was explosive. They melted into each other, lost in the thrilling new sensations of unfamiliar lips and tongues. The street faded away, the rumble of traffic disappeared, everything in the entire world narrowed down to the feel of this delicate-looking but surprisingly sturdy woman, the taste of her mouth (both sweet and salty), the brush of her blond hair against his cheek. He felt his prick grow hard and pulled away slightly so she wouldn't feel the pressure of his erection against her. To his surprise she pulled him closer, subtly shifted her body into his, let herself shift back slightly so he could tilt her head and kiss her even more deeply.

Finally, as if it had been rehearsed, they both pulled away at precisely the same moment, their breathing shaky. His hands rested lightly on her shoulders, he was unwilling to let her go.

"Well," she said. She traced the scar above his eyebrow with a fingertip.

"Exactly my thought," he replied hoarsely.

Suddenly she seemed to take stock of herself. She stepped back, slipping away from his hands.

"Look," she said, "I'm not so good at this part. I had a really nice time tonight, but I'm not going to ask you up, and I just want to be clear about that."

"I wasn't expecting to come up."

"Oh." She seemed a little disappointed.

"But I would like to see you again. Are you free tomorrow?"

The look of slight disappointment on her face transformed to a look of delight. "Yes. Yes, I am."

In the seemingly endless hours before he was to see her again, she tantalized his thoughts. Her hair, her scent, the curve of her waist.

The press of her body against his, her laugh, her clever mind. He felt light-headed with excitement when he saw her waiting outside the agreed-upon restaurant.

They ate Indian food and drank beer; conversation was effortless, the laughs plentiful. She kept surprising him. Her wit was sly, her sense of confidence palpable. She had strong opinions about current events and a real passion for her work designing playgrounds for a small firm that specialized in green construction.

At one point in the evening, as their conversation zinged and buzzed and tingled, Rob observed to Ellie that they had brain speed. Without missing a beat, she agreed, "We do, don't we?" Rob felt his shell splinter. Brain speed. His own private term for the rare instances when conversation with another person was so much on the same wavelength that all awkward pauses disappeared and the flow of words ebbed and eddied, peaked and drifted, dipped and crescendoed at an identical pace. The fact that she understood the term without explanation seemed just another example of how extraordinary their connection was. But as he relaxed with her more and more, his brain fired electric neon hazard warnings. He fought to quell them. Why wasn't he entitled to love and companionship? Why couldn't he have the things so many others took for granted?

He emerged from his thoughts to find Ellie studying him quizzically.

"Where'd you go?"

"Nowhere. I'm right here." He reached across the table and took her hand. He looked deeply into her eyes and had the sensation he was free-falling from a great height. Nothing had ever felt like this. Without another word, he signaled for the check. They left the restaurant and he put his arm around her shoulders. They fell into step with each other, as easily as if they had done it a million times before. At the corner they turned to each other and kissed. The urgency that arose in both of them was crazy—crazy good, crazy scary. By the time they were in the lobby of her building their hands were everywhere, their clothes loosening. A button popped off his shirt and landed on the tile floor with a ping.

As they pushed open the front door of her apartment after a frustrating fumble with the keys, he lifted her, and her legs wrapped around his waist, her small shoulder bag bouncing and swinging against her ass. He carried her, kissing her, not looking where he was going and not caring. The first room he found was the tiny kitchen and he sat her down on the little table. She watched him, her eyes wild, her hair mussed. She kicked off her shoes and yanked up her skirt, impatiently tearing at her tights until they puddled on the floor. Then she sat back a little, her bare legs open just a hint, her creamy white thighs an invitation.

"We need to be safe."

For a second he was bewildered. Had she somehow read his mind? Did she too know that safe was the last thing he was? But, no, she reached into her little bag, which was now on the table beside her, and pulled out a condom.

Relief flooded him. And the rush of that relief coupled with the heat of his desire left the events that followed a strange pastiche of sharp, discrete memories: the surprising sight of her strawberry-blond, neatly trimmed bush, darker than her hair color, the feel of her small breasts with their large nipples, kissing the jagged little scar that ran along her left hip, the feel of her mouth on his neck, on his belly, on his cock. How free she was with her body and with his.

Now they stood facing each other. A pause. An assessment. How far had they gone? How far were they going? She was naked; he still wore his button-down shirt. She slid it off his shoulders so they were both completely bare.

He laced his fingers through hers. Raised her hands above her head. Backed her against the wall, pinning her there, kissing her, hungry. Overpowering her, on the edge of domination, the brink of violence. He pulled away, teasing her, reassuring himself. She linked her arms around his neck. He wanted to look into her eyes, he was afraid to, he had to, he did.

She met his gaze evenly, openly. Fearlessly.

He saw intelligence and thoughtfulness, wit and spark, frank confidence and also vulnerability. The unasked but potent question: *If I let you in, will you hurt me?*

It was too much for Rob. He dived to kiss her again, then turned her to face the wall. He entered her from behind, rough. She softly bit his thumb. She boldly reached between her own legs to rub her clit as he thrust into her. Their rhythm increased. And then he was grabbing her hair when he came silently. The weeping sound, he realized, was Ellie, coming right along with him. It was sacred. It was profane. It was dirty and dangerous, wondrous and exalted.

Afterward, she took his hand and led him to her bedroom, gestured at the adjacent bathroom as if to say, "it's right there if you need it," and then took him into her bed. She fell asleep almost immediately. He lay there next to her, thinking how improbable and impossible this was, thinking that he had always believed that people are attracted to each other because they recognize each other's pain, and what did that mean about her? Because his pain was deep and wide, his past dark and ugly, and all of it tucked into a secret compartment that was rarely, if ever, opened.

So what was in her secret compartment that made her feel like home to him?

He looked at her delicate neck, crooked on a soft down pillow. So exposed. So fragile. He caressed it with his strong fingers. His large hand circled her throat. He could snap her bones. That would solve the problem, just like that. It wouldn't be the first time. He snatched his hand away, unnerved by the black smoke drifting virulently through his brain. He was a monster.

He contemplated stealing back into the kitchen, gathering his clothes, and easing away into the night. He would be quiet; she wouldn't even know he was gone until she woke.

Then he reached a tentative hand back toward her and cradled her skull gently, her silken hair and the smooth skin of her forehead, willing himself to be tender, to be loving, to be kind. She made him want to feel these things. They were desires alien to him, drawn from some murky, deep place, terrifying, thrilling. He watched the shallow rise and fall of her breasts, the ripple of her eyes beneath their almost translucent lids, the blue vein that pulsed next to her seashell of an ear. He should walk away. He knew this. He also knew that he couldn't. He wouldn't. He must. He stayed.

Now

It is a glorious day in Toronto, but as day edges into evening, the blue skies darken to gray, and an ominous bank of clouds rolls toward the city. The man, early fifties, head of thick salt-and-pepper hair, square jaw, square body, says good night to his co-workers on the Toronto Islands ferryboat for which he serves on the crew. He hunches his shoulders against the rising wind as he strides to his old Ford pickup in the dock's parking lot.

As he drives home, he reflects that life isn't too bad here in Canada. His job allows him routine and a sense of purpose while also keeping his disfigured face more or less private. He works belowdecks and doesn't come into much contact with the tourists. Even though it has been years since his disfigurement, and he has had reconstructive surgery, his mouth still curls in a perpetual sneer. He avoids his reflection.

Toronto itself is an attractive city, large enough to be anonymous, and that suits the man, fits his mood, his need for privacy. He likes his little place; he even has a patch in the shared yard where he grows tomatoes and snap peas. And although he is lonely (despite his occasional bedroom tumbles with Donna, a divorcee whom he met at the local plant nursery), he also recognizes that he has always been lonely.

The man sighs as he pulls up in front of his apartment, part of a fourplex that divides what was once a stately red brick bay-and-gable row house. He thinks about giving Donna a call. Just as he opens his car door, the skies open and plump, cold drops of rain begin to spatter. He covers his head with a newspaper and bolts for his front door. He drops the soaked newspaper on the doorstep to deal with at a later time. Stepping inside, he stoops to pick up the pile of mail that has come through the slot.

A padded envelope is among the bills and circulars. It is addressed to him in a handwriting he doesn't recognize, with a St. Lucia return address and postmark. His stomach lurches.

He takes a pair of scissors and carefully slits the envelope open, shaking the contents out on his Formica kitchen table. First, a post office box key slides out, hitting the tabletop with a metallic ping. Then a wrapped package, plastic wrap wound tightly around tissues. He ignores the key and unwraps the package. Buried inside all the protective swaddling is a severed lip.

Even with all the brutality he has seen in his life, the sight of the lip is a shock. He wraps the lip back up in its layers and shoves it into the padded envelope. He braves the rain, now turned icy and driving, to take it out to the trash bin in the alley. Back in his apartment, the man strips off his clothes. Leaves them in a wet heap on the floor. He pulls on a robe and fingers the mailbox key. Then he boots up his laptop to search for the next direct flight to St. Lucia.

Then

It was one of those days that makes New York shine. The streets were thronged with people, spring fever thrumming through their veins. Winter had held on well past her welcome this year, but today the city breathed a collective giddy sigh of relief.

The Union Square farmers' market was mobbed. Fresh vegetables, candles, soap, maple syrup, cheeses, pies, jams and jellies, eco-bags, wind chimes, and fresh flowers—it was life's rich bounty. As was the crowd. College students, young lovers, families with boisterous children, artists, that guy who is always there with his guitar. Punks and nerds, hustlers and homeless.

Ellie and Rob were walking off a late breakfast of assorted pierogi at Veselka, the twenty-four-hour Ukrainian coffee shop that had become their place, after a tequila-soaked night in the East Village had left them both ravenous at dawn. They had laughingly returned to an old debate: sauerkraut or cheese pierogi. Ellie had just proposed the Solomon's solution of a forkful that contained a bit of both when they reached the park. Rob lit a cigarette; Ellie plucked it away from him after one drag, and ground it out under her heel.

"You promised you were quitting."

"I am quitting." He smiled at her. "For you."

He tossed the pack into a trash can. Ellie grabbed his hand, leading him into the fray.

"Oooh. Look at those tomatoes!"

"There's basil too."

"I see a dinner plan forming."

"We just ate that huge breakfast."

"Are you pretending, even to yourself, that that is going to be your only meal of the day?"

"Look at those strawberries. Yum."

They made their way, loading up with produce, laughing, tasting cheese, sampling cookies. The day felt easy; everyone they encountered was in good spirits; Rob felt content. When he recognized the feeling, blood rushed into his head. He had to lay a hand on a table piled high with cucumbers to steady himself. It had been a very, very long time since he had felt content. Before his stepfather had come along.

A memory surfaced, long submerged. In the emergency room of the local hospital. Rob had been helping to groom his horse after his weekly riding lesson, learning how to use the currycomb, when something had spooked the animal. The horse bucked, and its metal horseshoe slashed Rob just above his eyebrow. An impossible amount of blood had spurted. As they waited to be seen by a doctor, Rob's mother held him on her lap and stroked his hair, murmuring her reassuring "it's all right, baby, you're going to be all right." Shock, fear, and outrage leached from Rob's body and his tears stopped. He laid his head on his mother's shoulder. Perfectly content, even as they were both spattered in his blood.

Remembering his mother knotted Rob's stomach. She had gone nuts when she realized her bastard husband was dead. She'd wailed, pummeling Rob with her fists, screeching she was going to call the cops, he was a killer, he was going to rot in hell.

Rob fled the house in shock. Not so much because he had just killed a man, but because his mother had chosen the bastard over him even in death.

He spent that first night sleeping in a park. If you could call it sleeping. It was freezing cold and he had left the house with nothing but the clothes on his back. He was covered in blood and felt conspicuous and exposed. Every bump and rustle jolted him awake. He heard sirens and was certain they were coming for him. As dawn broke, he sat up and cried, wrenching sobs that left him drained.

Finally, stony-eyed and hungry, he went over to Spencer's house. Shimmied up the drainpipe into his friend's bedroom as he had many times before. Spencer was not surprised to see him. Told Rob the police had already been there, that Spencer's father had forbidden Spencer to talk to Rob, that he was to let him know immediately if he heard from him. Rob's mom had called too, had told them that Rob was a homicidal maniac, a dangerous threat to society, that he had murdered her innocent husband in cold blood. Had blamed her injuries on Rob too, a revelation that sent a sick, icy shiver down Rob's spine.

Spencer gave Rob all the money he had ($1,586 that he had been saving toward a new guitar) and a duffel full of clothes. He believed Rob, he did, but he didn't see any way out of this other than for Rob to disappear. Rob gave his buddy a hard one-armed hug, teen boys not comfortable with physical affection. Then he pocketed the cash and hefted the duffel on his shoulder. Left his friend, his town, his life, intending never to come back.

Rob looked at Ellie, who was choosing rich orange blooms from a flower vendor. His heart clenched. What was wrong with him? Memories. Feelings. He had no place for these things. He focused on the "now," the people and challenges right in front of him. He moved from destination to destination, "project" to "project," avoiding his past as best he could. Compartmentalization was necessary for survival.

He should have just walked away, melted into the crowd, and disappeared from her life. Instead he walked over to her, dropped to one knee, and heard himself ask her to marry him.

She giggled and reached out to ruffle his hair. "Are you messing around?"

"Absolutely not."

She dropped her bundles and kneeled to face him, smiling. Around them shoppers surged and ebbed, some staring, most ignoring them.

"Was this on impulse?"

"Yes."

"Do you mean it?"

"Yes."

The smile faded from her face. Suddenly serious, she said, "Yes, then, I will marry you. I will become Mrs. Robert Beauman."

They kissed with urgency. Some passersby clapped. The guitarist hooted before breaking into a spirited version of "The Wedding March."

Now

Ellie realizes she has to pull herself together. People are staring. She had stumbled from the cab, breath short, half-expecting . . . What? A bullet to the back? All she knows now is that the merchants and shoppers, mothers and children, old men and even the wandering stray dogs seem to be staring at her in confusion. Take one step, then take another, she reminds herself. Figure out the first thing first.

There is the hotel Gold Tooth had directed her toward. She draws closer, unsteady, unsure whether she should follow his instructions, not certain what the alternative might be.

The smell hits her even before the man's presence. Pungent and ripe: sweat, dirt, salt, and ganja. The guy is impossibly huge, all muscled arms and a broad chest straining at his bright yellow Peter Tosh tank top, a knit cap in orange, red, and green crammed down on his wild and woolly hair.

"I have what you need," he says in a low tone.

"That I doubt," she retorts automatically, prepared to sidestep him. She's lived in Manhattan long enough; she knows how to evade this kind of simple menace.

He's quick though too, and falls into step beside her.

"No one on the island will give you the quality like me, pretty lady."

He flashes his wares, a sandwich bag full of reddish weed. In truth, she's tempted. She enjoys a cocktail or two but was never much of one for drugs. However, the idea of smoking or popping or even shooting something that would provide blissful vacancy from this nightmare has distinct appeal. On the other hand, she needs her wits about her.

"No, thank you."

"You change your mind, beauty, you come looking for me, Crazy B. Everybody know where to find me. Crazy B have *everything* you need." He gives her a lewd look, licks his lips.

"Not interested," she replies firmly.

The guy shrugs his massive shoulders. Nothing ventured. He bee-lines for a pasty couple in matching khaki shorts, cameras slung around their necks, fanny packs clipped around their bulging bellies. "I have what you need . . ."

Ellie crosses the street, enters the dinky hotel, and takes a swift peek over her shoulder before pulling the door closed behind her. The lobby is shabby and worn except for the spectacular and ornate gold cage that houses two fat parrots; the plaque affixed to the front of the cage announces them as "Royal" and "Ruby."

The names are apt: The parrots are majestic explosions of color—royal-blue heads that ombre into emerald-green necks and then into yellow, red, and lime-green feathered bodies and wings. The parrots are proud. They are the most beautiful things in this otherwise dingy little lobby and they know it.

There is a white rattan love seat with a couple of tropical pillows so ugly their faded condition is only a plus. A white rattan coffee table sits in front of it with a handful of flyers for taxis and snorkel rentals, Jet Skis and ATV rentals, restaurants and clubs. The lobby seems deserted, but for the parrots. Hastily, Ellie scoops up a flyer for a taxi company. She digs into her beach bag for a pen, thinking all the while of Rob's instructions. *Be clever,* he had written. *Try to leave hints about where you are and who you are with. I will find you, I promise.*

Ellie scribbles on the taxi flyer: *Blue Volvo taxi, 1 red door. Maison Mary Ann??*

She stuffs the flyer into the parrot cage, even though while doing so she feels absurd. How can this possibly help? She feels incipient despair welling in her gut, coupled with a weird desire to laugh. This is hopeless! She is well and truly fucked. She takes a few noisy breaths and tries to calm herself. Maybe if she could get some sleep? Maybe then she can figure out what to do next.

A Dutch door to the hotel office has its top half swung open. A pile of mail sits precariously on the ledge of it. Peering inside, Ellie can see the dyed blond head of an enormous woman, not only enormously fat, which she is, but also six feet tall at least. The blond hair is airily and fussily arranged, adorned with a delicate pink flower, a pretty reproach to the hamlike limbs and deep, straining gut that root this woman to the ground. The phrase "fairy giantess" pops without warning into Ellie's head. Ellie steps closer.

The fairy giantess doesn't look up, remains slumped over her untidy desk.

Ellie knocks lightly on the doorjamb. Nothing. Ellie knocks again, harder, and the pile of mail slides off the ledge of the Dutch door, skidding in every direction.

The fairy giantess jolts back abruptly, a startled look on her face, her eyes careening around madly to find the source of the interruption. It is only then that Ellie realizes the woman has been asleep.

"I'm sorry. Did I wake you? I wanted to see if there was a room available."

The fairy giantess exhales and surveys Ellie through narrowed lids.

"Not asleep." But as she says it, she wipes a string of drool from the side of her mouth with one hand and some sleep sand from her eyes with the other. "How long do you want the room for?"

"Tonight. Maybe longer."

"One twenty-five."

Ellie digs into her beach bag and pulls out her wallet. Counts the money out in cash. The hulking woman's eyes narrow again and then widen.

"Any other luggage?"

"No." Ellie pastes a persuasive smile on her face but doesn't elaborate. One thing she has learned in the last two days is that less is more when it comes to explanations. People often don't press, surprisingly, and she has come to realize that there is a kind of power in withholding. Plus, everything she says these days is a lie. And if one tells fewer lies, one is less likely to trip oneself up. Maybe that is why Rob has always been so tight-lipped about his past.

The fairy giantess hands her a key attached to a plastic fish. "Room 6."

Ellie takes the key and turns to go.

"Wait a minute!" the fat woman barks at her and Ellie nearly faints from terror. "You need to register." She pushes a dog-eared ledger book over toward Ellie. "Name and home address. And I'll need to see your passport."

Ellie hesitates, can't help the flush that spreads across her face and chest. Once again the fat woman's eyes narrow and then widen.

"It's okay, cupcake," she says. "If it's a man you're hiding from, you're good here."

Ellie stays silent. This woman could work for Quinn for all she knows. She could be one of the pairs of eyes Gold Tooth threatened were everywhere. The fairy giantess gives Ellie another appraising look and continues.

"No luggage, paying in cash, that scared rabbit look. Listen, I've been there. Husband?"

Ellie nods, and to her horror, a hot tear creeps from the corner of her eye. The fairy giantess pulls the register back toward her and slams it shut. "Never you mind, then. My name's Lou, if you need anything."

"Thank you, Lou."

Ellie turns away again. Lou calls after her, "Whatever your trouble, know it will pass. It always does." Lou's tone is genuine and unexpectedly compassionate. As Ellie makes her way down the hall to room 6, her eyes suddenly brim with tears. Her husband is missing, her entire life trashed, she has killed a man, for Christ's sake, but it is the simple (and possibly feigned?) kindness of a hulking fairy giant of a woman that finally brings down her defenses.

She turns the key in the lock and enters the room, closing and locking the door behind her. The room is surprisingly clean even if its décor is graying and faded. A so-tacky-its-funny print of leaping fish hangs brightly over the bed. Ellie flips on the ceiling fan and its breeze eddies the pale green curtains at the window.

Ellie looks out the window and down at the street. Crazy B, the drug dealer, flits from one tourist to the next, a bee scavenging flowers for pollen. Dogs loll in the hot sun, tongues spilling from their open mouths. A toddler in a bright pink sundress stumbles and falls, erupting in indignant wails as soon as her butt hits the ground. The little girl's mother scoops her up, offering soothing comfort. Ordinary life. Mocking her. Ellie draws the curtains tightly closed.

She lies down on top of the floral bedspread, and stares up at the rotating blades. *Whomp. Whomp. Whomp.* Each rotation beats a tattoo. Salty tears leak from the corners of her eyes and trickle down into the crease of her neck. She covers her burning eyes with her open palms, feeling the flutter of her eyelashes against her palms. Weariness suffuses her, a heavy, bone-deep, pervasive exhaustion. What she imagines the last conscious moments before drowning must be like. How easy it is to just give up. She surrenders herself to it. Sinks gratefully into a dreamless sleep.

Then

In the room where Ellie had dressed before the wedding, Rob popped the cork on a bottle of champagne. Ellie held two flutes at the ready. Franco's brushes and curlers still littered the dressing table. The simple white dress sprigged with yellow daisies that Ellie had worn to travel to the hotel was draped over a chair. They were remnants from before. Now it is after.

The wedding coordinator had told them they would welcome these few precious moments alone together, after the ceremony and before the reception. She was right. Ellie was grateful for the chance to commune privately and peacefully with Rob. They could hear the chatter and laughter of their guests in the ballroom trickle and swell. Rob poured them each a glass of bubbly. Ellie checked her watch. Eight more minutes to their grand entrance. She raised her glass to clink it against his.

"Let's just go," Rob said abruptly.

"It's not time yet."

"No. I mean leave. Just the two of us. Let's walk out without saying goodbye. Let's just disappear."

Ellie laughed. "My mother finally got to you, huh?" She saw the stricken look on his face. "Rob, darling, there are a hundred and eighty-seven people out there waiting to celebrate with us. We can't just walk away. Relax. The party will be fun. And then tomorrow—it's just you and me and sea and sand."

She straightened the single white rose pinned to his tuxedo lapel. Then, joking, hoping to lighten his suddenly somber mood, "I thought cold feet came before the marriage part, not the party part."

She kissed him. He lost himself in the softness of her mouth, the tenderness of her embrace. Then he pulled away.

"There are a lot of things you don't know about me—"

"I hope so." Ellie laughed. "It would be a pretty dull next fifty years if I knew everything already."

"I'm serious. I've done things."

"Okay, Mr. Mystery. What's the worst thing you've done? What are you hiding from me?"

No hesitation: "I've killed people." He gripped her forearms tightly.

Ellie's trill of amusement floated between them. "Okay, I am officially a-scared of you."

Rob didn't join in the laughter. Just caught up her hand and said softly, "So let's just go. *Now*." Ellie just blinked at him. Speechless. A question forming . . .

But then it was time. They heard the drumroll; the doors swung open.

"And now please let us welcome, for the very first time, Mr. and Mrs. Robert Beauman!"

Rob raised their clasped hands above their heads as they turned to face their guests. Ellie stared at his familiar profile. Suddenly he was a stranger.

Now

Rob emerges into consciousness, the sticky-taffy pull of the drugs he's been given slowing his reflexes, muddling his brain. Where is he? He would like to open his eyes, but it seems impossible just now. His lids are so heavy.

The air confounds him. It is hot and moist, although a soft breeze wafts, lightly scented: jasmine, roses, ocean. Ocean.

The realization of what he smells is a jolt. His eyes creak open and take in the room in which he lies. He struggles to make sense of what he's seeing. The room he sees launches from solid ground into midair, an optical illusion constructed from the confluence of glass and perfect placement on the apex of a cliff. It's spectacular. It's wildly disorienting. As if you could walk through the room and straight off the edge of the world.

The room itself is meagerly outfitted. A couple of cheap folding lounge chairs. A camping lantern. Remnants of a few hastily eaten meals. A pile of still-bagged supplies. No one is staying here long.

He pushes himself up. Winces. His body aches, sore from the beating Quinn has inflicted. Also from however his body was transported here. Where is here? He climbs stiffly to his feet and looks out the window. The vivid tropical paradise hits him like a slap.

St. Lucia? He doesn't remember traveling. The last thing he recalls is the suite at the St. Regis, watching Ellie walk away, uncertain if she would help him or leave him to his fate. Then bargaining with Quinn. Manipulating him, knowing that the surest way to get them down to the island was to tell Ellie to deviate from Quinn's plan. Rob has done everything he could think of to protect her. Has it worked? Is she here?

With stiff legs and shallow breath, Rob explores the rest of the house. Glass, steel, wood, and tile, aggressively modern in design. Empty rooms, once grand in aspiration, now looted of anything of value, defaced with graffiti, littered with broken glass, dripping with water, stinking of mold. The cold, ashy remains of a fire next to a filthy mattress in one bedroom, a nest of mice in another. But he is alone. No Ellie.

Thinking about her absence is painful. So Rob focuses on the sweet. He dives into the memory of the first time he slept with her. Not in the colloquial sense—the first time he really *slept*. It had been soon after she moved in. Accustomed to sleeping alone, Rob had found it impossible to do more than doze for a few hours when he and Ellie began spending nights together. He was always on the surface of sleep, floating, buoyant, wary, never deeply under.

The day preceding this magical night of slumber had been completely ordinary. It was a Friday. Rob had gone to work, and sure he was tracking his target, but he was also putting his fine mind to work in his cover job, juggling investments, bantering with co-workers, answering calls, shooting off emails. He felt productive, valuable, as if he belonged. The fact that he even had a target was playing in the background only.

He came home to find Ellie cooking dinner, roast chicken with rosemary and garlic, baked potatoes, sautéed spinach. She'd left work a little early to surprise him, she said. They both had been working so hard, relying too much on take-out and restaurant meals. He uncorked a bottle of light red and they chatted while she put the last touches on the meal.

Together they set the table. He lit the candles while she turned on some music. The food was delicious and homey, comfort food in the best possible way. There was a second bottle of wine and vanilla ice cream doused with limoncello for dessert. They left the dishes for the morning.

They tumbled into bed early that night, tired from their work weeks, sated with good food and wine, comfortable with each other, easy. Ellie fell asleep, instantly and deeply as she usually did. Rob watched her sleep, then felt the drowsy tug on his eyes, felt himself resisting it.

When he awoke, sun was slanting through the window. He could hear the sound of water running, the chink of china and glass, Ellie singing softly to herself as she cleaned the kitchen. Rob glanced at the clock. Just after ten—he had slept almost twelve hours! He stretched his limbs, luxuriating in how marvelously refreshed and revived he felt. Repaired. Then he walked into the kitchen and led Ellie back to bed.

Now, as he finds himself in an isolated ruin at the top of the world, he thinks about the emotions that had shadowed her eyes while he told her his history—shock, compassion, revulsion, disbelief, pain, betrayal, concern, and please God, let there also have been love, he isn't quite sure. He hopes she understands what she means to him, the change she has wrought in his miserable, corrupt soul. He hopes she has gone through with it, that she cared enough to try to save him, even as he dreads that she has, knowing what it means to cross that particular line of depravity.

He prays she will forgive him and love him, even as he prays she has walked out of the St. Regis and out of his life.

He prays she is still alive.

Then

"How come we never fight?"

"Are you complaining about that?" Rob asked with a smile.

"God, no. It's just my mother asked how we fight, said arguing well is the key to a healthy marriage, and I realized we just don't ever fight."

"Want me to pick a fight now? This street makes your ass look fat."

Ellie swatted Rob's arm playfully. "And here I thought it was an incredibly slimming street."

They had just had brunch with Ellie's parents, down from Vermont. A proper engagement ring had been purchased since the impromptu proposal in the park and Ellie's mother, Michelle, had *ooh*ed and *ahh*ed and plunged into wedding talk with a fervor that took Ellie's breath away. Her father had been quiet and gruff, but

Brian had enveloped Rob in a surprisingly warm bear hug as they said goodbye in the lobby of their hotel.

"Your parents are nice."

Ellie laughed. "You say that now; wait until Mom is in full-on wedding planner mode. I think she's been waiting for this since the day I was born, and I assure you there will come a time when we will both long to strangle her."

"I could never kill someone who loved you."

Ellie laughed again, then looked at him. He had sounded grave for a moment, as if he was saying a "real" thing. She shook off the slight unease his tone left lingering.

"You're sure there's no family you want to invite?" Ellie linked her arm through his as they continued down Park Avenue.

"I told you, there's really no one left. Just me."

"What did you do, kill them all?" Her tone was light but also probing. There was something she sensed, though she couldn't put her finger on what it was. Or why it bothered her.

Equally light, he replied, "Just the annoying ones." He turned her toward him and smiled at her full-on, looked right into her eyes. "You are my family now, darling."

She melted. This man was everything: smart, good-looking, romantic, successful. More important, he just got her.

He kissed her and they went on into their day, heading to a department store to pretend to register. Ellie marveled again at how amazing Rob was. It had been his idea to request no wedding gifts but instead donations to a foundation that helped homeless teenagers. He was giving her (and her mother) free rein on the wedding party, and lord knows, it was going to be a bash (!) but he had pointed out that between their two incomes they could buy anything they wanted. As long as he had her, he had all he needed. How could any girl not swoon over that?

The foundation had been started by a man named Matthew Walsh. Rob, who didn't talk about his family much, had spoken of Matt with genuine affection a few times. And Ellie hadn't pressed for more than Rob was willing to offer. Matt had seen something in him when he was young, Rob had said, had given him a chance when he was at his lowest.

Ellie wondered if her reluctance to push Rob more about his family history was grounded in the carefully protected secret she herself carried. Sharing should be reciprocal, and she knew she didn't push past a certain place so that he wouldn't in turn push her.

Still, she thought, as hard as she'd tried to look forward, things like her secret stained a person, they had to. She knew she hadn't escaped. She was marked; a specter of cold evil hovered over her. Could she marry this man without his knowing?

Sometimes she wondered if Rob would still love her if he knew her secret, then shoved that thought aside as fast as she could. And so, she allowed him his reserve in order to protect hers. Lovers, husbands and wives—they were allowed to have their private spaces, weren't they?

Now

Ellie wakes. The room is very dark. She's utterly disoriented. How long has she been sleeping? Where is she? Is it day or night?

Wow. She hasn't felt this rested in a long time. It's kind of a magnificent feeling. Then, as her eyes strain to discern objects in the darkness, she hears the soft *whomp, whomp, whomp* of the ceiling fan and she begins to remember. A floral bedspread. The funny print of leaping fish. The dozing fairy giantess. The parrots. Gold Tooth.

She jolts in fear, remembering him, and cracks her head on something hard. What the fuck? It is then she realizes she is standing up. Tentatively she reaches her arms out in front of her. She's shocked to feel a hard surface. Wood. Cautiously she lifts her arms above her. More wood. Her breath quickens. Is she in some kind of box? Rising panic. Is she in a coffin? She thrusts her arms out, palms squared and hard, and the front panel breaks away with a satisfying *crack*.

Ellie gasps air. It is humid, fetid. But at least she is freed. She starts to walk forward, into the shadows, toward the light, when she feels a strange, sticky pull from the base of her neck to the top of her ass. Terrified, she turns her head. Squints into the eerie darkness behind and sees her spine on display, mounted on the wood behind her, ropes of viscous blood linking her body tenuously to her bones. She opens her mouth to scream . . .

A meaty paw of a hand clamps down over Ellie's mouth. She shoots up, eyes blank with fear, to see Lou, gesturing to her to be quiet with the hand that isn't muffling Ellie's cry of surprise. The room is dazzling bright. Was she dreaming? Is she now?

"There's trouble," the fat woman whispers urgently. "Get under the bed."

Ellie shakes off the last cobweb tendrils of her sleep. She's still uncertain: Is the fairy giantess to be trusted? Or is she another puppet dancing to Quinn's commands?

Lou tugs at her. "Now! Go!"

Ellie does as she is told, slithering under the bed. There isn't time to argue or explain, ask questions or debate. Lou shoves Ellie's beach bag under the bed and Ellie clutches it to her chest. Then wills herself silent and still.

She hears the door open. She hears Lou call:

"Found the key to 6."

The giantess stands back to let in what appear to be two men, based on the shod feet Ellie can glimpse from her hiding place. Lou sits down heavily on the bed. The mattress sags low, pressing Ellie down, and she wills herself even smaller. Her heart is thundering in her chest, her fingernails bite into her skin.

"I told you. She came in but didn't have a passport. So I didn't check her in."

"When?"

Ellie recognizes the voice, the low, cultured tones of the man she saw at her wedding, the one who was calling the shots while her groom had the shit kicked out of him. The man she has come to know as Quinn.

"Not sure, exactly," says Lou. "Yesterday afternoon sometime. But you're welcome to check the rest of the hotel. I just don't want any trouble."

Lou shifts her bulk on the bed; below it, Ellie fights against the urge to cough. Once she notices it, the tickle in her throat becomes excruciating. She turns her head to peer out, hoping the twist of her neck will calm the need. Lou's heavy bare feet, solidly planted on the floor, block her view. Lou's heels are cracked and dry and red; they look painful. A shadow crosses Ellie's line of sight and there is the sound of footsteps retreating. Lou shifts her weight backward then rocks forward to hoist her bulk off the bed. The bedsprings creak loudly.

"Like I said, you can look around, but I'm telling you, she's not here."

Ellie watches Lou's feet shuffle to the door, following the intruders. She hears the scrape of the key and the satisfying *thunk* of the lock as it turns. Still, Ellie stays put, rigid with fear, breathing dust. A small hacking cough escapes her; she tries to swallow it down even as it surges in her throat.

Gradually, she relaxes, enveloped in the odor of musty, threadbare carpet. The immediate threat seems to have passed. She idly notes the ridges her fingernails have cut into her arms, the dull floral pattern of the box spring above her, the hem of the green curtains as they sway gently in the breeze.

Then she hears the key in the lock again. The door opening. Her eyes burn; her hands curl reflexively into fists.

"It's me. They're gone." The speaker is Lou.

Ellie inches her way out from under the bed. As she pulls herself up, one of her fake nails catches on the bed frame and cracks off. Ellie winces; it takes part of her real nail with it. She sucks on her finger as Lou offers her a hand up.

"How long have I been here?" Ellie is still disoriented.

"Since yesterday afternoon. I didn't hear a peep from you all night. Figured you could use the rest."

"Thank you," says Ellie.

"We girls gotta stick together."

Ellie looks up at the mountainous woman, she of the ridiculous girlish hair and the lumpy, lined face revealing she hadn't been a girl for many decades. Ellie doesn't know whether to laugh or cry. Laugh at the terrifying absurdity that has become her life or cry with relief because a stranger is showing her kindness.

Lou continues. "Do you want to talk about it?"

The last thing Ellie wants to do is talk about it. She weighs her options. Maybe she can still make it to the airport? Should she just go to the police and confess? Free herself from this nightmare, even if that means going to prison? She has been told to wait here for Quinn, but Lou has prevented him from finding her. Ellie knows enough of Quinn to know he is used to being obeyed. What will he do now that Ellie has disobeyed?

Lou settles back down on the bed, which protests under her girth. "I'll go first if you like."

"Sure. You go."

"I was pretty once, and young. And a hundred and twenty pounds soaking wet, if you can believe it now, looking at me."

Lou pauses. Her amber eyes dare Ellie to disbelieve she had once been young and beautiful. Ellie meets her gaze evenly, nods at her to continue.

"I met a man. I was only nineteen, he was forty-two. He seemed to know everything about everything—how to change a tire, wrangle free stuff from stores, tie a bow tie, play the piano. I had never been out of my hometown; he had been all over the world. I was a goner after ten minutes. Mad love. I ran away with him in the middle of the night—my mama would have never allowed it, and so I bolted. And . . . I loved him. In the beginning . . . well, it was wonderful. But then he began to clock how long I went out for, leveled crazy suspicions that I was cheating on him. One day, when I denied it, he came at me with a baseball bat."

Lou stops talking. Stares at the leaping fish as if this next part is too shameful to confess. Ellie is silent.

"I woke up the next morning. He had beaten me so bad I could barely move, but even so I was handcuffed to the bed."

Ellie doesn't speak.

"He kept me there for three years. Raped me. Starved me. Made me use a bedpan and gave me sponge baths. Used to murmur the same endearments at me whether he was fucking me, hitting me, or washing my hair." Lou laughs, a brittle sound. "Finally a UPS guy heard me moaning one day and called the cops. Saved by a man in silly brown shorts."

She studies Ellie. "I was twenty-four by then. I wanted to start over, but it was all in the news; everywhere I went I was 'that woman handcuffed to a bed for three years,' a goddamn headline, not even a person. Even worse, I became the butt of stupid jokes. So I came here, to the island. Just to get away for a time. But I found I didn't want to leave. I got a job, got fat, and eventually bought this place."

Ellie doesn't really know what to say. What can you say to someone whose life slid so spectacularly off the rails? She feels empathy, so much that it threatens to drown her. So she remains silent. Lou seems lost in her own thoughts. Finally, Ellie blurts out, "I'm sorry. It must have been awful."

Lou looks at Ellie, grateful to be pulled back from whatever dark place her mind had taken her.

"You know the worst part?" Lou continues. "I loved him. Really loved him. I still don't understand how I could have felt love that deep when all he felt was bat-shit crazy."

Ellie shakes her head. "Love doesn't make sense, does it? We fall in love with someone, and then as layers are revealed that don't line up with our feelings, we're in it already."

"So we lie to ourselves, that's what you're saying?"

"Not lie outright, I don't think. Color our perception of the flaws."

"Yeah, right—like the tiny little 'flaw' of being a rapist and torturer."

This hits a little too close to home. Ellie winces.

"You ever been really in love?" Lou asks her.

"I am in love," answers Ellie. She says it. She believes it. Maybe she doesn't, since it turns out she had no idea who Rob was. God damn it! She is furious at Rob for all his lies, even angrier with herself for being duped. If all Ellie's done wasn't for the sake of saving the man she loved, it was completely base. It was anyway—base, vile, hideous, repugnant, amoral, criminal—she knew this even while clinging to the shreds of her romantic idealism (but still, she needed something). "I am in love," she says again, with less certainty this time.

Lou sighs. "Well, that's your first mistake."

Ellie feels compelled to protest. "You don't understand—"

The giantess snorts. "Yeah, right, no one ever does. Until your nose is broke or your eye is black. But you know, I'm good now. I have friends here, a life—maybe not the life I expected, but it's okay."

"Were you ever . . . was there ever another man?"

The answer is flat, final. "Why?" A single word chiming with defiant resignation.

Lou's eyes widen as she takes Ellie's stock. "You, my poor girl, are a romantic. Even when it's clear you have some powerful trouble going on in your life. How to reconcile that? Or maybe you're just a damn fool."

Maybe she is.

The door to the room slams open.

The men holding guns are all too familiar to Ellie, the man from the wedding, Quinn, and the gold-toothed taxi driver from earlier.

Lou struggles to her feet, yelling, "Hey!"

Gold Tooth grabs a batik cushion and covers Lou's face. The barrel of his gun presses into the cushion and fires. A muffled bang.

Lou topples back, blood trickling slowly from the neat little hole in the center of her forehead. Gold Tooth drops the pillow and a few blood-smudged feathers float onto the bed. Ellie recoils from the gore of spattered brains and blood as Lou's head lurches forward. She whimpers.

Quinn smacks Ellie across the face, a sharp, stinging blow that splits her lip. She tastes blood.

"You have not followed instructions," he says, as he hits her once again.

Then

"You're still you, aren't you?"

Ellie and Rob sat across from each other on the bed in the Imperial Suite at the St. Regis. Their honeymoon suite. The complimentary bottle of champagne the hotel had provided lay sweating in a bucket of melted ice on the nightstand, untouched. "Of course I am," he answered.

Rob had just told her about killing his stepfather. He watched her face as she struggled to process. He debated continuing with his story but knew there was no time to wait. Quinn would not be a patient man tonight; Quinn never had been patient. She touched his bruised and swollen eye with her fingertip. Traced the split of his lip and the purple bruise bursting on his jaw. He thought he saw something like relief cross her face, but surely he must have misread that.

"But it was self-defense, right? And you were a minor? So what happened to you? Afterward?" Ellie's eyes were full of questions.

"Well, this is where things get tricky. Do you remember the day you took me to see your park for the first time?" Rob asked Ellie.

"Of course."

"That man outside. Spencer. He did know me." Rob continued, urgent and soft. "Do you remember after, when we went home?"

Ellie nodded. The intensity of their sex that day was something she would never forget.

"Spencer . . . he is from my life, but from a whole other life."

Rob continued his story. After leaving Spencer's, scared and certain he would be looked for at bus or train stations, Rob walked for six straight mind-numbing days before he began to hitch rides. He was too dazed to think; he just needed to move. He drifted from town to town, finally seeking anonymity in the relatively large city of Cleveland. The money Spencer had given him didn't last long. For twenty-nine months, he lived on the streets. He endured days of frigid cold and nights of icy despair, the swelter of August days when his sweat and angry tears commingled, brisk fall mornings with their promise of a change for the better (a change that never came), soft April evenings racked with loneliness. He begged for change, scrounged Dumpsters behind restaurants for food, and occasionally picked up day laborer work, welcoming the harsh soreness in his muscles that meant he was bulking up. He got beaten up twice, one a mugging right after he got paid cash for a grueling day loading bricks, the other the sport of a gang of homeless kids he looked at the wrong way. Soon after that, he picked a fight with a hopped-up crackhead that left his victim bloody and broken and left Rob both exhilarated and soul-sick.

Rob grew hard in a way he never expected, but also in a way he began to relish. For the first time, he could rely on himself. Fuck anyone and everyone else. He liked how street-smart he became. He liked also that if he cleaned up a little, he could still twist a stuffy maître d' around his little finger. He dined and dashed on a few occasions. Once, when he was caught on his way out the door, he spun a compelling tale about having been meant to meet his estranged father, who paid the bills but who had once again stood him up. The restaurant bought him his dinner that night. Emboldened by his success, he used that particular ruse a number of times, the thrill of putting the con over even more enjoyable than the delicious food it netted him. He began playing other angles. He filched clothes from expensive shops and resold them on the street, and, he admitted, hooked up with girls whom he played for a place to stay before disappearing on them, along with any cash he could wrangle and easily disposable electronics or jewelry. He blew most of the cash he netted on drugs (pharmaceuticals mostly, a callback to the days of stealing Vicodin).

Living on the streets required survival skills, and he learned them and honed them, but he had always been smart and he wanted more. He began to think he needed some way to come out of hiding and get more of a "real life," whatever the fuck that meant. His first step was to clean up. Withdrawal, well, let's not talk about it; it wasn't pretty. But when it was over, he was even more motivated to get off the streets.

He was over eighteen by now, too old for social services or youth shelters, and they asked too many questions anyway. The homeless shelters where he occasionally crashed were scary places, filled with the desperate and mentally ill, so he tried to stay away unless it was really frigid or wet outside. But on one rainy, miserable autumn night, Rob had reluctantly taken refuge at a shelter, and without warning, things suddenly shifted. There was a guy at the shelter, P.J., a little younger than Rob. Despite the fact that his parents had kicked this kid out of the house at fourteen, P.J. had a vibrancy to him, life in his eyes, swagger and hustle. They ate navy bean soup and smoked cigarettes together, swapping lies.

P.J. told Rob he knew of a place that was hiring. The work wasn't glamorous or easy; it was with a moving company. P.J. had started there a couple of months before, and the work was hard, but the pay was steady. He was hoping to have enough together to rent his own place pretty soon. The guy who owned the company had been homeless once too, and had taken it upon himself to hire homeless kids who needed a break. If Rob wanted, P.J. would take him over there tomorrow when he went to work.

Rob wanted. P.J. introduced him and Rob got a job. Cash payment. Backbreaking work, but Rob got stronger and stronger. His body transformed, he became ripped, a man, no longer a boy. Earning his own money and providing for himself made his mind and spirit stronger too. Finally he had enough money together to lease a crappy studio apartment. It was a shithole, but it was his shithole.

He and P.J. became friends. Rob liked his boss, Matthew Walsh, a no-bullshit guy with a tough exterior and a big heart. Matt didn't talk much about what his life had been like before he got to the place where he owned a business, or why he felt compelled to help the kids who were society's detritus, but he was quietly empathetic to Rob and all of his employees. Rob liked it this way. He felt understood, grateful for the opportunity, but not compelled to volunteer much information about his own life either.

Soon, the past began to fade. Rob worked hard, humping boxes and furniture. Ate a lot of ramen noodles. Occasionally, he went out with the boys from work and drank himself stupid. But not that often. He knew he couldn't really chance being stupid. P.J. hooked him up with a guy who got him a fake ID. Suddenly he was Vincent Murphy, age twenty-two. Sometimes he forgot he had ever been anyone else.

Here Rob paused. Then he confessed to Ellie this was the first of many identities he had acquired and discarded along the way before he became Rob Beauman and came to New York. He watched as the importance of this registered on Ellie. There was no Rob Beauman. The man she had married was a fiction.

Gradually, he and Matt became real friends too, if that was the right way to describe it. It was really more like Matt became his

mentor, a kind of surrogate father for the kid who had killed his surrogate father. Matt took him to ball games, they went bowling; he
treated Rob to a fancy steak dinner. Rob began to confide in Matt a
little about where he had come from (not the details of his stepfather's death or his mother's crippling insecurity, but enough that
Matt began to see Rob's intelligence and potential). As their relationship grew, Rob also confided he had dreams. Plans. Matt told
Rob he saw a bit of himself in him. If he had done it, escaped the
streets, so could Rob. Rob began to think he might be able to build a
life worth living.

One day he got a call from Matt to come in early; there was something he wanted to talk about. Matt sounded serious and Rob was
nervous. He racked his brain. Had he fucked something up? Was he
getting fired? His heart raced as he entered through the moving office's loading bay. The place was shadowy and quiet. He made his
way back to Matt's office.

A tall man, very pale, leaned casually against Matt's battered
desk. Gaunt but ropy, with the coiled energy of a snake. Close-
cropped hair. Powerful hands. Rob could see the hint of a tattoo, two
bony skeleton feet on his inner wrist, emerging from the cuff of his
butter-soft leather jacket. The stranger's eyes were so dark they
looked black; if eyes were the windows to the soul, this man had sold
his soul to the devil for chump change a long time ago.

He introduced himself as Quinn, Rob told Ellie, with an acknowledging nod at the man hovering just a few feet away from the
bedroom suite in which they now sat.

Matt was behind his desk, his usual easygoing demeanor gone; he
rocked in his swivel chair and drummed nervously on its arm with a
pencil.

Rob looked back and forth between the two men, waiting, on
edge. Finally the tall man began to speak.

He told Rob that he had been looking for him for a long time.
Then he proceeded to recount details about Rob's past life: the name

of his grandparents' estate, the names of the elite schools Rob had attended prior to his stepfather's "unfortunate death."

Rob listened, shock radiating through his body. He had thought this past dead and buried, any connective tissue to his old life ruthlessly snipped. He had not used his real name for years. He was physically transformed; a muscular young man had replaced the scrawny teen. He had bleached his hair and grown a goatee. He had tried to make himself into a new person; he believed he had succeeded.

In his calm, controlled voice, Quinn explained the reason for his search. "I know this will come as a shock, but I'm your father, your biological father."

Shock was an understatement. Rob had of course spun numerous fantasies about his biological father (what fatherless boy doesn't?), daydreams in which his father was a CIA operative or a race car driver or a rock star. But this stranger emanated danger, the thin-skinned threat of effortlessly ignited violence Rob recognized instantly from having lived with his stepfather all those years.

Matt interjected, asking Rob if anything this man said rang true.

Rob swallowed nervously; he couldn't speak. The information was all correct. Could this man be his father? What did it mean if he was? Quinn hadn't directly said that Rob's stepfather had died at his hand, but he had danced close enough to the edge. Something in his eyes when he spoke about it (a hint of merriment perhaps?) made Rob fearful.

What did this man know? What did he want? How had he found him? Why now? Rob cast an uneasy glance at Matt. He wanted to keep his job; he wanted Matt to like him. What would Matt do if he learned Rob was a wanted man?

As if he had heard the questions Rob was too stunned to ask, Quinn continued. He had always wanted to know his son, he said. Rob's mother's family had put a stop to his attempts. But after Rob had disappeared, Quinn no longer had to breach that gate.

"How did you find me?" Rob demanded.

"I have resources" was Quinn's reply. Quinn smiled, but it was not a smile that reached his eyes.

There was an uneasy silence as Rob struggled to absorb this. Matt placed himself protectively between Rob and Quinn and suggested that Quinn leave his number and give Rob a little time to think things through.

Quinn replied that that was not an option. He wanted his son to come with him now. Hearing the word "son" sent Rob's stomach lurching. Matt settled his bulky body more firmly in front of Rob. Once again he suggested Quinn leave.

Then Quinn casually shrugged off his soft leather jacket. He moved swiftly, a hard sucker punch into Matt's gut that sent him reeling. Matt cried out in pain and toppled back into his chair, his hands clasped protectively, tears streaming. Quinn seized a box cutter, then tipped back Matt's head. Matt's wail of shock and agony as Quinn sliced off his lower lip echoed in the cavernous space.

Rob stopped here and took a breath, needing to see how Ellie was taking this. She averted her eyes, wouldn't look at him.

"Ellie, it's been agonizing, having secrets from you, that's why I started telling you—"

Ellie interrupted, angry. "You think casually mentioning you've killed people in the *middle* of our *wedding* was the way to handle this?"

"Please try to understand. When it all went down, when I left home, Spencer—he was the only person who had believed me and helped me and I had to walk away and pretend I didn't know him. It was a wake-up call. I knew then that I needed to tell you the truth. You've healed me, Ellie. Changed me. But I was so scared of losing you."

Now she looked at him and he could see fear, even disgust in her eyes, but yes, also the desire to understand. Or in his desperation was he imagining that?

In a tight voice she asked: "But I take it the story doesn't end there? In a moving company office in Cleveland?"

"No. But before I continue, I ask you to have compassion for the boy I was, and also ask if you can somehow keep that compassion for the man I became." She gestured, a noncommittal shrug. She would try, no promises.

Then his new bride took a long shaky breath and said: "What's your real name?"

Now

Poor Lou. A first love corrupted by insanity and violence. Then public humiliation. Followed by a retreat—not only from the world she had known, but also from her brutally betrayed, lithe young body. Peace, finally, in a wallow of fat and obscurity—only to have her brains blown out by a sadistic fuck. Poor Lou.

Ellie aches with sadness. And resigned helplessness about her own fate. Quinn and Gold Tooth hustle her out of the hotel, Gold Tooth's gun jammed into the small of her back. Ellie clutches her beach bag protectively in front of her chest. She expects she will die soon. Also that it won't be swift or easy.

But life goes on out here in the streets of Vieux Fort. The street is throbbing with tourists and vendors; reggae music blasts from a bar a few doors down. Piquant chicken spits and hisses on a barbecue. The smell of the food brings a sudden rush of saliva to Ellie's mouth.

Ellie spies Crazy B hawking his wares to a young couple with rucksacks.

"Hey, B, Crazy B! I changed my mind!" she calls to him impulsively.

The drug dealer pivots, a broad smile lighting up his face. "Beauty! Whatever you want."

"Shut up," Gold Tooth hisses in Ellie's ear.

"Going to shoot me in the middle of the street?" she hisses back. Then, louder, to the dealer, "Let's you and me go somewhere together."

"You got it, beauty." Crazy B sidles over to her, all sweat and muscle, his forehead creasing as he notes the blood trickling from the side of Ellie's mouth. He looms over Gold Tooth.

Gold Tooth flashes enough of his gun to make a point.

Crazy B just smiles broader. With a tug of his tie-dyed T-shirt he reveals the automatic weapon shoved into his waistband. "The lady wants to come with me." The island lilt in his voice makes him sound sweet, despite the madhouse glint in his eyes.

Ellie glides away from Gold Tooth and toward Crazy B's outstretched arm.

Gold Tooth glances at his own single-round handgun and then at Quinn, panicked.

Quinn's hand reaches into his pocket. "The girl has nothing to do with you."

"Like I said," Crazy B insists, "Beauty wants to come with me."

Quinn glances around at the crowded street. Back at Crazy B. Quinn's bony face looks skeletal; his skin goes paper white. "Let's go," he murmurs to Gold Tooth. Then to Ellie, "We'll catch you later. Count on it."

Gold Tooth hurries into the driver's seat. Quinn slides in next to him and the Volvo churns to life.

As Ellie turns to face her savior, dread rises in her throat. Crazy B's eyes are bloodshot; a wild heat spirals off his muscular body.

Has she jumped from the proverbial frying pan into the weed-reeking fire?

Then

Was this terrifying stranger his father? Rob got into Quinn's car and drove away with him, insisting he call 911 for Matt. Quinn seemed amused by this gesture but allowed it. Then he tossed Rob's cellphone out the car window.

Quinn changed clothes in a rest stop bathroom, discarding the clothes still damp with Matt's blood into a Dumpster. He kept Rob with him all the while but didn't initiate conversation. They went to the airport, and traveled first class to Miami.

Quinn's behavior on the flight gave no clue about the horrific act he had just committed. He sipped the proffered champagne, flirted with the flight attendant, made observations about fellow passengers to Rob. When they landed, a chauffeured car awaited them. They were driven to a modern beachside mansion, with floor-to-ceiling windows overlooking the ocean. The décor was black and white and steel gray, with a few splashes of startling red (the kitchen counter, a patterned area rug in the dining room, an enormous abstract painting that swallowed up most of one wall). Rob was burning with questions and Quinn gradually doled out answers.

Quinn had loved Rob's mother, and she had loved him, but her uptight WASP parents were never going to accept a man of Quinn's type. What type was that? Rob wanted to know.

Quinn took the long road in answering this question. His origins had been impoverished, his upbringing lonely and insecure. He was working as an errand boy for a drug dealer by the time he was ten, dropped out of school at fourteen. He moved up in the ranks, started side businesses that flourished. At twenty-four he met Rob's mother, a college senior from Bryn Mawr down in Miami for spring break. A year later she had Rob, at which point her parents got involved, separating them with an iron hand. He tried to see her, tried to see his young son, but was thwarted at every turn and eventually gave up. Until he heard that Rob had been accused of murder and had disappeared. Then Quinn had started looking for him.

It was a time for fresh starts for both of them, Quinn insisted. Rob gathered his courage to ask about Matt. Why had he, you know, felt it necessary . . . ? To his astonishment, Quinn hugged him. He had waited long enough to know his son, he answered simply. He added nothing more.

The next few days passed like a dream. There were girls in neon bikinis, lavish meals prepared by Quinn's private chef, the ocean and the pool and the hot tub. The spectacular sunsets: crimson, gold, and magenta, palm trees silhouetted against the exploding sky. Quinn came home with gifts for Rob: new clothes and shoes, an expensive watch. He had a girl come to cut Rob's hair and shave off his goatee, an old-fashioned shave with a straight-edge razor. There were drugs, and Rob couldn't help himself, one bump of coke leading to another. Rob wasn't a prisoner, not exactly, but Quinn seemed to travel with a posse and one of his men was always visible a few feet away.

Just as Rob had compartmentalized his life into neat, hermetic compartments in the past (one, before his stepfather; two, after the abuse started; three, after Rob killed the bastard and was homeless and friendless; four, working for Matt), he now allowed himself to pretend this new phase was all he had ever known. Why not? The living was easy, the best he had had since the long-ago compartment number one.

He surfed the Internet looking for information about Matt Walsh. No obituary, no crime reports. It suited him to believe Matt was fine and so he did. He had plentiful food and a comfortable bed, all the material comforts he could desire. He had the father he had never known. He had what he had always wanted.

Quinn was casually frank about the illegal nature of his businesses, and even though Rob was on the alert for it, he didn't see another incident where a trickle of menace spiraled into a flash flood of violence. So what if his father was a criminal? Rob asked himself. His stepfather had been a card-carrying Republican, a respected and respectable member of the country club set, and he had been an abusive monster. Who was Rob to judge? People did what they needed to do to survive.

Days drifted into weeks. And then one morning, as a thunderstorm raged outside the windows, Quinn told Rob he wanted to put him to work.

Quinn had a job for Rob that would play to his particular skills. Surprised, Rob asked what Quinn thought those skills were. Quinn painted a flattering picture. Rob was special. Intelligent, but more important, both street-smart and society-smart; he had the healthy all-American good looks that opened doors. He had charm and he had hustle. He could think on his feet and had quick reflexes. Here Quinn tossed a beer bottle at him. Rob snatched it midair and Quinn smiled.

Rob felt a swagger flood his bones. This was more like it. This was who he was.

The first job was easy: checking into a swank hotel and leaving behind a satchel when he checked out. In fact, Rob felt a little deflated afterward. Sure, he engendered respect from the hotel staff when he checked in with his hip clothes, Louis Vuitton suitcase, and twenty-dollar tips. But how was this using what was special about him?

Quinn sensed Rob's disappointment and teased Rob that he had to walk before he could run. Rob realized this was his first ever father/son pep talk.

There were more simple drops. Then Rob was brought in on a meeting regarding Quinn's pipeline for smuggling counterfeit designer goods. Soon he was handling some meets all on his own. Cash drops. Drug pickups. A cache of guns.

He was also hitting the clubs. Young, good-looking, and moneyed in Miami, what else would he do? He met a girl one night, a fun girl, Cuban American, Solana. Her name meant sunshine, she told him. They danced a little, kissed a little. Rob had to step out to the parking lot to meet a guy. He told Solana he'd be right back.

From the moment he saw the guy, Rob sensed trouble. He was high on meth, for one thing, cagy about the fact that his payment was light. They were getting into it, standing by the open trunk of Rob's car, when Solana, tipsy and flirtatious, teetered into the exchange on her canary-yellow stiletto sandals.

It was all so fast—the guy had a gun in her face, he was twitchy and shouting and shaking. Rob grabbed the tire iron in his open trunk and smashed it into the guy's head. The gun clattered to the pavement. Solana stared at Rob in horror as the meth head slumped to the parking lot pavement and blood spattered her strappy yellow shoes and her perky toes with their optimistic poppy-colored nail polish. She began to cry.

Killing the meth head was a rush. It was terrifying. It was thrilling and awful, empowering and dreadful. It felt like his destiny.

Quinn cleaned things up. Gave Solana a few grand to keep her mouth shut, got rid of the corpse. Quinn seemed proud, like Rob had popped his cherry. And so began Rob's lessons. His induction into Quinn's world.

Now

Ellie desperately assesses what she knows. Maison Mary Ann. It's really the only clue she has. And where she has directed Matt Walsh to find her, in the note left at Lou's.

Ellie lays out a proposal to Crazy B boldly, spinning the shiny threads of fiction as fast as she can invent them. She had come to St. Lucia to make a major drug buy, she tells him. The losers he scared away ripped her off. But she knows where the drugs are, and also the hundred grand they have taken from her. The dealer's eyes widen at the mention of the number and Ellie knows she's got him on the hook. If he will help her find the place, she continues, share his local knowledge, she will make it well worth his while. He's already seen the men she's dealing with are pussies. The two of them will be able to take back the money *and* score the drugs.

He seems all in until she mentions Maison Mary Ann.

"No, no, no," he mutters. Ellie has to jog to keep up with his long strides as he hurries away from her.

"Please," she says, putting her hand on his arm. "Why not? Tell me."

Crazy B pivots and stops. He had known Marianne; she had gone to school with his sister. She had been a stunning girl, full of life, blessed with the warmest heart. But then seduced by a rich American and murdered by his jealous wife. Who then killed her husband and herself! Now Marianne is a tortured soul, haunting that twisted place, searching for her lost lover. Strange things happen to the people who dare to go there. There is no way he will.

Ellie digs into her beach tote and counts out ten crisp American hundred-dollar bills.

Crazy B stares at the money, torn but tempted.

"This is just a down payment," she promises. "We'll split the money and drugs fifty-fifty."

Later. The siren call of cash successful, Ellie clings to Crazy B's broad back for dear life, as his battered motorcycle wends its way up the one famously bad road that encircles all of St. Lucia. He turns off this main road onto a new one, which is in an even sorrier state. The bike shudders up the rutted, winding dirt path, hitting rocks, lurching into potholes. Glimpses of the ocean flash in and out of view as they climb higher and higher. In the distance, Ellie can see the Pitons, the two huge outcroppings featured in virtually every St. Lucia promotional photo, stunning in their abrupt rise from the sea. The sky is sapphire blue and cloudless, the sun hot; a sultry breeze perfumes the air. Another fucking day in paradise.

Abruptly, Crazy B pulls the bike off to the side of the road. They seem to be in the middle of nowhere. Ellie shivers with panic. Her body will never be found here.

But Crazy B tilts a crooked smile at her as he dismounts. "We best walk from here," he intones, as he gestures up the hill. "So they don't hear us coming."

Crazy B parks the machine off the path. Makes sure it's hidden by foliage. The sun beats down on them as they creep around the next bend. A wrought-iron gate half off its hinges creaks open into a long crushed-shell driveway.

Crazy B stops at the gate. "Maybe I leave you here." His huge body seems to shrink in his fear of the place.

Ellie pretends a nonchalance she doesn't feel. "If that's what you want. The money and the drugs, though, they're all mine, then."

Crazy B hesitates. Then murmurs a prayer and crosses through the gate. They trudge up the driveway without speaking, the crushed shells crunching beneath their feet. As they go, Ellie wonders if she should have let him leave. After all, who is to say he is less of a danger than Quinn and Gold Tooth? Her mind races. She's anxious; face it, she's terrified. Of both the known and the unknown. Operating on instincts that she's not at all sure she can trust.

A massive house with soaring arches and vast planes of glass looms into view. It's perched on what looks like the edge of the world, positioned to best exploit the view, designed to look as if it is soaring off the cliff and about to take flight. The vista is shockingly beautiful: dramatic mountains, lush green tropical plants, drooping flowers like yellow bells, hot-pink blooms, the deep blue ocean meeting the horizon of the pale blue sky. A covered porch encircles the house, empty of furniture except for one weather-beaten teak deck chair, snapped in half.

A majestic marble fountain sits smack in the center of the circular drive. The fountain is dry.

Ellie scans the house. There don't seem to be any signs of life. No cars in the driveway. It looks like the abandoned house Crazy B described. She fights back tears. What if she is wrong? What if her overheard reference to Maison Mary Ann meant nothing? What if she heard wrong?

She reassures herself that at a minimum it's the clue she has left for Rob's trusted friend Matt Walsh. Walsh will find her here. If he's coming. If he's smart enough to retrace her steps and decipher the scribble left for him. Despair overwhelms her. She has done everything exactly as Rob had instructed. Ignored Quinn's instructions to get Carter out on his boat and kill him there, tipping the body overboard. Left him in a high-end hotel where he would be found, so that the police would be looking for her. Sliced off his fucking lip, for Christ's sake. She shuddered. Barbaric. Mailed it to Walsh, her supposed savior. Changed her look and tried to hide until Walsh arrived. And all of it was futile. An innocent woman who had tried to help her was dead. Walsh could be a phantom.

What will she do when Crazy B wants his piece of the $100K she has promised but can't deliver? Why on earth did she think it was a good idea to use false assurances to enlist an armed drug dealer? It was the only alternative that occurred to her, but now she berates herself. She is a fool.

Panic swamps her. And fury at Rob. This is all his fault.

Crazy B shifts from side to side, uneasy. "What do we do now?" His eyes dart to the colossal house, and Ellie follows his gaze.

She sees a shadow cross one of the upstairs windows. Someone is here. Crazy B sees it too. He bounces back and forth on his heels, skittish. "We best be going. No one here but that ghost."

With a conviction in her voice that masks her deepening well of uncertainty, Ellie decides, "No. We wait."

Then

The first time Ellie killed someone she was twenty-three. She didn't actually kill him, although the coma was likely to be permanent, and so he was really as good as dead, wasn't he? He would never again walk or talk, fight or laugh, love or hate. He lay suspended, not really dead and never really alive, maintained by complicated machines that inflated his lungs and pumped his heart. His parents couldn't let him go, even after the doctors had strongly advised turning off the life support.

Of course she hadn't meant to kill him. She hadn't even meant to put him in a coma. It was all a horrible accident. That's what everyone said—"a horrible accident," as if those words could explain away the fear, rage, and remorse that tormented her still, all these years later. When she didn't keep all those emotions in a little box, tucked away in a corner of her mind, a box that rarely opened. Everyone said that she was not to blame, but she knew it was her hand that had pushed him.

When Jason had shown up at her apartment, she had been surprised—first that he was there at all, and second that he was very drunk. It was two years after they had broken up and they hadn't been in touch. Or at least Jason hadn't been in touch with Ellie. She had sent him Christmas cards, and an ecard on his last birthday; he replied to none of them. Ellie had decided, finally, to let it go. There was the occasional wishful thinking on her part—the "what if" game she played with herself late at night after she burrowed into loneliness. "What if" Doug hadn't killed himself? "What if" Ellie had let Jason go to him that night when he called instead of slamming the door shut? "What if" she and Jason had been able to move past what happened to Doug and continue on with their relationship? Would they be married? Would she be happy?

She liked living in Manhattan and was building a community of friends, shaping her career, doing all the things she was meant to be doing, but there remained a hollow space in her. She missed being in love. She liked the automatic status a boyfriend gave her, the steady movie-night date, the regular sex, the sense of certainty that walking in anywhere with a handsome man provided. She dated sporadically, sure; as a young beautiful blonde in New York she had a plethora of suitors, but she hadn't clicked with anyone the way she had with Jason.

Sometimes she got angry. Angry at Doug, that selfish, stupid weakling who through the narcissism of his suicide had destroyed her first love. Sometimes she got angry at Jason. When he had to choose between Doug and Ellie, he'd chosen Doug, the freaking dead guy! Over her, a live, loving woman. Mostly, this anger stayed buried, rising up in a crushing red tide only after a deep loneliness hit. Then, weeping and inconsolable, she would beat her pillows or smash a plate, one time stepping on a leftover shard the next morning and ending up in the emergency room with four stitches in the ball of her left foot.

But the day Jason showed up, two years later, stinking drunk and wholly unexpected, Ellie was cheerful. She'd come back from a run, feeling invigorated. It was a clear autumn day, crisp and golden. She planned to make soup and as she sprinted up the steps to her apartment, she thought with pleasure of the onions, carrots, and celery that needed chopping, the beans that had soaked overnight, the organic chicken she had splurged on, the fragrant fresh herbs that lay waiting. It seemed a very grown-up thing to do, cooking soup. She planned to make a big pot and eat it all week, adding noodles one night, maybe rice the next.

When she reached her floor, she saw the hunched body in front of her apartment door and instantly turned wary. Had some homeless person gotten into the building? An addict? But as she cautiously neared the huddled form, she recognized something in the shape of the hand cradling the man's forehead.

He looked up when he heard her and she could see that he had been crying. His clothes stank of alcohol. His eyes were bloodshot, his nose dripped. He wiped the snot on his sleeve as she approached, sending another waft of whiskey in her direction.

"Jason! What are you doing here? What's wrong?"

He hauled himself unsteadily to his feet. "I needed to see you, El."

Her heart surged, she felt her face go hot. Was this the moment she had been dreaming of? The day Jason realized, declared his love for her, came back? She was suddenly and painfully aware of her sweaty running clothes and flushed face.

"Of course," she said. She stepped past him and unlocked the door. "Come on in."

Once inside, Ellie cast a quick look around and was pleased with what she saw. She had created a warm, welcoming home out of her little apartment. She sat Jason down at one of the two chairs flanking the café table in her tiny kitchen. She gave him a glass of water and a box of tissues. She excused herself and went into the bathroom, where she splashed cold water on her face and combed her hair. She studied her reflection in the mirror and added a quick slash of lip gloss. No time to shower and change, but at least she looked more presentable.

In the kitchen, Jason had drained his water glass. He held the glass out for a refill.

She was determined to let him guide whatever conversation they were about to have. To keep her nerves under control, she set about her plan to make soup, pulling the cutting board from the drainer by the sink, taking the carrots and celery from the refrigerator. She allowed herself a small smile as she decided to wait on the onions, too pungent for the tantalizing scent of romance and reunion she felt in the air. Then she set to work on the celery, chopping and dicing in a smooth, methodical rhythm.

"When did you get to New York?" she asked as he continued to look off into some distant place.

"I've been here a couple of days."

"So what is it that's brought you to town?" She kept her tone light.

Jason mumbled something.

"You're meeting who?" she asked, confused.

Finally he looked at her. "My fiancée's family."

Fiancée. He had to be kidding. This was not how this was supposed to go. And if he had a fiancée, what was he doing showing up at her place unannounced?

Still, Ellie kept it light. "Well. Congratulations. But if that's what you're doing here, then what are you doing *here*?"

"I wanted to talk to you about Douglas."

"What is there to talk about, Jason? We've gone around and around this a hundred times. You're not responsible. I'm not responsible. The stupid fool killed himself! And over what? One failing grade in college? Frankly, I never even understood why you two were such great friends."

Another mumble. Ellie's patience was eroding. "What is it you are trying to say?"

This time Jason said it loud and clear. "We were lovers. Doug and I. That's why he killed himself."

"What are you talking about? You're not gay." Ellie gripped the handle of her knife so hard her knuckles ached.

"No, I mean, I don't know . . ."

"You have a fiancée." She said it as a statement of fact. Then, "A woman?"

"Yes, a woman. Olivia."

"And does she know?"

"She knows I . . . experimented. So has she. She doesn't think it means anything." Jason grimaced. "She doesn't know it was Doug. That he was the 'dead best friend' and the 'male lover.' She thinks it was nothing."

"But it was . . . something?"

Jason was silent. Ellie stared at him. He had put on a little weight; it suited him. He looked less the boy and more the man. Jason looked quickly at her, then down at the table. He began to run his thumb across the grain, and Ellie suppressed an involuntary shudder of, what?—lust? revulsion?—as she suddenly remembered him running his thumb down her naked spine in the same manner.

"It was everything."

He said it simply and quietly and Ellie felt a chasm crack open deep inside. She had long suspected something ugly about herself. This admission confirmed her worst fears.

"Everything? What the fuck do you mean it was everything?"

"I was in love with him."

"So you were sleeping with Doug while you were sleeping with me?"

Jason gave a guilty nod.

"The whole time we were together?" She couldn't help the shrillness that crept into her voice.

"Even before."

"Oh. And how do you think your betrothed will feel about all this? Or don't you intend to tell her?"

"Ellie, I just want to make sense of it . . . Things seemed simpler then . . . and—"

"And what? You lied to me! To yourself! And now you want to lie to what's-her-name, Olivia? For pity's sake, if you're gay, you're gay. Live your life."

"I don't know what I am. Doug's the only man I was ever with . . ."

"So what the fuck are you doing *here*, Jason? You're engaged to another woman, to whom you haven't come clean, but you dropped by to—what? Humiliate me? Get some kind of absolution? What is your point?"

"I don't know . . ." He looked genuinely miserable, and for a brief second Ellie almost felt sorry for him. Almost. "I don't want to live a lie anymore. We were together, the three of us—"

"No! Let's be clear. The only person in a threesome was you. And the only one in the dark was me! I was the stupid idiot who was the butt of the joke! Did you and Doug laugh at me together?"

"It wasn't like that!"

"No? Go fuck yourself."

Ellie felt rage rise like bile in her throat. The first time in her life she had thought she was in love and it was all bullshit. She felt nauseous as she realized he *had* picked Doug over her—just way before she thought. Even sicker, as she realized the depth and breadth of her own stupid self-deception.

"I think you ought to go."

"Ellie . . ."

"What do you want from me? I loved you! I've never loved anyone else. And you decide that you want to 'come clean'? Why? So you feel better and I feel like shit?"

"You loved him too—" Jason staggered to his feet.

"I didn't! I never did! He was your best friend, so I accepted him . . . Get out, Jason! I can't stand the sight of you—"

"I want you to understand . . . I cared about you too, Ellie, I really did—"

"If you had cared about me, you wouldn't have lied to me. You wouldn't have started up with me when you were already fucking Doug."

Jason began to snivel. "I'm so messed up!"

"Well, don't look at me. I have nothing to offer you. Get out!"

Jason didn't move. Something in Ellie snapped. "Go! Go ask your precious fiancée for understanding! See if she can help."

Jason just stood there, limp and sobbing.

"Oh, I see. You're not going to tell her. You're confessing to me so you don't have to. What a fucking coward you are! If you have any feelings for this girl, tell her. Don't destroy her down the road, when you suddenly decide to live in truth. Don't do to her what you did to me."

She shoved him.

"Ellie, come on, just let me talk to you—"

"No!" She pushed him again.

The tip of her knife nicked his jaw. She hadn't even realized she still gripped it. He touched the blood on his chin in wonder, then stretched his glistening fingertips toward her, grabbing at her T-shirt.

"But Ellie, I need you to—"

"It's too late, Jason! There's nothing I can give you. Go! Just go, goddamn it!"

And then it all got crazy. She stormed past him, elbowing him aside, sick of the sight of him. She flung open the front door, kept shoving him back toward it, desperate to be rid of him. Finally, in the doorway, Jason dropped to his knees, scrabbling at her, trying to grasp her around the waist. Struggling to get away, Ellie pitched right over him and fell. Face planted. She felt her nose erupt in blood. She dropped the knife and swiped at the blood. She tried to crawl down the hallway, away from him, but Jason pulled her back, her cheek scraping along the carpeting. He kept bleating her name.

"Stop! Let me go!" She grabbed for the knife and he did too. In the struggle her hip was sliced. Blossomed a crescent moon of blood.

She tore away from his grasp and scrambled to her feet. He grabbed at her again. Ellie shoved him, frantic to be away from him.

"Stop it! Leave me alone!"

"What the devil's going on?" A neighbor appeared on the stairway, peering up, frowning.

Jason turned, lurched toward her. When Ellie remembered it later, she was never quite sure if she had pushed him, just a little, or if he had simply lost his footing before he pitched down the stairs. Ellie's neighbor jumped back to avoid him as he tumbled. There was a hollow, reverberant *crack*.

"Oh my God. Oh my God. What happened?" Jason's body lay sprawled at the foot of the stairs. The neighbor's face was ashen. "Are you okay?"

Ellie burst into tears. Even as she did, though, a small, private part of her brain began to spin. She felt both in the moment and—bizarrely—like she was watching herself from a distance. Her hysterical sobbing was real, but so was her spiraling sense of guilt and fear. She stared down at Jason's motionless body. She had done that. This was her fault. "My ex showed up drunk . . . attacked me . . . call 911."

Ellie told the police, Jason's parents, her neighbor, and all her friends the identical story. That Jason had shown up uninvited, clearly wasted. That she had given him some water and tried to send him on his way. But he had insisted on his love for her, swore to her that he was engaged but had realized it was the biggest mistake of his life. That he wanted her back. When she'd told him she had moved on in her life, he had become enraged. He had attacked her. She'd acted in pure self-defense, and was devastated by the entire encounter. She adopted a pious tone at this point in the story. Of course she had loved him, once, long ago. But they were just kids at the time. It was so tragic that he turned to violence when she rebuffed him.

Jason's blood alcohol level bore out her story. As did the snippet of their exchange the neighbor had witnessed—Jason pursuing Ellie, her pleading with him to leave her alone. And there was Ellie's broken nose and bruised face, the knife wound along the curve of her hip, his bloody prints on her shirt. Ironically, even Jason's fiancée's story contributed to the picture Ellie painted: Jason had called Olivia, drunk and incoherent, to tell her he would be late meeting her, that he had unfinished business with an old friend, but there was a darkness in his tone that she had never heard before, one that had frightened her.

Ellie began to believe her own fabrications. She shut down the truth about Jason and Doug, the deception and betrayal.

But she knew it was a small, leaking poison in her, this secret. The bitter shame, the horror of its ending, the pride-salving, ugly lies, all seeped and festered deep in her soul.

Now

Detective Lucien Broussard is not happy. Two murders in two days. Both expat Americans, although Lucien is hard-pressed to find a single connection between them. He reviews what he knows about Louise Butler. She was sixty-three years old at the time of her unfortunate acquaintance with a bullet. She had been a resident of St. Lucia for almost forty years and had owned and operated her small hotel in Vieux Fort for thirty. Lucien studies the pictures of the beautiful young waif that Louise had been, photographs a quick Internet search has turned up in connection with her abduction back in the States years ago. He finds them hard to reconcile with the bloated mountain of flesh he has just seen. Time can be cruel.

Two murdered Americans in two days, even if they were residents of the island and not tourists. Incredibly bad for business. Bonnaire is rabid; Lucien has to come up with some answers soon.

One killed with a knife, one with a gun. One mutilated after death, the other not. One murdered in a luxury hotel that ran along the most exclusive stretch of beach on the island, the other in a dumpy bed-and-breakfast in the small town of Vieux Fort. One victim reportedly seen with a blond American, the other, no particular link to a blonde of any kind. Lou was found by a middle-aged couple from Nebraska who had traveled to the island for a second honeymoon. They had come to Lou's straight from the airport, and were at first surprised to find the hotel empty, then horrified to stumble upon the dead proprietress.

Lucien reflects on his next steps. He has been a cop long enough to know that people mostly kill people they know. He decides to head back to Vieux Fort and ask some more questions.

Lucien spends five hours interviewing street vendors and locals. He encounters a not-unexpected resistance to his questions. Tensions have been high in Vieux Fort; with a police crackdown on illegal street vendors in play, Lucien knows he is the enemy. And then there is the angry group, furious about the authorities perceived indifference to the island's four missing boys. Their discontent roils and spreads. Lucien begins to fear their anger will billow into something violent. But the angry mutterings dip and simmer in the face of Lucien's quite genuine and shared frustration.

And let's not forget, gossip is gossip, enjoyed by most. People like to talk. People want to be heard. They tell some wild stories: The four abducted boys have been stolen by the devil, one old crone swears, she has a magic powder that can bring them back; the American killed at the Grande Sucre was a CIA agent, double-crossed by a Russian informant. It's all drug-related, insists one old man with a gray Afro, his pocked and scarred arms held out to testify; he should know. A frightened mother clutches her two young children to her side and whispers that she's heard the missing boys are imprisoned by the angry ghost at Maison Marianne. Did the detective know Marianne was pregnant when she died? She's stealing boys to replace her own lost child.

Lucien is patient. He speaks to everyone. He listens with considerate attention. He promises to check the drug angle, the political rumors; he assures the scared mother that they have checked Maison Marianne, but even so, promises to do it again.

Each time he is able to bring the topic back around to Lou. He learns that the fat woman was well liked, known for a soft heart and a generous hand, and as he expresses his determination to bring her killer to justice, more tongues are loosened. He finally finds one woman, a beneficiary of Lou's kindness, who is not only willing to talk, but actually has something of value to say.

The woman, Camille Allard, has a stand on the same street as Lou's hotel from which she peddles an astounding array of junk: cheap T-shirts bearing the slogan "No Pressure, No Problem, St. Lucia," plastic sunglasses, rag dolls clothed in the local madras, hats formed from woven banana leaves. Camille also has a black eye, faded now to a purplish bruise. Camille tells Lucien that Lou had taken her in when her boyfriend hit her, didn't charge her, had been kind. If she can help find who murdered her, it would be a way of repaying that debt.

Lucien asks if she had seen a blond woman the day of Lou's murder, but Camille is adamant she hadn't. But she does have something odd to report. The day before, she insists, a taxi had let off a woman—no, not blond, hair very dark. Camille remembered this woman not just because she seemed so agitated but because she had these crazy fake fingernails encrusted with crystals, which Camille considers a stupid American affectation. Camille didn't see the dark-haired woman enter Lou's hotel, but she had headed off in that direction.

Lucien presses her: Is she sure the dark-haired woman was American? Yes, she was. How does she know? Did she speak to her? No. But Camille has been selling on this street since she was fifteen; she knows an American when she sees one. And the taxi? Could she give him the color? The model? A Volvo, she thinks, an older model, not new. Blue. With one red door.

The next day, Camille saw the same taxi return. She remembered it because of the one red door. Then Camille beckons him closer and whispers, "The men in the taxi tried to take her, but the American woman went off with Crazy B." Camille shakes her head.

This revelation only confuses Lucien more. He knows Crazy B (legal name Benjamin Rossier) as a low-level street dealer. Why would the American go with him? Camille shrugs, indifferent to the strange ways of American tourists. Who knows why they do half the things they do?

Lucien scans the street as he walks back to Lou's hotel. No sign of Crazy B, and the other dealers he might have expected to be working this stretch have also vanished. No surprise really, given the police presence on the street since Lou's body was found. Lucien nods at the uniformed officer who is standing watch at the hotel and heads in, ducking under the crime scene tape, passing under the flickering neon turtle. He nods at the representative from a local bird sanctuary moving Royal and Ruby into a cage for transfer and makes his way to room 6. Lou's body is gone—off to the morgue—but the forensics team is still there, dusting for prints, combing the room for any scrap that could be evidence.

Lucien stands in the doorway, watching them work. A breeze lifts the shabby green curtains away from the window; sunlight floods the room and an iridescent blue lizard skitters across the floor and under the bed. Following the lizard's trajectory, Lucien catches sight of something. He steps into the room, kneels, and peers closely at the shiny object glinting on the floor just under the bed. It is a crystal-studded fake nail.

So. The woman Camille saw *has* been in this room. Instinct tells him the two murders are linked. But still he can't see how. How many women can be killing people in hotel rooms in St. Lucia in the course of forty-eight hours? Is one of them Eleanor Larrabee? Or are the blonde and the dark-haired woman one and the same?

Then

There are an astonishing number of ways to kill someone, Rob learned. There are poisons and garrotes, guns and knives, the opportune push from a window. Staged suicides, overdoses, and accidents.

The key was in the planning. The observation of routines and habits, the assessment of opportunities and weaknesses. Because not only must the intended victim unequivocally die (no last-gasp revivals or trips to the hospital) but either he or she must disappear without a trace, or the death must be an unsolvable crime. Rob had done well in a crisis, Quinn assured him, but killing is an art.

Quinn, for example, had a favored routine, as Rob learned over the next weeks. Quinn's victims were brought to him, snatched away by his carefully trained muscle, so it was as if his victims simply vanished off the face of the earth. He liked them bound, and Rob came to recognize that it was this particular part of the sadism that Quinn relished most, the utter and complete helplessness of those whose lives he was about to snuff out. Quinn was verbose. He liked to talk to his victims while he tortured them. His weapons of choice were knives. And every single death, he took a trophy: an ear, a toe, a nipple, a lip. After he was done, his victims were dropped out at sea under the cover of night.

Quinn's brutality was horrific, but there was always an explanation, some grievous betrayal that was being righted. Rob's father could be vicious, but also charming and expansive; he had elegance and taste. But most important, he wanted Rob in his life, and that was like a drug for a young man who hadn't ever felt wanted.

When Quinn thought he was ready, Rob was told to kill someone. The victim was not likely to be missed, a thug of low intelligence but high hubris. The thug had thought he could skim from Quinn without Quinn noticing. That was his first mistake. His second was bragging about it. The thug, known on the streets as Monkey, was an unpleasant fellow, brutish and ugly. Monkey enjoyed inflicting pain, which had made him an effective collector for Quinn, but despite this utility, his greed and stupidity had made him a liability.

Rob observed Monkey for several weeks, just as Quinn had taught him. Monkey was a creature of habit. Every morning, he shambled from his apartment to the coffee shop on the corner. There, he ate waffles, bacon, and coffee and chatted up the pasty-faced waitress, whom he also banged every Thursday night when her husband went to his AA meeting. After breakfast, Monkey started his rounds.

He broke for lunch, rotating a pizza joint, a Chinese restaurant, and a deli. His orders were always the same: two slices of pepperoni with a Coke, beef with broccoli, a pastrami sandwich with a side of potato salad and a Cel-Ray soda. After lunch, a few more pickups.

Monkey's evenings were only slightly less predictable than his daytime habits. He stayed at home most nights, the flickering light of his TV set sparking through his blinds. Sometimes he hit the Irish pub down the street for a few shots of whiskey and boozy bar camaraderie. Thursdays of course were devoted to the pasty-faced wait-ress, an arrangement that seemed to suit them both.

Quinn wanted Monkey dead, but this time he wanted the body found. It was to be a message to any of his other employees who figured they could get greedy.

One sultry night, the air thick as cotton, Monkey emerged from the pub, stumbling drunkenly. Rob slid from his car and followed him discreetly, waiting until Monkey turned off the main avenue and onto a side street.

As he quickened his steps, Rob's thoughts raced in a million dif-ferent directions. He congratulated Quinn on his methodology; his insistence on observation and planning was paying off and Mon-key's devotion to his routine was making this easy. But beneath his logical appreciation of the plan raged more powerful feelings.

Self-disgust, fear, and repulsion, as well as a sense of hopeless inevitability. He was a killer. He had killed twice already. It was what he was meant to be. He was his father's son.

The cacophonous roar in his head flared into a mushroom cloud. Softly, Rob called, "Hey, Monkey." Monkey turned. Then Rob did just as Quinn had taught him, wielding a knife with force and preci-sion.

That night Rob didn't sleep. The few moments he did were poi-soned by toxic dreams. His mother flitted in and out of them; in one dream she floated peacefully in a pool of warm water and when he dove in beside her, the current turned fast, the water icy. She pulled him to her, nuzzled him to her breast, then held his head below the freezing waves while she laughed and he drowned. The next morn-ing, hollow-eyed from lack of sleep and guts gnawed with fear and shame about the man he was becoming, Rob scanned the news for reports of Monkey's death. Nothing.

Rob told Quinn he wanted to go away for a few days; he had never been to Vegas, maybe he would check it out. But at the airport he switched his ticket. He went home to Pennsylvania.

Rob rented a car at the airport and drove to his old house in Devon. It was a compulsion, a siren call he couldn't ignore. He felt hypnotized. Seduced. His eyes went to the bay window of the master bedroom. The room where everything had changed. A family emerged, the parents packing their two little boys into car seats, loading a double stroller into the trunk of their Audi. The parents were loving, the little boys happy. Rob drove away; their domesticity felt like a punch.

He stopped at Trinity Episcopal Church. It was where his mother had married his stepfather. Rob took a seat in the shadowy recesses of the nave and watched a baptism, the baby wailing as the water spilled across her tiny velvet head.

It was years later, but the memory flooded in, clear and crisp.

Eight-year-old Rob had served as ring bearer at his mother's wedding. When the minister requested the rings, Rob fumbled the platinum bands. They dropped to the stone floor and rolled in opposite directions. The assembled guests tittered. Rob's mother covered her initial flush of mortification with a pat on Rob's head. But it was his stepfather's face Rob remembered. It had mottled an angry red, the first harbinger of the temper that was to destroy them years later.

A quick Google search at the Philadelphia library revealed his mother's new address. But it took Rob a couple of days to gather enough courage to drive to her new house. She was living in a large elegant colonial, not far from where he had grown up. The house was set back deeply from the street, with a sweep of manicured lawn, lush plantings of flowers, old-growth trees. A brand-new silver BMW was parked in the driveway. He circled the block several times without stopping, unsure of his intent. Would he ask her about Quinn? Would she tell the truth if he did? What did he want from her? He wasn't at all sure.

Over the next three days he drove past the home numerous times but never stopped. Then, on the fourth day, impulsively he parked across the street. Killed his engine and lit a cigarette. Idly kept watch on the house, chain-smoking, as late afternoon oozed into dusk. The house was hushed, the shades drawn.

He was about to pull away when the front door opened and there she was. She wore a gunmetal silk dress with high black heels. An Hermès scarf was tossed about her shoulders and she carried a Prada handbag. She was, he had to admit, still a good-looking woman. She pulled out a compact and checked her cherry-red lipstick, wiping an invisible smear of it from her teeth; her formerly broken mouth now flashed a perfect smile. A car pulled up, a late-model Lexus. She got in the passenger side. Rob noted her date hadn't opened the car door for her. He couldn't see the man clearly but watched their shadows as she leaned over and kissed him.

When the Lexus pulled away, Rob almost packed it in. But instead he decided to follow them. They drove to a nearby restaurant, a high-end steakhouse; the bar at the front had a cozy, clubby feel. As his mother and her date made their way to a table in the dining room, Rob took a seat at the bar.

He ordered a dirty martini and then another. His mother and her date, a silver-haired man, seemed familiar with each other, although Rob thought she was working too hard to be charming. Her companion didn't seem to mind.

"Does she ever wonder about me at all?" Rob didn't realize he had spoken out loud.

The barfly next to him, navy blazer with a gold crest on the pocket, beet-red nose, looked puzzled. "Who you talking about?"

Rob blinked. "Uh, no one. Sorry."

"Your ex, I bet. Am I right? Fucking crazy how a girl can get under your skin. I oughta know, I have two exes myself. Left in a room with them, I still don't know if I'd fuck 'em or just fuck 'em over."

The barfly delighted in his crudity and laughed until he choked. The bartender brought him a glass of water as he sputtered and pounded on his own thigh, completely secure of his charm. At the sound, Rob's mother pulled her attention away from her dinner companion and stared right at them. Rob's eyes met hers. He held the glance a beat too long, his breath snared in his chest. Would she recognize him? Shouldn't she recognize him, her only child?

But his startled gaze was mistaken for quite a different intent, he realized with horrified disgust. She dipped her head at him with a coquettish bob, and adjusted her neckline to best show off her décolletage. Rob pushed blindly away from the bar, slapping down a handful of bills. Out on the street he puked up the martinis.

He drove directly to the airport. Returned his rental car and got on the first plane back to Miami.

It wasn't really a surprise that Quinn knew Rob had gone to Pennsylvania. So when Quinn quizzed him, asked if he had found what he had been looking for, Rob nodded and copped to the trip. "I don't need to go back again" was all he said.

Now

Lucien is in the morgue. The building is very cold; the air feels shocking after the dense heat of the day. The thick perfume of formaldehyde, rotting meat, and bleach assaults his nostrils. Lucien listens to his old friend Alphonse Dafoe, the coroner. Alphonse is as loud, warm, and cheerful as his workplace is gray, sterile, and bleak, but his reports do not help Lucien's investigation much.

Williamson had been drugged with a hefty dose of Seconal before his stabbing. This accounts for the lack of evidence of a struggle in the room. Lou, well, Alphonse figures she was probably taken by surprise and also that a woman of her size would have had slow reactions to a perceived threat. She had been shot at close range, through a pillow. Alphonse confirms that the nail Lucien found was not from Lou's fingers (no adhesive was found on her nails, or evidence of a torn nail matching the piece still affixed to the fake), and while he has sent the torn piece out for DNA processing, there is a weeklong backup at least. Lucien thanks him and begins to leave, but Alphonse clears his throat.

"I've got one more good one for you."

Lucien waits expectantly, looking at his old friend's mischievous brown eyes, as round as his shiny bald head, his neatly trimmed gray mustache. This is their ritual.

"Three nurses working in a morgue discover a dead man with a hard-on. The first nurse says, 'I can't let that go to waste,' and rides him. The second nurse does the same. The third nurse hesitates and says she has her period but does him anyway. Then the man sits up! The nurses apologize, saying they thought he was dead. The man replies, 'I was, but after two jump-starts and a blood transfusion I feel better than ever!'"

Lucien gives an obligatory guffaw, and Alphonse looks delighted.

As Lucien emerges into the bright sunlight, he automatically checks his cell. There is no reception in the morgue, and he is annoyed to see he has three missed calls from Agathe. Doesn't she know the kind of pressure he is under? He feels petulant and resolves not to call her back, but before he can even begin to delete the calls, the phone rings again. Agathe.

"Listen, Agathe, I am in the middle of two murder investigations. I don't have time for this right now—"

Agathe cuts him off.

"Lucien, listen to me."

There is a ragged hitch in her voice, she sounds hysterical, but he instantly hears the seriousness in her tone, the urgency.

"Yes? I'm listening."

"I was at the park with the baby and Gabrielle and Thomas."

Gabrielle is Agathe's sister; Thomas is Gabrielle's six-year-old son.

"Someone took Thomas, Lucien! Thomas is missing! We only had him out of our sights for a minute!"

"Where are you?"

"Still at the park. We—"

"I'll be right there."

Lucien clicks the phone off. A deep, agonizing pain stabs through his brain; it feels like it will split his skull right open. His palms sweat; his cell slips from his grasp and clatters to the pavement. The screen cracks. As he bends to pick up the phone the faces of the missing boys swim before his vision. Olivier Cassiel. Pierre Deveraux. Jacob Abellard. Sebastien Durio. Please, God, not Thomas too. Please.

Then

"You can't not care about cake!" Ellie glared at Rob as if he was well and truly insane. She looked so truly affronted and disbelieving that he burst out laughing.

"I'm not much of a sweets guy."

"But this is wedding cake! Our wedding cake." She gave him that smile, the one that was so brimming with love and faith in their partnership, it sucked him in a little deeper every time.

"So what's involved exactly?"

"Um, we go to a bakery and eat cake? Decide what we like?"

Gravely, Rob said, "It sounds complicated."

She shot him a look; saw the small secret smile tucked in the corner of his mouth.

"So I can make the appointment for next week? Thursday after work, maybe? Or would you rather do it on the weekend?"

"Thursday's fine." He kissed her lightly on the lips, pulling her to a stop in front of François Boucher's painting *A Lady on Her Day Bed*. He leaned in close to the painting, to better study the subject's face. Then glanced at the placard that accompanied it.

"The artist's wife. She's saucy. I can tell. Just like you."

Next to them, a security guard cleared his throat.

"Keep your distance from the painting, please, sir." In a musical Jamaican lilt.

They were in the Frick, Ellie's favorite museum in New York. She had brought Rob here for the first time on their fourth date. They had been so shivered through with desire, so drawn to touch each other, so distracted and elated, they had raced through the museum and straight back to bed. Today they moved more languorously, still magnetically attracted, but their passion was now dipped like a wick in layers of wax, a candle in the making—a warm, thick coating on an incendiary core.

Ellie had explained her love of the Frick to Rob the first time she had taken him there. It was like walking through the looking glass into a part of New York life that was in the shockingly near past given how much the world had altered. What would the mighty coke and steel magnate Henry Clay Frick think of the tourists meandering through his former home with their iPhones and tablets, sweatpants and sneakers? It was also that the collection and the building itself were so personal to its founder. Only paintings Frick found "pleasant" (no nudity or war), the enormous dining room he designed to host lively dinner parties at least twice a week, its gilt-edged cream walls vivid with graceful paintings of women of noble birth, the wood-paneled library filled with leather-bound first editions and dark-hued paintings of men of note—all of it made Ellie feel like she was spying through an inverted telescope, stalking the home's long-dead family.

There were certainly museums with better collections, with art and objects more to Ellie's taste, she had explained, but she always preferred the Frick. She was thrilled when Rob seemed to appreciate it too. What Rob hadn't told her was that he had been to the Frick as a child; that his mother's family was distantly related to Henry Clay himself; that being back there unleashed a torrent of memories about his lost life that left him feeling deeply unsettled.

They made their way through the round golden music room, its rows of empty chairs fruitlessly waiting for patrons eager to be dazzled by virtuosity. Rob felt itchy and anxious. He fell into what he knew had become a default coping mechanism—the adoption of a persona not his own. He strode to the front of the room and faced the rows of chairs. He took three deep bows, one to audience right, one to audience left, and one to center, an impresario acknowledging his audience. A pair of teenaged Chinese tourists peeked in just as he swept his arms in a flourish, conducting an invisible orchestra, and they scurried past, giggling. Ellie laughed, and Rob linked his arm in hers. They strolled on.

No visit was complete without a stop at the small gift shop. Nothing elaborate, but there were gift cards and books, stationery and posters, umbrellas and mugs, silk scarves and caps, totes and journals. Ellie browsed, admiring a selection of chinoiserie-inspired gift items. Rob flipped through a stack of framed posters, then moved on to the books.

There on the shelves, in a section of books about the gilded age, was a reproduction of the New York Social Register of 1910, the bible of everyone important in American society at the time. He flipped through. There were the Fricks: Henry; his wife, Adelaide; and their daughter, Helen. And then there he was: Charles Buckingham Scott, Rob's maternal ancestor, the cousin of Frick's his mother had been so proud to name each time she brought Rob here as a child. He remembered the feel of his small, hot hand intertwined in her cool, elegant fingers, the pleasure she took in showing him the art and objets of the collection, the frozen hot chocolate she bought him at Serendipity afterward as a reward for his good behavior. Money, privilege, access, society—they were all supposed to serve as a protective barrier from the harsher realities of life. They hadn't shielded his mother, though. They had corrupted her. Her investment in appearances had led her to cover her external bruises with makeup and long sleeves. And her internal damage had led to her betrayal of her only child.

"What was that you asked?" Rob's voice was suddenly not his own. Rob finger-combed his hair into Henry Clay Frick's neat side part, as he drew Ellie's attention. "You want to hear about the assassination attempt? Well, certainly, if you have the stomach for it."

Rob planted his feet wide apart and put his hands on his hips. "It was July 23, 1892. Inspired by his lover and lifelong friend Emma Goldman, the anarchist Alexander Berkman busted into my office, murder on his mind. I sprang to my feet, immediately sensing danger, as he pulled a revolver and shot at me! The bullet hit my left earlobe . . ." Rob stroked his left earlobe as if caressing Frick's scar from this event, before continuing, ". . . penetrated my neck, and lodged in my back, tumbling me to the floor."

Rob reeled, imitating taking the bullet in his neck.

By now the handful of other museum shop browsers and its two employees were all paying attention, even those who were pretending they weren't.

"The bastard shot at me again while I was down! Blood everywhere! But then my esteemed colleague John Leishman—surely you've met him? He's now the president of Carnegie Steel?"

Ellie played along. "Yes, of course, I am acquainted with the gentleman."

"Leishman grabbed his arm and prevented a third shot, which surely would have proven lethal! I struggled to my feet and Leishman and I charged at Berkman! The three of us crashed to the ground, a tangle of limbs and fury. This was when Berkman pulled the sharpened steel file he had secreted about his person. He stabbed me four times in the leg, before we managed to subdue him."

"My goodness," Ellie murmured with admiration, as Rob struck the noble pose of the martyred survivor.

"I was back to work within a week." Rob-as-Frick shrugged. "But do you know the shocker? Berkman tried to kill me in retaliation for those dirty low-down strikers killed by the Pinkertons I had hired to disperse picketing at our Homestead Steel Works." He gave a snort of a laugh. "They were keeping men who wanted to go to work from honest labor! Un-American! Stopping the march of progress! It had to be done. But ironic, isn't it? The bad publicity from Berkman's murderous attempt collapsed the strike. Twenty-five hundred men lost their jobs. And we were able to pay those who remained half their wage."

By now everyone was openly rapt. Even those who had known of this chapter of the industrialist's life were captivated by Rob's imper-sonation. And perhaps a little disturbed by the pleasure Rob-as-Frick took in the collapse of the strike.

Only later, when they were long out of the museum and sipping cappuccinos, did Rob reveal that during his performance he had pocketed two boxes of note cards, a tin pencil case, and a pack of playing cards. Stealing the souvenirs had felt like a delicious fuck-you to his mother, her lineage, the whole notion of the society from which he had been ejected.

"I'll send a check to cover the cost and then some. But did you see? How I got everyone to look at one thing so they never looked at another? The perfect distraction. If anyone asked them later, all they would remember would be the performance."

"Shoplifting? Really? Any other dark secrets you're hiding, dar-ling?"

Rob felt perversely pleased by Ellie's shocked amusement, even as he promised he was otherwise an open book.

And then he told her lies. That his father had died of cancer when he was three and a half, that his mother had never remarried. That she struggled valiantly to provide for him but died in a car crash right after he turned twenty-one; that he didn't like to talk about these things because what was there to say, really? He had no other family. Until now. Now he had her.

And that, at least, was the truth.

Now

The square-jawed man with the salt-and-pepper hair stares out the window of the plane as it descends toward Hewanorra International Airport in St. Lucia. The Pitons, two extraordinary pyramids of rock emerging from the sea, are every bit as impressive as the tourist photos had promised. As the plane touches down with one bump and then another, some passengers squeal, the scared/excited release of safely alighting from the sky with just a touch of peril.

Everything goes smoothly. He clears customs, picks up his rental car, and plugs the address of the post office into the GPS. The skies are azure, the sun scorching. He opens the windows, letting the salty breeze and tropical scents stream through the car as he drives.

He finds the post office branch with no problem. Slips inside and locates the box number, 143. Uses the key he received in the mail and unlocks the box. There is an envelope inside. The man slips it into his pocket, nods cordially at the post office clerk, and steps back outside.

He gets into the rental car and, just to be safe, pulls away from the post office and drives to a beach down the road. He parks. He walks out onto the beach, turning the envelope over in his hands. He sees a small wrecked sailboat a few hundred feet down the beach and walks to it. He needs to read this letter, he wants to, but he knows it will also require action, thought, strategy. He is tired from traveling, not fully ready. A few people circle the overturned boat, a curious fixture on the beautiful beach. The man peers into the wreckage: leopard skin–patterned sheets on a waterlogged queen-size mattress, a turntable, vinyl records (Crosby, Stills, Nash, and Young; Jethro Tull; Yes; the Grateful Dead), plastic plates and cheap cutlery. An incense burner, charred with use. The faint scent of patchouli. Some old hippie's boat gone to hell.

The man sighs, takes a seat on the sand, and slits the envelope open. The letter inside is handwritten, the penmanship spidery, shaky, hurried.

> *Dear M,*
>
> *You don't know me, and I don't know you. But Rob has told me that in this situation you are our only friend. He also asked that I tell you how sorry he is that we have had to call on that friendship. He had hoped you would be able to live on in peace. But if you have received this letter it means you have traveled to St. Lucia. And you know that we are in mortal danger.*

Then

Ellie stared at the unopened bottle of champagne, the puffy pillows on the bed, the full skirts of her wedding dress that now felt heavy and constraining. This was not how she had envisioned her wedding night. "What's your real name?"

"Kevin."

"Kevin what? Is Beauman a lie too?"

"Kevin Palmer."

Ellie rolled the name silently over her tongue. Kevin Palmer. And then, fingering her wedding ring, she thought, *Does that make me Ellie Palmer?* Her brain was reeling.

"And how long ago was that? That Quinn found you?"

"Seven years."

"And in that time . . . how many . . . ?"

He was silent.

A sour smile twisted her lips. Yes, probably better not to know.

"What you have to understand, Ellie," insisted Rob, "is that you changed everything. You gave me the reason to get out. And I was out. I made a deal with Quinn."

"If you made a deal, what happened? Why did he come to our wedding?"

"Quinn changed his mind."

"So what happens now? What does he want this time?"

"He wants you to kill someone."

"Me? No! I won't. I can't."

Rob gripped Ellie's hand. She shuddered and pulled away.

"El, do you remember the day we moved in together?"

The tenderness in his voice, the way he looked at her. It was impossible to reconcile those emotions with all she was hearing.

"Our discussion about the coffee cups?" he persisted.

"The coffee cups?" she echoed, bewildered.

"Remember I told you to always put them facedown? So the dust doesn't get in? This is just like that. If we keep things as clean as possible, it will be all right. I promise you. I swear to you it will be all right."

"What do we have to do?" she whispered, searching his eyes with hers.

"Obey."

She squeezed her eyes shut. She was in shock. Terrified. Exhausted. Yet exhilarated in a weird way she couldn't define.

Till death do us part. Had she said that phrase only a few hours ago?

Ellie opened her eyes.

"So," he said, kissing her lips, "just do what you're told. Obey. Remember that if you can figure out the first step, you can figure out the next step. Okay? And never forget that I love you."

Quinn escorted her to the door of the suite, giving her instructions. If she didn't follow them, Rob would die. She believed him.

She left the hotel, got into a yellow cab, and went back to the apartment that had been their sheltered nest. She was numb.

Their cozy apartment felt like a stranger's, with piles of unopened wedding presents splayed every which way. Ellie caught sight of herself in the hall mirror. Still in her wedding dress, her carefully applied makeup and coiffed hair a ruin, she looked like a desperate clown. She wanted to weep but no tears came.

She peeled off her dress, leaving it a cumulus cloud draped carelessly over boxes. She stripped off her corset and Spanx and pantyhose, unclasped the pearl necklace at her throat. She fingered her diamond engagement ring and the brand-new gold band that now nestled beside it on the third finger of her left hand. She removed both, dropping them into a little porcelain dish on Rob's dresser.

The first thing was a shower. If you can figure out the first thing, you can figure out the next thing. As she showered, her thoughts raced. She could still call the police. She could stop this. She didn't have to follow Quinn's instructions. But would he kill Rob if she didn't? She believed he would. And probably kill her too.

She wrapped herself in Rob's terry cloth robe and wandered the apartment. She inhaled the scent of him from the robe's collar. It was dawn.

Ellie thought about Rob's reference to the coffee cups. Her bare feet padded over to the cabinet with the coffee cups. There they were, on their shelf, open sides down. Methodically she pulled each cup from the shelf, inspecting the inside of every one. Nothing.

She shoved them back into the shelf, frustrated. One of them, a Central Park Zoo polar bear mug, crashed to the floor.

"Shit!"

Ellie stooped to pick up the shards. She gathered the big chunks in her hands and as she straightened to toss them in the trash, she froze. She dumped the broken pieces and felt underneath the shelf on which the mugs sat. There was an envelope taped to it.

Quickly, she sliced at the tape with a steak knife and freed the envelope. Two pages were inside. She unfolded the first:

My darling Ellie,
I am so, so sorry.
Please follow the instructions enclosed with this
letter exactly and it is my fervent hope all will be fine.
You are my love, and always will be, believe that.
You are everything.

Rob

Ellie unfolded the second piece of paper and began to read.

Now

When Lucien arrives at the playground, the park is buzzing with hysterical mothers and scared children. Two patrol cars are already there and the uniforms are taking statements. When Gabrielle and Agathe spot him, they sprint over, Agathe clutching Bertrand close to her chest.

His sister-in-law bursts into speech. "He was out of my sight for maybe three minutes—Agathe was changing the baby on a bench, I was talking to her, but we were right here!" Her voice is shrill. Lucien sees his wife shudder.

Lucien lays a soothing hand on Gabrielle's shoulder. "Listen to me. It is important you remember every detail. So breathe. Calm down, and think. Was there anyone or anything unusual at the park this morning? Anything at all that you noticed?"

Gabrielle shakes her head. Her lips tremble.

"Has Thomas ever run off before? Is it possible he's playing a game with you? Hide-and-seek perhaps?"

"No! Listen, Lucien, he just wouldn't. If anything, he's timid, he doesn't like strangers, so he never strays too far!"

Lucien turns to Agathe. "Did you see anything unusual?"

Agathe looks down at the sleeping baby safe in her arms, then at her distraught sister. She raises her eyes to her husband's.

"There was one thing . . . although I don't know if it means any-thing . . ." She falters.

"Anything might help us," he assures her.

"There was a taxi, blue, an old sedan? Boxy . . . maybe a Renault? I'm not sure. But it was idling near the corner of the park. It was here when we got here, and I noticed it was still there about an hour later."

"Which corner?"

Agathe points.

"Okay, that's a help. Gabrielle, what was Thomas wearing?"

"A red shirt with a dump truck on it. Tan shorts, sneakers—you know, the kind that light up . . . he loves those sneakers . . ." Gabri-elle's eyes overflow with tears. "Oh, Lucien . . ."

Lucien pulls his wife aside. "Take Gabrielle home. There is no point in you staying here."

Agathe begins to protest, but Lucien puts a finger to her lips to quiet her. "There's nothing more you can do here, Agathe. But I promise you—"

"That you'll find him?"

"That we'll do everything we can."

Lucien sees the pain this answer gives his wife, but he doesn't want to make promises he isn't sure he can keep.

He escorts Agathe and Gabrielle to their cars, taking care to strap Bertrand into his forest-green velour car seat himself. He kisses his son's damp forehead, the tip of his nose. He watches until Agathe's car is out of sight. Then he confers with the uniforms about the statements they have collected. Two other women had noticed the blue taxi; one of them seems pretty sure it was a Volvo and had one red door.

Surely this couldn't be a coincidence? But how could this taxi be connected to both the murder in Vieux Fort and Thomas's disappearance? And was it connected to the Grande Sucre murder as well? Was this mysterious taxi driver so stupid that he didn't realize that a blue car with one red door would be conspicuous? Or was he so brazen he didn't care?

Then

Ellie stared at herself in the three-way mirror. The satin dress, embroidered with seed pearls and delicate sequins, clung to her body, hugging the curve of her waist before cascading in an elegant bubble of the lightest chiffon. The dip of the neckline demonstrated solemn respect for the sanctity of marriage while hinting at the delights of the wedding night to come. As the saleswoman placed a veil on her head, Ellie was certain. This would be her wedding dress.

"Are you ready to show them?" the saleswoman asked. Ellie's mother and Marcy were waiting, sipping the complimentary champagne and making polite conversation. The last four dresses had been soundly rejected. The first her mother deemed too sexy, the second all agreed was overwrought, the third definitively proved to Ellie that she was not interested in a mermaid gown, the fourth was just not special.

Ellie wanted a moment. She closed her eyes and imagined Rob's face when he saw her walking down the aisle toward him. She opened them and again contemplated her own reflection. This dress was perfect. She felt like a princess.

Ellie stepped into a pair of white satin loaner shoes. The high heels emphasized the arc of her back, the length of her neck.

"You look beautiful," the saleswoman cooed as Ellie stepped out of the dressing room.

Marcy loved the dress. She *ooh*ed and *ahh*ed and asked Ellie to give them a twirl. She earnestly debated the veil options with Ellie: fingertip or floor-length? A tiara instead?

Ellie turned to her mother, a hopeful smile on her face. Her mother was accepting another glass of champagne.

"So, Mom? What do you think?"

"It's very nice." There was a slight slur in Michelle's voice, one Ellie was accustomed to hearing, although not usually at eleven in the morning. *Very nice,* thought Ellie. From Michelle, that was high praise indeed.

"I'll take it."

Marcy squealed with delight. The saleswoman summoned a seamstress. Ellie stepped back into the dressing room and onto the platform before the three-way mirror. The seamstress measured and pinned, wrote notes and complimented Ellie's figure.

Ellie watched herself in the mirror, feeling happy, daring herself to trust that emotion. The seamstress tweaked the position of the two side mirrors. Suddenly Ellie was confronted with an infinite number of her own elegant reflections receding into endless space. Ellie smiled and her reflections all smiled with her.

Now

It's been a long few hours. First Ellie had to talk Crazy B into staying at Maison Marianne. Then she had to negotiate a hiding place that she felt gave them a decent vantage point from which to observe the house, but that he felt was far enough away from the mansion (and its angry ghost).

They have crouched in the heat, hidden in the overgrown tropical landscaping, without water, flicking away insects. Crazy B has lit and smoked spliff after spliff, talking all the while. Ellie is light-headed, thirsty, hungry.

Crazy B regales her with lurid tales about the house. How after the American couple's bodies were shipped back to the States, locals came to loot the place but were scared away by slamming doors and oozing bloodstains on the walls. How the pool was drained but fills again and again. Even after the water was turned off. How Marianne's ghostly, dripping body roams the mansion, leaving trails of water and slime.

Ellie tunes Crazy B out, willing her brain to decide what to do next. This wait seems fruitless. There's been no more movement at the house. She wonders out loud if she imagined that shadow in the window, a question that unleashes Crazy B's next round of stories.

At least she feels somewhat safe here. Ironic, feeling safe while on the run from both the police and ruthless killers. Not to mention camped outside a haunted house with a delusional drug dealer. A bitter smile flickers across her face.

Crazy B mistakes her smile for invitation. Suddenly his meaty hand is on her thigh.

"Stop it." Ellie's tone is sharp. She scoots away from him.

"Come on, beauty. We've got nothing but time."

"Stop!" The word is only a squeak and she curses herself. "Stop," she says again more firmly. "Don't you ever touch me again," she spits. She clutches her beach bag, remembering the pointy tip of the screwdriver hidden inside. It's the only weapon she has.

The merry, crazy glint in Crazy B's eyes goes dark with rage.

There's the creak of the gate. The whine of a car.

"Listen!" she exclaims, desperately relieved. "Someone's here." He's heard the car too. She ducks behind the thicket of birds of paradise that screens them. Peers out.

Ellie sees Gold Tooth's taxi rumble onto the crushed-shell driveway.

The taxi draws to a stop. Quinn exits. Followed by Gold Tooth, who opens the back door and pulls someone—a small child—from the car. The boy is crying, shouting for his mother. Ellie hears Gold Tooth curse and then, "The little fucker *bit* me!" Whoever that kid is, he's fighting back; good for him.

Gold Tooth shoves the boy into Quinn's arms. "I'm not staying here," he snaps. "There be no amount of money that make me stay at this house!"

As Gold Tooth pulls away in the taxi and Quinn wrestles the boy to the front door, Crazy B exclaims in horror, "It's not drugs, is it? It's those children! Those missing kids!"

Before Ellie can reply, the front door to the mansion swings open.

Ellie gasps, a sharp, painful inhalation. Framed in the doorway is Rob.

Then

Marcy and Ethan Clark were delighted that their matchmaking had been successful. Soon the two couples were double-dating often, taking full advantage of all the city had to offer people with a bit of money and few family encumbrances. They hit up the latest restaurants, the bars in the meatpacking district, Broadway plays, and concerts. They argued over the best pizza to be found below Fourteenth Street and above Seventy-second. They agreed Chinatown's best dive was Excellent Dumpling, with its wonderful soups, and launched a fruitless quest for good Mexican food. The foursome took a long weekend road trip together to Vermont, where they marveled at the changing leaves and gorged themselves on local cheeses and pancakes with real maple syrup.

Rob welcomed the rhythm their group activities afforded, and also his burgeoning friendship with Ethan. Ethan was a bright guy, a born-and-bred Park Avenue New Yorker, savvy about the city and well connected. Ethan always knew someone who knew someone who could score the tickets they wanted for a sold-out show or a reservation at the hot new restaurant. Rob genuinely liked Ethan, his smart conversation, his commitment to team building at the office, his open affection for Marcy, his easy self-assurance.

But Ethan was his assignment. And Ellie was part of his access to Ethan. It was bad enough he was falling in love with her; true friendship with his victim was impossible.

Now

The clerk at the taxi commission confirms to Lucien that a blue Volvo with a red door had been registered at one time, but has been decommissioned as a taxi. Lucien runs a check on the title and registration. The Volvo had been sold to Carter Williamson's company. Lucien has issued an APB for the taxi, but it has not yet turned up.

Lucien now sits across from a very anxious-looking Pascal Jarett. The American has answered every question put to him in the last twenty minutes with an unwavering, "I don't know what you're talking about, man."

Lucien leans in toward him and speaks kindly.

"Listen to me, Pascal. Your partner is dead. A car registered to this company is potentially linked to another murder and to the abduction of a child. What is it you're not telling me?" Lucien's eyes narrow, his tone shifts to one of nuanced threat. "Do we need to beat it out of you?"

Pascal's Adam's apple bobs up and down in his scrawny neck. "You're the police. You can't just beat me up."

"Don't you read the papers?" Lucien asks with quiet menace.

Pascal squirms back in his seat. His fingers twist a dreadlock. There have been several instances of police brutality reported lately, young men of the island who have been badly beaten in the course of their arrests. Violence begets violence. Just a week ago there had been a riot in one of the slums. Rocks and knives. Gasoline fires. Guerrilla fighters against uniforms until the fire department hosed the instigators down. "But I'm—"

"What? White? American? You live in St. Lucia now. Our rules. My rules."

"I swear. I don't know anything."

Lucien's cellphone bleats. He glances at the number. "Yes?"

He listens, and his face changes. Fear clouds his features.

"I'll be right there."

He clicks the phone off.

"What do you know about your partner's boat?"

"Carter's boat? Not much. He keeps it at Rodney Bay."

"He ever take you out on it?"

"Nah. He used to joke it was his love shack. I think he took girls out on it so he could keep Cookie in the dark."

"That's not all he was keeping in the dark."

Then

Her fever was high, he could tell just by touching her forehead. This morning, when Rob had left for work, Ellie had groaned and said she was going to stay home again, it was the second day in a row she felt flu-ish. But now, coming home, he was unprepared for how sick she seemed. He tried to urge her into a sitting position so that he could get her to swallow some water. Her body felt like dead weight in his arms. He held the cup up to her chapped lips.

"Sweetheart. Please try to drink."

She moaned and batted limply at the air in front of her with her hands. "Stop the arrows! They're coming at me!"

"Baby, there are no arrows. It's just the fever. Come on, drink some water."

He got her to take a sip, before she collapsed back against the pillows. She was soaked in sweat and Rob tried to remember whether this was good—did it mean the fever was breaking?

"The arrows! They're hurting me," Ellie moaned.

Rob flashed on the tattoo that graced Quinn's wrist, a dancing skeleton gripping an arrow. Quinn had pressured Rob to get the same tattoo, a rite of bonding, he had said. But Rob had resisted. He was more effective, he argued, if he had no permanent marking that could betray him. Now Rob grimaced. It was as if his hidden past was piercing its way into her subconscious.

Ellie lapsed back into restless sleep, her face ashen, her breathing shallow. Rob touched her forehead again. She was burning. He got up to see if they had any canned broth in the kitchen, his anxiety over her illness giving rise to a need to do something, anything, to help her. As he heated a can of chicken noodle soup, he heard a *thump*. He ran to the bedroom. Ellie had fallen to the floor. Her eyes looked sunken in her skull; her face was filled with fear.

"Make it stop! Make them stop! Please!" She clawed at him desperately.

Her eyes rolled back in her head and her body jerked. He scooped her up in his arms and, cradling her shivering body, ran.

They rushed her in at emergency.

After she was out of danger, the ER doctor told him he had done exactly the right thing. Ellie had been dangerously dehydrated. She could have died. That night, as Rob stood by her hospital bed and watched her sleep, saline drip in her arm, Rob was assaulted by a dire realization. He could have lost her.

"A tale of woe," that was the phrase that defined today. The expression was one he had first heard in L.A., where he had last lived before coming to New York. Directors and producers, executives and lawyers, actors and writers all used the phrase as they launched into laborious tales of projects gone south.

It had been Rob's first time in L.A. He expected to hate it, but he loved it immediately. Loved the weather, loved his house in the hills with the swimming pool, was delightfully amused by the absurd self-importance of industry people in an industry town. The women were beautiful and easy for a man with an expensive car and a lot of cash. He had the use of a Ferrari, and a wardrobe of luxurious casual clothes. He jogged on the beach, hiked in the hills, and spun stories that allowed him to infiltrate the circles he needed to. He killed someone there.

The man he killed, Ken Corcoran, was a money manager with a wife and three young kids back in Idaho. Corcoran had somehow finagled a position as a CFO with a start-up production company (through a college connection, long attenuated but recently and opportunistically exploited). Ken had big aspirations, and a rapacious taste for all L.A. had to offer. He flew private to Vegas, fucked hookers, and snorted blow in his office on the Sunset Strip. He wrangled premiere invitations, hit all the clubs, and stretched his lavish expense account to the breaking point.

Hollywood folded Ken in (to a point); some access is easy with a business card labeling you an executive with a company bringing fresh money to town. Ken was admittedly clever about money, but he didn't have a creative bone in his body, nor much emotional intelligence (but to be fair, hustle and swagger have gotten many people pretty far in this world, not just Ken).

At a network party, he picked up a hot young chick, took her home, and banged her senseless. He recorded the whole thing. Looking at trade coverage of the party after she was gone in the morning, he discovered the chick was the daughter of the network head. Ken took a little time to process the angles here (as noted, creativity was not his strong suit). Finally he tried blackmailing the network head (not for cash, nothing so crass; he wanted a production deal). Unfortunately for Ken this backfired big time. The network chief told Ken to go ahead and release the sex tape; his daughter was only sixteen. Ken would be tried for statutory rape and his daughter could get a reality show off the publicity ("This is a win-win for my family, you cocksucker" was how he ended the call). Ken buried the tape and kept his mouth shut.

But the network head was an old friend of Quinn's (arms dealing back in the day, was the rumor) and so six months after the blackmail attempt, Ken Corcoran was buried under the newly renovated pool in Rob's backyard.

When the job was done, the "For Sale" sign posted on the house he had owned just long enough for his needs, Rob was restless. He had loved L.A. but now he felt repulsed by his time there—the befriending of Ken Corcoran, the steps taken to assure all copies of the sex tape were destroyed and that nothing could connect Rob or Ken back to the network head (who insisted on coming to spit on the body before it was folded into wet concrete).

Rob had money, he had women, he had everything he was supposed to want. But a malaise was creeping into his cells, seeping into his bloodstream—a disgust at himself, the knowledge that he was weak when he appeared to be strong, ugly when he appeared to be beautiful, a twisted, corrupt old soul who looked like a handsome, healthy young man. He thought about Solana, the cute Cuban girl, who had washed ashore, drowned, not long after he had killed the meth head in her presence. He wondered if Quinn had had a hand in her death.

Rob thought about a vacation. Cabo maybe, or Hawaii, places about which he had heard L.A. residents wax rhapsodic. But he was fearful time away would allow him introspection (and what was the use of that?), so he was relieved when Quinn told him about New York. Back to work, figuring angles, executing them—this absorbed Rob, this was what he was good at.

But then there was Ellie. Ellie changed everything.

Now

Lucien strides into the Rodney Bay Marina, searching for *The Whimsy*, Carter Williamson's boat. Restaurants, cafés, and bars catering to the "yachting lifestyle" hug the shore. Lucien's eyes scan their patrons: ruddy complexions, plaid shorts, thick gold jewelry, deck shoes. Salsa music bleeds into the hot air, live music from the Ocean Club. Through the windows he sees a few couples dancing, laughing, drinking. He takes in the large, elegant yachts, the diving boats, the catamarans. Seabirds swoop and shriek in the breeze; the bold ones stay close to al fresco diners. There is so much life here. And now, death.

Dirty gray clouds clutter the sky, an ominous harbinger.

A uniformed cop, a young man Lucien knows well, Frank Jessup, sees Lucien and strides over to greet him.

"Red T-shirt, shorts, sneakers." Jessup says it without preamble.

Lucien feels queasy, remembering Gabrielle's description of his nephew's bright red shirt with its dump truck. "I need to see for myself."

Jessup's lips tighten, but he nods. "Of course."

"Lucien, I heard . . . about Thomas." It's Alphonse. The coroner grasps Lucien by the arm.

Instinctively, Lucien steels himself for the gallows humor. But Alphonse surprises him. "I'm praying it's not him, Lucien," the old man says.

Lucien blinks back sudden, scalding tears. "Thank you. Have you examined the body yet?"

Alphonse shakes his head. "It's tight quarters in there. The techs are still at it."

"I need to take a look."

"Of course."

Jessup escorts him onto the boat. It is a Carver 466 Motor Yacht, pretty fancy. Three staterooms, a state-of-the-art stereo system. In the galley, Lucien notes a washer/dryer, a microwave, an electric oven, and a refrigerator/freezer. The door is ajar. The techs see Lucien and part respectfully. Lucien stops. Steels himself to look inside.

Who will it be? Impish little Olivier? Tiny, frail Sebastien, hardly more than a baby? Chubby little Jacob? Skinny Pierre with his knobby knees and big ears? Please not Thomas. Please not some other poor young soul Lucien isn't even aware has gone missing.

Lucien peers into the refrigerator, expectant and afraid. He sees the body of a small boy. The child's limbs are contorted, stuffed into the refrigerator at an awkward, clumsy angle. He is wearing a bright red T-shirt.

Lucien shudders.

This little boy has a halo of soft frizzy curls, café-au-lait skin. Not Thomas. Thank you, sweet Jesus. But Lucien swells with sorrow and rage. The boy is Olivier Cassiel. Lucien flashes on the cocky little smile, the way the child had shown off his muscles in the photograph his terrified parents had provided. Now Lucien must tell them their prayers have gone unanswered; their son is dead.

Then

Ellie stood next to Jason's bed for a moment before sitting down in the room's ugly orange guest chair. The machines that kept him alive clicked and hissed relentlessly. Ellie shuddered. Then she reached over and touched Jason's forehead, gently.

"I've come to tell you something," she began. "Do you remember, Jason, when we used to feel invincible? How we used to joke that our only quest was how to feel more pleasure, living as we were in the House of Pleasure? Everything was ours for the taking then. We had so much goddamn hope."

Ellie took his nonresponsive hand in hers. Her engagement ring sparkled even in the green-tinged fluorescent light.

"When you told me about Doug and you—I wish I had been able to show you more compassion. If I had, everything might have been different. So I've come to tell you I'm sorry."

Ellie fell silent, lost in the memories of the girl she had once been, the love she had shared with the man who was now consigned to a hospice, lost forever to what the doctors called a persistent vegetative state.

She took a breath. "And I've come to tell you I'm getting married. His name is Rob. Rob Beauman. He's made me feel healed, Jason. And I've debated it back and forth in my head a million times and I've decided I just can't tell him about you and Doug and what really happened between us at my apartment that night. And I'm sorry about that too. I wish love meant complete honesty, but I'm scared, Jason. If I tell him, he will see me as a monster. You claimed to love me, yet you kept a secret from me, didn't you? So you understand, right? I just can't risk it. I can't bear the thought of looking in his eyes and seeing revulsion, not love. So this will be my last visit to you, and I'm sorry for that too. I won't come back, ever again. I have to look forward to my future, and tell you for the last time how sorry I am I robbed you of yours. Please forgive me."

Ellie blew her nose and swiped at her eyes, struggling to regain her composure. A stocky, Filipino male nurse entered to check on Jason and glanced at her sympathetically.

"Sorry to interrupt. Do you need a moment?"

"No. Thank you. I was just going."

As Ellie passed the nurse on her way out, he touched her arm. "It's good you come every week. But I know it's hard to see him like this. You're a young woman. You gotta get on with your life."

Now

Lucien emerges from his captain's office, his eyes swimming. He has just been put on compassionate leave, despite his protests that nothing conclusive links his missing nephew with the two murders or even the other three missing boys, for that matter. Bonnaire does not see it that way. The captain believes there is a strong probability that Lucien's nephew, Thomas, has met the same fate as poor little Olivier Cassiel.

"No!" Lucien had snapped. The thought of Thomas dead is unthinkable. In Lucien's mind all of the missing boys are alive and in need of rescuing. And it is his job to do just that.

But the captain has insisted: Lucien should be at home with his wife and her family during this extremely trying time.

Lucien had seen the look in Bonnaire's eyes. Pity. Determination to set Lucien straight. Delivering the hard truth for Lucien's own good. It was infuriating.

Lucien had come close to rank insubordination as he argued with Bonnaire. They have a lead on the taxi. He is looking deeper into Williamson's partner. Interviewing the girlfriend again. Lucien has work to do. He doesn't want to go anywhere.

The captain was stunned by Lucien's vehemence but held firm. The island is exploding with press. The deaths of two expat Americans have inflamed a salacious journalistic hunger. The pressure on Bonnaire is intense and intensifying. He needs men at the top of their game, he informed Lucien. Not a distracted uncle.

As Lucien paces the corridor, his emotions speed from shock to disbelieving grief. Go home! Sit and wait! Impossible!

A square-jawed American man with salt-and-pepper hair talks to the desk sergeant, drawing Lucien's attention from his own agitation. The man is insisting he speak to the detective in charge of the investigation into the death of the American man found in the Grande Sucre Hotel. This in itself is not unusual; every high-profile case brings its fair share of tipsters, psychics, nut jobs, and false confessors. What catches Lucien's eye, however, are the faint scars on this man's face. They betray that once upon a time, this man might have had his lip sliced off.

Then

Rob tried to still his fidgeting fingers. He cracked his knuckles once, decisively, and then folded his hands on the table in front of him.

He was early. He had his back to the wall and a clear view of the door. The restaurant was quietly elegant. Rob dreaded this meeting, even though he had called it.

When Quinn came through the door, Rob's heart started pounding. Quinn spotted him and waved off the hostess. Strode over and pulled out a chair and sat.

"You're looking well."

Rob didn't reply.

"Must be love."

"I saw you, you know. That day at the department store. It's not like I'm hiding it from you. It's why I asked to see you today."

Quinn smiled at him. "I'm kind of hurt, actually. You're not asking your own father to the wedding?"

"Look, it's not that I'm not grateful. I am. For everything. But I love this girl, and I see a chance for a different kind of life. Surely you want that for me too?"

"I've always been invested in your happiness."

Hope sprang up in Rob's heart. "So you agree? We can go our separate ways?"

Quinn put his hand lightly on Rob's wrist. "It may not be as easy as you think, this life you want with a white picket fence, brats in the yard, and an SUV. Can you deny you get a rush from the work we do, the way we live?"

"Maybe I did. Once. Not anymore."

"But you have a job to finish, yes?"

"I can't do it."

Suddenly Quinn's fingers tighten. "You can and you will. You will finish what you started. Don't forget just how much I know about you. How many murders I can link you to if I choose."

"And if I do?"

"And then, just one more thing."

"What?"

"You remember your old friend? Matt Walsh?"

"Of course I do." The shock on Matt's face, the rush of blood spurting down his chin.

Quinn leaned across the table and beckoned Rob to come in closer. "The one outsider who can link the two of us. He's moved. Changed his name. But I've found him. And you will kill him. And then, son, I will let you go."

Quinn released Rob's wrist. Rob looked down at his arm where Quinn had gripped him; a bruise was already starting to stain his skin.

Rob thought of Ellie's delicate bones, her tender heart. He looked up and met Quinn's gaze.

Now

"Listen, bitch, I don't know what kinda shit you trying to pull . . ." Crazy B is furious. "First you drag my ass out to this haunted-as-fuck house! Then you parade your skinny white behind all over the place . . ."

Ellie bites back her indignant retort.

"And now those missing kids!" He takes a step toward her. "You ain't nothing but trouble!"

Ellie raises her hands in supplication. "Listen to me. I want to rescue that boy. Others, if they're in there. It's why I brought you here."

Crazy B's bloodshot eyes blink. "And the money? The drugs?"

"There is no money. No drugs. I lied to you. But these people are stealing and selling children. And I needed your help."

He stares at her. "I still do," she says, struggling to keep her voice level and her mind clear, to meet his gaze. "I need your help."

"I'm out of here." He wheels away from her. "Who needs this crap?"

Ellie can hear the little boy sobbing, an aria of misery. Her eyes rake the house. If she can get up onto the roof of the porch . . . Maybe she can access the room from which the cries emanate.

"I'll give you another five hundred. Just to boost me up onto that roof." This at least stops Crazy B in his tracks. She points. Crazy B's eyes twitch to the house, then slide back to lock on hers.

"But I'll give you a grand if you wait for the kid and get him out of here."

"Let me see the cash."

Ellie digs into her bag and fans it out. A thousand dollars in American hundreds. "We have a deal?"

Crazy B only gives her a noncommittal shrug.

Ellie edges over to the porch. The weeping above is making her heart ache. Crazy B joins her, his eyes darting. One wrong move, she knows, and he'll be gone. She can smell his fear.

Ellie hands him the cash. It's most of the money she has left, but what can she do? The dealer pockets the bills and makes a lattice out of his hands. Ellie slings her bag over one shoulder and steps up into Crazy B's boost. He hoists her up. She grabs the drainpipe and pulls herself on top of the porch with a thud. She freezes, holding her breath. But all she hears are the child's soft sobs, the breeze scuttling through the dry tropical scrub.

After a wait that feels interminable, she exhales. She scrambles up the slope of the roof, heading toward the room from which the boy's cries rise and fall. She glances back down when she reaches the window. Crazy B has disappeared.

Rivulets of sweat snake down Ellie's body. She peers into the broken window. In a shadowy corner of the empty room is the small boy, his knees tucked up to his chest, thin arms wrapped tight around his bony knees. His disconsolate wails stop abruptly when he sees her. Ellie puts a finger to her lips. "Sshhhh."

She climbs through the window and crouches next to the little boy so their eyes are level. "My name is Ellie," she whispers.

The child stares back at her, his amber eyes wild with panic. Her heart starts to trip-hammer. She is terrified he will scream.

"I'm here to help you," she whispers urgently. "What's your name, sweetheart?"

He gnaws on his knuckle, silent. Then he whispers: "Thomas."

"Thomas," she says. "I'm here to help you," she repeats.

His eyes stay blank with disbelief.

She rises and strides back to the window and gestures for the boy to follow her. "Do you see how the roof of the porch is low over there?" She points and, after a second, he nods. "That's how I climbed up here to get you. I'm going to help you climb out the window, Thomas. Then I need you to crawl as quickly as you can to that side of the porch. Then all you'll have to do is drop to the ground. Can you do that, Thomas?"

The little boy looks panicky, unsure. His eyes skitter from her face to the window.

"It'll be just like the jungle gym at the park. You can climb the jungle gym, right? A big boy like you?" The boy nods. "When you get down, run away from the house. I'll be right behind you, I promise. Okay?

"But we have to go *now*, sweetheart. I'll help you out the window. And then, just like the jungle gym. And when you get down, you run. Run as fast as you can down the drive. There will be a man waiting for you with a motorcycle. You can trust him, I promise. He'll take you home. Do you know your address, honey?"

"Of course I do. I'm *six*."

"Six? You are a big boy. I know you can do this."

She lifts the child. She's surprised at how little he weighs. Tenderly, she sets him on the lip of the window. He hesitates, looking at the drop below, and squirms in her arms. She smiles at him. Unexpectedly, he smiles back. She touches his cheek and nods. Trustingly, he crawls down the slant of the porch roof. Ellie swings one leg out the window to follow him and then she hears a sound that freezes her soul.

The boy has fallen. He slides down the roof, his little hands scrabbling at the tiles. A whimper of fear escapes his lips as he slips over the edge of the roof. His fingers clutch at the drainpipe.

Ellie sees his hands straining as he dangles, his tiny knuckles going white.

"Thomas!" she commands, as loudly as she dares. "Thomas, listen to me. Listen to me, sweetheart. Fall. Can you fall?"

He is mute. Breathing heavily, rigid with fear.

"Thomas," she croons. "Listen to me. You need to trust me, honey. Just fall!"

Still no movement from him.

She flings herself onto her belly and hurtles down the roof's steep incline. Reaches a hand for him, but comes up short, in danger of falling herself. She scrabbles backward, desperate for better purchase.

"Don't let me fall. Please!" The plea is so quiet she almost doesn't hear it. She looks down into the boy's terrified face. His small hands strain. He stares at her with desperate, pitiful eyes.

His hands start to slip treacherously down the drainpipe. He whimpers. Ellie lunges for him. She misses, clutching only air. She tries again, her fingers closing miraculously around his red T-shirt. It comes away in her hands as he falls, the boy's thin body slipping through the oversized garment.

She doesn't know which is the most terrible. Is it the boy's howl of pure terror as he drops? Or the sharp cry of pain that erupts as his frail body hits the crushed-shell driveway?

Or most horrible of all, the hollow, vacant silence that follows?

The boy is a broken bird, splayed motionless on the ground. "Thomas! Sweetheart!"

He doesn't stir. She crumples the red T-shirt in her fist, fighting back a sob.

Then

Rob was late. Ellie glanced at her watch and smiled apologetically at her parents and the hotel's event coordinator. "I'm sure he'll be here any minute . . ."

Ellie decided she would give it another ten minutes before she began to worry. In the meantime, they could get started, as Rob had graciously (and laughingly) ceded control to Ellie's mother weeks ago. Ellie smiled, remembering how he had thrown up his hands in surrender and conceded that, yes, Ellie had been right, her mother was an unstoppable and scary force.

She turned to her mother. "I was thinking I liked the silver and white tablecloths, what do you think?"

Her mother's lips pursed. "I was thinking the lavender."

Ellie coughed to hide her giggle. Of course she was thinking the lavender, if Ellie was thinking silver. Once again she wished Rob were here, in on the joke.

Across town, Rob checked the time and silently cursed Ethan Clark. Normally the guy ran like clockwork and if he had maintained that admirable quality, Rob could be safely uptown debating linens and flowers with Ellie and his future in-laws. Instead, he was on the crowded platform of the uptown 6 train at Union Square, hiding behind a copy of the *New York Post*.

Finally. Ethan came down the subway stairs in a hurry. His tie was loosened, his cheeks flushed. He bumped into a squat black woman with an Afro and mumbled an apology. Clearly he had had a couple of drinks. Ethan had been feeling the pressure lately and had not been shy about opening up to Rob. Three nights ago, at the bar while waiting for their table, Ellie and Marcy had talked wedding plans, and Ethan had pulled Rob aside and spilled his guts. Marcy's thunderous ticking clock regardless, they had not managed to get her pregnant. They had recently begun the seemingly endless series of tests designed to determine whose biology was at fault, and Ethan was scared to get the results as well as a bit over the entire thing. Sex was supposed to be fun, wasn't it? Babies were supposed to come easily, right? Ethan had friends who had struggled with fertility. He had watched how it had sucked the joy out of not only sex but also entire relationships.

Ethan didn't know, of course, that Rob knew all too well the source of the other pressure Ethan was feeling. Rob reflected that having "mislaid" a million dollars of Quinn's money might be an even bigger source of anxiety than infertility issues.

Rob thought about the people he had "handled" for Quinn over the years. A cavalcade of lowlifes and gangsters, idiots and fools. The scum of the earth. Their baseness made Rob's work easier to reconcile, at least in the light of day. Rob went where he was told, did what he had to, and moved on to the next assignment. He availed himself of the sensory pleasures of life: superb food and wine, excellent accommodations, fine clothes, expensive watches and cars. Vacations in exotic locales, blissfully alone and achingly lonely at the same time.

It was deep in the night that his nightmares flared.

As Ethan lurched over to the edge of the platform to peer down the tunnel for the train, Rob mused that it really was too bad about Ethan. Rob liked him. And his wife, Marcy, had been the one to insist he meet Ellie. But it was going to be difficult enough to be a young widow, let alone a young widow with a baby. Their infertility was surely a blessing in disguise.

And if Rob had any hope of getting out, this last job must go forward. He would figure out something to do for Marcy, he promised himself, and quashed the knowledge that after killing her husband, her college sweetheart, nothing he could do would possibly compensate. He had thought he could never love anyone, and yet, there like a miracle was Ellie. Surely Marcy could love again. Even as he thought this, he knew he was bullshitting himself. He rocked back and forth indecisively on his heels, torn. Fuck. How could he do this? Could he kill a friend? Even with all he had learned about Ethan, it didn't make it easier.

Rob glanced at his watch once more. Fuck again. Ellie was going to be mad.

Finally, the roar of the approaching train. Ethan swayed unsteadily. Two tattooed, too-cool-for-school Puerto Rican girls rolled their eyes. One gave Ethan the finger. Leaning over the yellow warning line, Ethan peered into the tunnel. The train rumbled and screeched its way into the station. Like Quinn had taught him, it was a matter of preparation and timing. Rob switched into autopilot, moved alongside Ethan. Spoke his name, "Ethan," loudly enough for the drunken man to hear, softly enough that no one else on the platform heard him. As Ethan pivoted, a question in his eyes, Rob pushed, hard and fast.

Ethan tumbled onto the tracks in front of the onrushing 6 train as Rob walked swiftly across the platform and jogged up the stairs. He heard the screams of watching passengers, the high-pitched screech of the train, the thump and tear of Ethan's mangled body.

Rob emerged into Union Square, flicking his lighter and gratefully inhaling on a cigarette. If he got lucky with a cab, he wouldn't even be too late.

Now

Lucien leads the American out of the station and into the humid glare of the noisy street outside.

"Where are we going?" the man wants to know.

"Someplace quiet. Where we can talk."

They stride along the crowded streets of Castries in urgent silence. The scents of spices clog the air: cinnamon, turmeric, sea moss, pepper. They pass candy-colored shops catering to tourists. Tables set outside the shops feature beaded necklaces and handbags, shells painted colors not found in nature, intricately woven baskets, crafts and paintings by local artists, shot glasses and bottles of rum. Flyers stapled to telephone poles scream: MISSING CHILDREN, with blurry photographs beneath the blaring headline. HELP US FIND THEM! Lucien will not avert his eyes from the children's images. One of those boys was Olivier Cassiel, indeed found, indeed dead. And now one was little Thomas, his nephew. Guilt and frustration gnaw at him.

Lucien ushers the American into Castries Cathedral of the Immaculate Conception. The dull brick of the exterior belies the richness of the interior. Emerald green and deep purple walls are stippled with gold leaf vines. There are lavish displays of tropical flowers, bright purple altar cloths, carved and gilded columns, painted panels depicting biblical scenes, and numerous flickering red glass candle holders lit by the devout and hopeful. The red-and-gold ceiling is cantilevered to best display stained-glass panels so exquisite they could convert a nonbeliever. One depicts a beatific, haloed, dusky-skinned Madonna. She gazes lovingly at the black baby Jesus she cradles in her arms.

Lucien gestures to one of the carved wooden pews, then sits next to the stranger. He realizes he hasn't been in this church since his mother's funeral. After her untimely death, Lucien lost the comfort his faith had once provided him. It comes as a surprise to realize he thought of taking the American nowhere else.

The American wears jeans and a powder-blue windbreaker, too hot for the weather. Scuffed deck shoes. Crumbs of sleep gather in the corners of his eyes. His body is composed; his hands hang loosely, the wrists draped over his knees.

Lucien stays silent, not certain he can trust his own voice but also knowing that silence is sometimes the best way to get someone to talk. The American meets Lucien's appraisal with a frank inquiry of his own.

"Is there a reason you wanted to talk in a church? Rather than at the station?"

The questions take Lucien by surprise. "If you have legitimate information to share, I suggest you do it now. Let's start with your name."

The stranger shrugs, an acquiescence. "My passport says my name is Marshall Weston. But my real name is Matthew Walsh."

Lucien lifts an eyebrow. It isn't often people blithely announce they are traveling under a false passport. He nods for the American to continue.

"In order for you to understand what I am about to tell you, I need to go way back, to my own beginning. Is that all right?"

Marshall Weston (née Matt Walsh) had been born to a junkie mother, father unknown. He was placed in foster care and bounced from home to home until he was eleven. Then, unable to stand it, ("it" being his life in general, his foster parents in particular, and most particularly the sounds almost every night of his foster father in the room next door with his seven-year-old foster sister), Matt stuffed a knapsack with some clothes, a carving knife he filched from the butcher block in the kitchen, a can opener along with three cans of tuna, two apples, and fifty dollars he stole from his foster mother's secret stash in the laundry room. Then he hit the streets.

He lived on his wits and occasionally on his back. But every single shitty thing that happened to him made him more determined to change the course of his life. He was not going to be a junkie like his stupid bitch mother; he was not going to be a creep like his stupid-ass foster father. He learned that he was not only street-smart, but very smart.

When he was sixteen, he got a job with a moving company that was looking for cheap off-the-books workers. By the time he was twenty-six he had launched his own business, and was committed to hiring homeless people who needed a hand up.

He felt like a success but didn't allow himself to get cocky. He realized, as he grew his business, that his was one of many tragic stories, with a happier ending than most. He felt grateful but humble. He kept his expenses low, his head down. Until of course the sociopath he had since come to know as Quinn showed up at his place of business.

Lucien interrupts. "Quinn?"

Matt strokes his scarred mouth. Then he tells of arriving at his company garage one morning. Of being told a story of a long-lost father and a missing son and being asked to call a young employee, Rob Beauman, into the office. How Quinn had tortured Matt, cut off his lip. How when he regained consciousness he found both Rob and Quinn gone.

After the horror of that morning, Matt had been hospitalized for days. He told the police he had surprised a robbery in progress. The perpetrator, he insisted, had been masked. Fearful of Quinn's promised retribution, he told the cops he never saw his attacker. He protected Rob and never mentioned the young man had been present. Lying. It was one of many survival skills Matt had honed while living on the streets. After a time, the detectives interviewing him moved on to new cases, ones with a better chance of a solve.

Plastic surgery partially repaired his lip but the scars didn't mar just skin. Matt lived in fear that the maniac who had mutilated him would return. So he relocated to a new city, assumed an alias, started a new business; people always needed movers, he just had to hustle. He still hired kids from the streets, but he befriended them less often. He thought about Rob, wondered where he was, how he was, what he was doing, if he was even still alive.

One balmy spring night, when he locked up his garage, he found Rob standing in the shadows, waiting for him. At first he didn't recognize him. Rob was older of course, but different in other ways too. Harder. Wary. Weary. But also lighter. It was contradictory, but true.

Over rancid black coffee and overly sweet peach pie, in the unforgiving light of the crummy diner down the street, Rob explained why he was there. He was in love with a woman, Eleanor Larrabee. And she in turn loved him. He felt like he was home when he was with her. This naked admission gave Matt's heart a surge of envy; never in his life had he felt that way.

Rob went on. Quinn was willing to let Rob go to be with Ellie, but only if he killed Matt. Matt interrupted to ask why—after all, it had been years since Matt had even seen either one of them. Rob explained. Quinn had told him it was because Matt could link Quinn and Rob, but Rob was convinced it was really just a part of Quinn's twisted sadism. A way to punish Rob before letting him go free. Rob, however, had a plan. Matt had changed his identity once; Rob proposed he do it again.

Within days, Matt had sold his business, claiming he wanted to retire early and do some traveling. He took the money from the sale of the company and divided it. He hid one half through a series of complex bank transactions in order to set up his new life. With the other half he created a small endowment to help homeless kids and teenagers in his original name. At least a part of Matt Walsh would live on that way.

He bought a ticket for Indonesia, claiming Southeast Asia was first on his bucket list. The night before he was to leave, he took his former employees out for drinks. He toasted them again and again, seemingly in excellent spirits, leaving only when it was certain that many witnesses would be able to attest to his inebriated state.

Rob met Matt at a secluded spot near a stretch of sharply curving highway known locally as Devil's Run. Matt couldn't look at the body in the passenger seat of Rob's rented Dodge. The corpse was about Matt's age, weight, and height; even his hair color was a close match. He was naked. Rob had stripped him bare and disposed of his clothes.

Matt stripped off his own clothes, climbed clumsily into the new clothes and shoes Rob had bought for him. The silence of the night was cut only by muttered phrases—"Lift his arm." "Push." "That's it."—as they wrestled the clothes Matt had discarded onto the dead man. They positioned the corpse in the driver's seat of Matt's pickup truck.

Matt snapped his watch onto the dead man's wrist and then, for the first time, he faltered. The man was already dead, but what they were about to do was repugnant. In a brusque voice Rob said, "Wait in the rental. I'll take it from here."

Later, Rob drove Matt to the airport. They didn't speak. But as

Rob left Matt at the terminal for his flight to Canada, the two men hugged. Matt could smell smoke and oil on Rob's clothes and something more, the charred stench of burnt flesh.

Matt's death was attributed to drunk driving.

Lucien broke in here. "What about the body? Didn't they try to match dental records? DNA?"

Rob had assured him, Matt answered, that someone who knew the needed result, if not the reason why, would conduct the body's formal identification.

Matt moved to Toronto, became Marshall Weston. He started all over again.

Here Matt pauses. Then, looking steadily into his eyes, he tells Lucien about coming home from work yesterday and receiving the severed lip in the mail.

Lucien Broussard has heard many stories in his years as a cop. The one the man sitting across from him has just told is crazier than any of them.

"We had agreed that Rob would only reach out to me if and when his life was in danger, his life and that of the girl he was going to marry. I owe him that. He saved my life. That's why I'm here."

Lucien plucks at a loose thread hanging on his shirt cuff. A button tumbles to the church floor. "So if what you say is true, then you believe Rob Beauman and his wife are here on the island."

"Yes. At least his wife is."

"And this Quinn is on the island too."

"I don't know for sure. But I believe so."

"So you don't have any idea where they might be?"

"None. As I told you, Ellie sent me a package. It held a key to a P.O. box here on the island, in which there was a letter. The letter didn't give me much more detail. But I will tell you this: Rob and I had agreed that the plan would be to leave further information. Bread crumbs creating a trail."

Lucien studies him appraisingly. Then he asks, "And the severed lip?"

This telling little detail about the murdered Carter Williamson still hasn't been released to the press.

Matt's fingertip touches his mouth. He grimaces. "In the letter she said it was the lip of the man she admitted killing."

"Pretty insane, don't you think? Slicing off a man's lip just to send a message?"

"The world of Quinn is insanely dangerous, Detective. Computers can be hacked, letters intercepted, phones have GPS. A lip in an envelope means nothing, except to me and to Rob. Until I opened that post office box, I thought the message to come here was from Rob."

"Why are you telling me all of this? Are you saying that your friend and his wife, despite being killers themselves, are, what? Worthy of rescue? That we should find them and then ride in, guns blazing, and save them from this devil Quinn? And then what?"

A priest enters the cathedral from one of the side doors. He makes his way to a confessional booth. Matt blots the sheen of sweat on his forehead with a handkerchief. "I just want to find them. I swore to Rob that I would help him."

"You do understand that they have committed crimes? From what you have told me, Mr. Beauman has been working for a criminal organization for years. And you say that Eleanor Larrabee admits she murdered Carter Williamson and then mutilated him. She is also a person of interest in connection with another murder here on the island."

"You do what you need to do, Detective. All I can ask is that you understand this: Some people are born into darkness, some people fall into it over the course of their lives. To find a man like Rob Beauman, who suffered both, but maintained loyalty, kindness, his essential humanity—I refuse to believe he is irrevocably broken. And if he loves this girl, she's not broken either."

"You are a loyal friend."

"I have also known my fair share of darkness."

The tale is extraordinary, fanciful, bizarre . . . and yet it rings true. And what other options does he have? Officially on leave, Lucien knows he must follow this lead through.

"So what do you suggest we do now, Mr. Walsh?"

"Take me to the last place Ellie Beauman was known to be. If Rob taught her what we had worked out, she will have left a message."

Then

The day was appropriately overcast, the gray headstones of the cemetery bled seamlessly into the steely sky. As the rabbi spoke about Ethan, Marcy wept quietly into a crumpled tissue. Her mother-in-law sat next to her, her face a frozen mask of grief.

Toward the back of the small throng, Ellie and Rob stood together, clad in black. Ellie swayed a little as her spike heels sunk deep into the moist earth and Rob placed a steadying hand on her elbow.

The rabbi signaled it was time to lower Ethan's coffin into the cold, dark earth and Marcy rose to place a handful of dirt on its lid. This act snapped her thin veneer of control. She began to sob.

"It's so awful," Ellie murmured into Rob's ear. "Who would ever do such a sick thing?"

Rob shook his head. His hand tightened on Ellie's elbow, the same hand that had shoved Ethan to his death.

They offered their condolences to Marcy, to Ethan's parents and three brothers. Milled about exchanging the awkward pleasantries that funerals seem to demand, rendered even more so because of the abrupt and violent nature of Ethan's death. Finally they took their leave, relieved and guilty. Relieved to be away from the presence of naked grief—guilty, in Ellie's case because death hadn't chosen them, in Rob's case because it had, and because Ellie must never know.

In the car back to their apartment, they clutched each other's hands but did not speak.

As soon as they were inside, they tore at each other, frantically ripping at buttons and tugging at zippers. They made love often, but never before had it been like this, this ferocious, visceral attack, the brutal need to lose themselves and the memory of Marcy's heartbreak in the affirmation of each other's living, breathing bodies.

Later, they lay together, entangled on the floor. There was a thick smudge of blood on Rob's shoulder where Ellie had bit him. Blood smeared her lips and chin. They were both breathless, shocked at their own ferocity, unwilling to speak of it.

Now

Death. It follows her, swallows her, spits her out on the other side. Leaves her chewed and broken. And then circles back for another vicious bite. Ellie is almost used to it. Resigned.

But Thomas. Hardly more than a baby.

Ellie closes her eyes. Maybe she will never move from this spot again. Maybe she will just lie here. Burn in the sun. Let the tropical rain pound, the lightning flash. She will freeze in the cold dawn, stare down the stars in the inky night as she starves and dies. She deserves death. Her carcass will be pecked at by birds and nibbled by rats.

Sunspots swim against her shuttered lids as she thinks about all the different ways girls she knows have debased themselves for men. Drunken texts. Facebook stalking. Midnight booty calls. Turning a blind eye to cheating, gambling, a drinking problem. Forgiving that first angry punch and thereby becoming ripe for the next one. She thinks about poor Lou.

It hits her like a slap. She's more pathetic than any of them. She's let people lie to her her entire life, but she's been complicit. She's been a victim and blamed everyone else. And now she has willingly destroyed her own life for the sake of her husband. For Rob she chose to kill and mutilate a man. Now a child's death is on her hands. All for a man who has done nothing but lie to her. The hell with Rob Beauman, or whatever the hell his name is. She owes him nothing.

She seethes with fury. How the hell did she lose control over her own life?

Before she goes to prison, or dies (both seem equally likely), she needs to reclaim herself. Redeem herself.

Ellie's eyes snap open. Thomas is no longer splayed on the ground below. There is, to her bewilderment, no sign of him.

For a moment, she's convinced she has hallucinated him. Was he nothing but a figment of her tortured imagination?

Wait. Is that a rustle in the whispering beach grass? Her eyes narrow against the sun. She can't tell for sure.

Maybe the ghost of poor betrayed Marianne snatched him up, Ellie thinks wryly as she drops from the roof to the ground, landing painfully, staggering upright.

Wherever he is, she's going to find him and bring him home to his parents. She will not leave behind a boy who trusted her. There's been too much damage done. She will not let another person become a victim, especially not a child. But are there other children inside? She needs to check.

Ellie slips into the house through a shattered French door. She finds herself in a sunroom of gracious proportions. The house is cool and smells of mildew. There is a soggy patch of ceiling from which water drips steadily and arrhythmically.

Ellie tiptoes into the main hallway. She knows she needs to avoid Quinn and Rob as she searches, so she moves stealthily. Broken glass from skylights litters the once glorious wide-plank floors, now buckled and rank. The light is fractured and bent. Misshapen discolorations mar the painted walls.

As she creeps deeper into the house, she finds cracked tile floors, whole chunks missing, graffiti. Evident looting; a bathroom gapes with ragged holes where fixtures and copper piping once dwelled. Water drips and puddles in unexpected places. Maison Marianne lives up to its eerie reputation. The formerly grand palace is sodden with grief.

Ellie hears the faint murmur of men's voices and dips away in the opposite direction and up the stairs. She's in a hallway, three closed doors in a line.

A pitiful, mewling sigh floats through the air. The cry of a child? Ellie shudders. Flings open the first door. A bedroom probably, empty now but for one battered armchair. Opening the second door she finds only a stained mattress, dozens of empty beer bottles, charred wood and ash.

Her ears straining, Ellie clutches the handle of the third door and twists it, only then noticing the deadbolt. With trembling fingers, she unlocks it. The door hinges release an ugly screech of protest as she swings it open and she freezes, heart racing, certain the sound will bring Quinn and Rob running.

She finds herself staring into the very room from which she freed Thomas. Empty. Sun slanting in, dust motes dancing. There, by the window, is her beach bag, abandoned in her fruitless attempt to rescue Thomas.

And then from behind her, that cry again, full of despair and longing. Ellie whirls.

No one is there.

Then

The morning of his wedding to Ellie, Rob woke in his hotel room, reaching instinctively across the bed for her warm body. It took him a moment to remember where he was and why. As the realization hit, he smiled, a goofy grin of liberation.

He had done it. He had fulfilled his obligation to Quinn, as least as far as Quinn knew. He had killed for the last time. He was free to start his new life. He felt happy, a foreign emotion and therefore hard to trust. But already his mind was leapfrogging to all the delicious possibilities of what could come next.

As he showered, Rob wondered, and not for the first time, if Quinn had told the truth when he claimed he and Rob were father and son. In his heart Rob just couldn't believe they were tied by blood. Or maybe he just hoped that was the case. So what if he had no family at the wedding? So what if his mother and grandparents would never know? He was about to start his own perfect family.

Rob turned off the shower and smiled. Today he would marry Ellie. As he toweled off he made himself some promises: From here on out, his life was going to be a clean one, a good one, one that atoned for all his many wrongs. From this day forward he would love Ellie and take care of her.

As he stepped out of the bathroom, Rob saw Quinn. He was sitting on the edge of the bed idly toying with the gold cufflinks Ellie had bought Rob as a wedding present.

"Here to wish me well?" Rob asked the gaunt man evenly.

"Always," said Quinn, with that smile that never reached his eyes.

"We had a deal, Quinn. I did what you wanted."

"What do you really know about her?"

"I know all I need to."

"You disappoint me, son." Quinn's tone was mild, like a father rebuking a son for a minor infraction—ditching school or getting caught with a pack of cigarettes. "I don't think you're really thinking things through. She's a good-looking American woman; she would make an excellent mule."

"I won't get her involved."

"But I ask you—what kind of woman do you really think could love you? Don't you realize she must be as damaged as you are?"

Quinn let that question suspend between them for a good long beat. It hit a bitter nerve. Rob had wondered why he and Ellie felt so drawn to each other. But surely she was accessing his light? Surely he was not liberating her darkness?

"Violence is in you," Quinn continued softly. "Your mother welcomed it, didn't she? Even reveled in it. And you took your raw inclination for it to new heights once I schooled you. You can't escape who you are. And either your little bride senses it in you and wants it, or she is going to get the shock of her life when your true nature is revealed."

With sickening dread, Rob realized he might never be free of Quinn. But he had one last card to play.

Rob told Quinn that he knew where Ethan Clark had hidden the money he had stolen, that even better, he knew with whom Ethan had been colluding.

This pricked Quinn's interest. He asked for details.

"I took care of Ethan. Of Matt Walsh. I've always been loyal to you," Rob insisted. "If I give you the rest of the information, I'm asking you, please, let me go."

Quinn tossed the cufflinks from hand to hand. Finally, he gave a curt nod. "I need to know."

Ethan had teamed up with Carter Williamson, one of Quinn's men in St. Lucia. It began with Ethan diverting funds from Quinn's smuggling operations to Carter, money that was now snugly situated in St. Lucian bank accounts. Rob had traced the money, knew the account numbers and passwords.

Rob withheld the kicker for the finale. Ethan and Carter Williamson had been trafficking children into the U.S. for the black-market adoption industry. Using Quinn's pipelines without Quinn's knowledge or consent. They had betrayed Quinn, something he, Rob, had never done.

The revelation that Quinn had not been in total control was even more infuriating to him than the stolen money.

"Carter Williamson. I never would have thought he had the balls." Quinn's fist tightened around the cufflinks.

"Okay?" asked Rob. "Are we good?" He held his hand out for the cufflinks.

Quinn tossed them on the night table, ignoring Rob's outstretched hand. "Thank you, son. You've done well."

Quinn left the room, closing the door softly behind him. Rob rushed to the door. Flipped the security bolt and cursed himself for not having done it earlier. But although Quinn was gone, Rob didn't believe this was the end of it. He had been under Quinn's dominion too long to fool himself. But he also knew Quinn now. Could predict how he would react. Rob checked the clock. Ellie was due at the hotel in an hour in order to get her hair and makeup done. The wedding was in four hours.

He had time.

Now

Lucien and Matt drive to Vieux Fort in silence. Bertrand's favorite stuffed caterpillar is in the backseat of Lucien's Ford Taurus, a silent rebuke, a painfully cheerful totem of children and family. Lucien prays for his nephew. Then prays for himself, keenly aware that for the first time in his career, he is coloring way outside the lines. He has always prided himself on his ethical behavior. Even the threat of the thrashing he had leveled at Carter Williamson's partner, Pascal Jarett, had been no more than a ploy. Despite the recent hue and cry about frequent brutality on the force, this is not Lucien's way. He has fired his service weapon fatally only once in the course of his career, a shooting the resultant inquiry declared a clear case of self-defense. He has respected the rights of the criminals he has apprehended, even when the sons of bitches were really asking for it.

Now as they pull into the town, he glances at the American sitting next to him, wondering at the man's silence. Not many people, particularly Americans, have the ability to be so self-contained.

"First time to St. Lucia?" Lucien asks.

"Yes."

Matt volunteers nothing more. Lucien maneuvers his car into a parking space in front of Lou's shabby little hotel. The half-lit neon turtle sputters and flares.

"This is the place. We have reason to believe Ellie was here."

In the lobby, Matt's eyes skim the décor, the white rattan furniture with its faded cushions, the pile of brochures for local vendors on the coffee table, the Dutch door leading into what had been Lou's office, the now-empty parrot cage with its plaques announcing the names of the birds.

"We found Louise Butler's body in room 6."

Matt nods and the two men make their way over to that room. Lucien breaks the police tape crisscrossing the door so they can enter.

"I assume your people went through the room thoroughly?" Matt asks.

"Of course."

"And found no message of any kind?"

Lucien has to hide his irritation. He has encountered this attitude before from tourists. A kind of condescension toward the local police, as if being from the island meant they were playing at being cops.

"No. We had a witness statement that put her in the vicinity and then found in this room a piece of a fake nail that she had been reported as wearing. We haven't confirmed that she was actually here, but it's our best lead so far."

"Mind if I look around anyway?"

"Be my guest."

The American opens the night table drawer, peers under the bed. Stands on the bed and examines the blades of the ceiling fan. Runs his fingers along every inch of the green curtains. Lucien watches by the door. His cellphone rings. Agathe.

"I need to take this. Let me know when you're done."

Matt nods his assent. Lucien walks back to the lobby to take Agathe's call. He wants to keep his business private. He glances at his watch. With each passing minute, the odds of finding his nephew alive diminish. He tugs at his collar, which is suddenly choking him.

Agathe is surprisingly calm, given her hot temperament, and Lucien realizes his wife is keeping it together for the sake of her sister, whom he hears keening in the background. Lucien's heart aches as he thinks of the crumpled little boy stuffed into a refrigerator on Carter Williamson's boat.

Calmly he explains they are doing everything they can. He is reassuring about Thomas's well-being even though, deep inside, he is no longer optimistic the boy is still on the island or even alive. He is suffused with a kind of tender pain. He loves his wife, he loves his family. If Thomas is dead, he knows none of them will ever be the same again. He has seen violent death shred families too many times to believe his family will be any different.

He does not mention he has been pulled off the case. He does not say he is engaged in a desperate wild-goose chase on the basis of information provided by a stranger he has no reason to trust. He had vowed to protect his wife when they married. He will do so as long as he can.

Matt comes back into the lobby. He shrugs. Nothing. Lucien watches as the American wanders over to the empty parrot cage. The parrots are gone, but a curled, blood-red feather wavers atop the filthy newspaper at the bottom of the cage. Matt opens the cage door, idly plucks up the feather.

Lucien's last slim clue is a bust and he is suddenly, irrationally angry with this American and his wild stories. Agathe's voice rises in her distress, spilling rancid through Lucien's phone and into the moist air. Lucien raises a finger to indicate he needs another moment on the call. Turns his back to Matt. Tries to soothe his wife, and feels only shame.

Then

She supposed it was ridiculous, this hat perched on her head, festooned with ribbons, white ostrich feathers, and glittery letters that spelled out "Bride." But her girlfriends had insisted. And several margaritas in, Ellie was enjoying it. Men at the bar were blatantly offering to take her for "one last spin"—she hadn't paid for a drink all night. The flirting was outrageous, good-natured, flattering. She had wanted a girls' night out, a bachelorette's debauch rather than a shower, and her friends had delivered. Ellie was tipsy, happily rooted in ritual.

She knocked back the last of her current drink, and excused herself for the restroom, dancing her way to the back of the bar. There, she peed and flushed, washed her hands. She repaired her makeup in the mirror, a touch more lipstick, a fixed smudge of mascara.

She felt so blessed. Her bridesmaids were here: Tara, her best friend from childhood, and Collette from college—funny how they had gotten so much closer after. Six other girls she had met since moving to New York. They had a limo for the night and nowhere to be in the morning.

Ellie was sorry that Marcy, who had set her up with Rob in the first place, hadn't made it. Still, Ellie understood. She couldn't imagine living with the pain Marcy must be feeling now. Ellie sloughed off the thought; she would call Marcy tomorrow. Tonight she was going to party.

Now

Lucien swallows but nothing dislodges the lump in his throat. He knows he has to join his family, he is on his way, but he is sick at heart and dreading seeing them. On leave, powerless and empty-handed, he can't bear the sense of impotence and passivity that overwhelms him. If at least that peculiar American had brought him a useful clue with respect to the hotel murders, he could be back at the station, in the mix, hearing the latest on the search for Thomas.

Lucien wonders, and not for the first time, if a single thing the American has said is true. What a bizarre story! But at least the missing boys are back in the foreground. A cop's nephew and suddenly the department is paying attention again. Lucien drums his fingers on the steering wheel, full of fury and despair.

As he turns the corner that will take him to his sister-in-law's house, Lucien sees a sea of bodies standing in the street. What is this? But he realizes the crowd is peaceful: singing, swaying, holding flickering candles and photographs of the stolen boys.

Lucien can see his wife at the front of the crowd, dry-eyed and resolute, her arm wrapped protectively around her sister's shoulders. Gabrielle's husband and parents stand behind the two sisters. Baby Bertrand is cradled in his grandmother's arms.

Lucien parks his car. Weaves through the crowd toward his family. He sees Olivier Cassiel's mother, Yvette. She is slumped across her boyfriend, Rudy, their little girl hollow-eyed between them. Rudy strokes Yvette's back, trying ineffectually to soothe her disconsolate sobs, and Lucien is relieved to see that grief has leached the violence from him. Lucien sees the parents of the still-missing boys: Sebastien's scrawny, teenage single mother, comforted by her own mother; Jacob's parents, solid and stalwart, surrounded by their four other children; Pierre's petite mother with her milk-coffee skin and electric blue eyes, dwarfed by her darker-hued and burly husband.

Agathe meets his gaze as he nears them; she stretches out an imploring arm. The frank need in her eyes stops Lucien in his tracks. He has never felt so inadequate. He embraces his wife, lifts his sleeping son from his mother-in-law's arms. Lucien buries his face in the crook of his son's neck and inhales his powdery baby scent.

Then

The night before their wedding, Ellie stayed alone at their apartment, while Rob took a room at the hotel hosting their reception. They had decided to spend the night apart, a nod to tradition, not superstition. But as Ellie wandered the apartment, unable to sleep, she wished Rob were there.

It really was their place now, as opposed to his, and would be even more so once they integrated the mounting piles of wedding presents—things that would be "theirs" rather than "hers" and "his." Gift boxes filled the apartment, despite the fact that they had requested donations to the Matt Walsh Foundation instead of wedding presents. Ellie had convinced Rob that they should return most of them, but choose a few to keep as symbolic of their new life together.

She knew she should sleep, but her mind skittered about. She felt elated and not at all tired. She thought about how much she loved Rob, even as she worried about the distance he kept between them, the deft way he circumvented questions about his past.

He had embraced her friends, her parents, and her world with ease but hadn't merged much of his life into hers—with no family to speak of, just one cousin who lived overseas, and few friends in New York, he seemed to exist as an island. And he teasingly deflected most of her questions about his upbringing. His rationale—that she was all he needed, that their life together was the only life he wanted to talk about—was simultaneously thrilling and a bit terrifying. He seemed to accept her dark secrets without her having to admit them, to be able to calm her anxieties without her naming them. Weren't they bound by an intoxicating combination of affection, connection, lust and thrills, intellectual stimulation, and laughter? What was love, anyway? Who really knew? Why couldn't she be happy with what she had?

Yet, as the night lengthened, her uneasiness built. What did love mean to her? Loss. Her sister, Jason, even Hugh . . . She remembered their final night together.

It had been a night of crossed purposes. Ellie had been steeling herself to tell Hugh she loved him. She hadn't said this to a man since Jason, but after almost eight months with Hugh, she wanted to proclaim it. He had been a little odd lately, alternating between distant and very attentive. But then he had bought her a beautiful necklace for her birthday, intricately worked silver set with turquoise, moonstone, and carnelian. And as he had kissed the back of her neck with utter tenderness when he had fastened the clasp, Ellie decided the necklace was the declaration of his feelings. She was now ready to pronounce hers.

As always, the specter of Jason hung over Ellie. She was nervous, drank a little too much wine at dinner. So when the dessert was served and Hugh had clasped her hand in his and started to speak, she had shushed him and plunged on impulsively.

"I love you."

"What? Ellie, listen to me—"

"You don't have to say it back, I know you feel it."

She fingered the silver necklace; she had worn it precisely for its affirmation.

"Ellie, you don't understand."

There was something of shredded steel in his voice; it was the only way she could think to describe it. Impervious, yet torn.

"What is it? Hugh? What don't I understand?"

"I haven't known how to tell you."

A decision had been made; she suddenly felt it in her bones, a decision that was about her, about them. And she had not been a part of the process. She felt dizzy with fear. "Tell me what?"

"I'm being transferred. To London."

Oh. Was that all it was? Okay. A long-distance thing. They could work it out. Hugh was extremely ambitious about his career; she liked that about him. She tried to keep her voice light.

"When do you leave?"

"Five days. But I've known for a month."

"Why didn't you tell me? This is terrific news, isn't it?"

"It is terrific news. But it's also really made me think about us, and if I wanted to, you know, continue on. Given the distance and all."

Ellie felt her cheeks burn. She had just blurted out her confession of love. And now he was breaking up with her. Why couldn't she have kept her stupid mouth shut? Why had she drunk so much?

"It's not like you're not a great girl—"

"Compliments through double negatives. Fantastic."

"Come on, Ellie, don't make this harder than it has to be. We've had fun—"

"Did you not hear me just tell you I love you?"

"Well, yes, I did. But I think we both rather wish you hadn't, am

I right? So why don't we dial it back and just finish our dinner like the friends we are—"

Ellie scraped her chair back and rose, jerking on her sweater and fumbling for her handbag.

"Don't be like that, Ellie."

She hadn't replied. She had left the restaurant and stalked home. The night was chilly, but she didn't feel the cold. Her head was pounding. How stupid could she be? Why did she always get it so wrong? She wanted to be in love, to be loved, but she just couldn't manage to read the signals correctly. What an idiot she was! What was wrong with her? How could she not have seen this coming? Could Hugh somehow see the black stain on her soul that was Jason?

Finally on her corner, she stopped. Without thinking, she reached up, unclasped the silver necklace, and tossed it into a trash can. She wanted no reminders: not of Hugh, not of her humiliation, not of her deepest belief—that she was fundamentally damaged. That she was—and always would be—unlovable. Unloved.

Now, on the eve of her wedding to Rob, she looked at her wedding dress, a ghostly presence dangling from a hook over the bedroom door. Within hours she would bring that phantom to life, and in it, marry the man she loved wholeheartedly. In doing so she would lay down the revenant that was Hugh—she would lay down all the ghosts of her prior relationships. But even as she thought this, a menacing shadow crept through her thoughts. Was there such a thing as love without reservation? Was that truly how she felt or had she just been swept along in a foolish romantic tide? Should she be worried by Rob's reluctance to talk about his past? Was she repeating her pattern of not seeing what fit the world as she so desperately wanted to view it?

Fingering the frothy lace of her wedding gown, Ellie smiled. Rob loved her. He told her so all the time. Rob was going to marry her. She wasn't damaged, as she had feared.

She was going to love him and be vulnerable to him, she was going to take care of him and let him take care of her. It was all going to be wonderful. It was going to be perfect. She was going to fall into her life with Rob, arms and eyes and heart wide open.

Tomorrow was her wedding day. From now on, she was getting her happily ever after.

Now

Rob paces in front of Quinn, who leans against the wall in the near-empty room, watching him. Water drips from the swollen ceiling. Sky and sea stretch beyond the window, infinitely blue, achingly beautiful.

"Why shouldn't I take advantage of a deal that's already in place?" Quinn's tone is biting. "That was built on the back of my business?"

"Because it's *children*." Rob's agitated. "I was taken from you. Surely you understand what you're doing to these families?"

"But I'm also creating new ones. People who desperately want children are getting them." Quinn sounds pleased with himself. "I'm conducting acts of profitable altruism."

Carter Williamson is dead. Ethan is dead. Quinn has punished the guilty and seized what he deems rightfully his. Rob knows that neither he nor Ellie is needed anymore. Despite Quinn's promise that he has sent his man out to get Ellie, Rob knows at this point they are now both only liabilities.

"This is what is going to happen," Rob insists, fighting the dread rising within him.

Quinn laughs, genuinely delighted. "You think you're in a position to be giving me orders?"

"I'm going to turn myself in for the murder of Carter Williamson. Ellie is going to go home to New York a free woman."

Quinn replies with a dismissive gesture. Pulls one of the chaises away from under the *drip, drip, drip* of the water. "Why would I allow that to happen?"

"Because if it doesn't, an anonymous tip is going to expose everything you've got coming in through Miami. Come on," Rob baits him. "Wasn't it you who taught me about a time-release guarantee?"

Rob watches Quinn suppress a twist of a smile, one at war with the thinly veiled anger Rob's ultimatum has sparked. Flattery always has been a bit of a weakness for Quinn. But predictably, the anger wins. Quinn's eyes and voice go cold. "Hector will find her. Then we'll see."

Three distinct heavy thuds echo through the house.

"What's that?" Quinn cocks his head, feral, hunting.

"I don't know."

There is a swell of quiet. The ceiling drips. The tropical breeze blows through the dingy room carrying with it the scent of brine and flowers.

The air is split by a plaintive cry, pierced with anguish, cracked with pain.

Quinn's visibly unnerved. "Is that the kid?"

"How should I know?"

"Come with me." There is a crumple of red at the other end of the main hallway, near the bottom of the stairs. Quinn strides over to it. Kicks it flat with the toe of his shoe. It's a child's T-shirt, a dump truck emblazoned on the front.

Another thud. A single one this time, reverberating like a meditation bell, its last vibrations tapering off into eternity.

Just as the last faint tremor fades, another loud keening cry, laced with suffering, doused with longing. It sounds like it's coming from upstairs.

"Enough," Quinn snaps. His bony shoulders hunch in irritation as he ascends the stairs.

A child's ball comes tumbling down the steps and past his feet, navy rubber with happy red stars.

Bounce. Bounce. Bounce.

Quinn twists his head to follow the ball. There's a thick, dull thud. An explosive grunt of surprise and pain. Quinn slumps facefirst onto the stairs, limbs splayed.

Rob stares down at the dark crimson liquid flowing from the back of Quinn's head. There is a clinking sound. Rob lifts his gaze.

A piece of copper piping, one end smeared with Quinn's blood, falls down from the shadowy landing, clanging its way down the steps until it comes to rest at the bottom.

Silence.

Rob ascends the stairs slowly, stepping gingerly past Quinn, whose breath is shallow, whose wound is ugly.

At the landing, it takes Rob's eyes a moment to adjust. So much of this house is flooded with light, but this hallway is thick with shadows.

"Ellie," Rob breathes.

She's pressed up against the wall, receding in the gloom, practically a ghost herself.

Between them, mere flickers of eye contact. Rob feels tentative and fragile, excruciatingly aware of the heavy layer of exhaustion coating them both. The oppressive weight of unasked and unanswered questions. He takes a step toward her.

"We should see to that child," he says.

"He's not here," she replies. "No one else is here."

"Are you sure?"

"I got the boy out. No one else is up here."

Ellie pushes the hair away from her eyes. "I heard what you said," she murmurs. "You would have done that for me? Turned yourself in?"

"Yes. Of course . . . I can still do it," he offers impulsively. "Turn myself in. Let you go home."

"I was going to walk away. Never see you again."

He knows in his gut this is what he deserves.

"We've come this far," she says hoarsely, then falters.

She's alive. She's well. She said "we." Could she still love him? He longs to kiss her. He doesn't dare.

Quinn moans and stirs.

"What are we going to do with him?" Ellie asks.

Rob doesn't answer. He descends the stairs quickly, drags Quinn onto one of the chaises in the great room. Roots in the bags of supplies next to the chairs and finds duct tape and a folding utility knife. Tapes Quinn down tightly as Ellie creeps down the stairs, watching. Then he drops the knife. Backs away from Quinn.

His eyes meet Ellie's.

Then

Rob paced the anteroom, his cellphone pressed to his ear. The ball-room was mere steps away, full of plumed and perfumed guests. Rob could hear the string quartet. The processional was to begin in twelve minutes. He exclaimed into the phone, asked questions, his face registered disappointment.

There was no one on the other end of the line. This was all a show for the benefit of his tux-clad future father-in-law, who stood a discreet distance away, allowing Rob his privacy.

Rob said goodbye to his nonexistent caller. Turned to Brian. "He's stuck in Dallas. Flight's been canceled."

Rob had planned this elaborate ruse for weeks. When the subject of a best man had arisen, Rob was flummoxed. Who could he ask? The convention of a best man to stand up for him at the wedding was a detail he hadn't considered when making his impromptu proposal. Ellie knew his friends in New York were recent, none of them particularly close. He had endured a moment of wistful thinking about his old mentor, Matt Walsh. If anyone should be beside him today it should be he, although that was sadly impossible.

So he had created a first cousin. Jake Beauman. Jake was a romantic figure, a world traveler who had taken a stint in the Peace Corps and turned it into a passion for teaching drought farming in Africa. Jake was a free spirit who came and went unexpectedly, who lived out of a rucksack.

Ellie had been thrilled when Rob told her Jake had agreed to be his best man and was flying in for the wedding. Then there had been weeks of updates: Jake had booked his flight; Jake had sent his measurements for the tux; Jake had to change his flight but would still arrive the day of the wedding. Rob had taken the false measurements to the shop, and paid for and picked up the charcoal-gray tuxedo, which now hung in Rob's hotel room, always and forever a phantom.

"You must be disappointed." Brian clapped a hand on Rob's shoulder.

"Of course." Rob's distress was real enough. "What should I do? What do I tell Ellie?"

"How about this? I walk Ellie down the aisle, then come and stand with you instead of taking my seat? I'd be happy to stand up for the man who has made my daughter so happy." With a smile, "After all, I already have the boutonniere."

Rob was genuinely touched. He shook Brian's hand and thanked him. Problem solved. Except for the difficulty of adding to the many falsehoods he had already told his lovely bride. At least the lies about the mythical Jake Beauman were relatively harmless.

Now

The candles have been snuffed, the hymns concluded. Still the street is awash with people—chatting, commiserating, gossiping, and speculating, but also comforting the families of the missing boys, offering prayers and meals. Lucien is grateful the gathering has been a peaceful one. He stands alone now in the small yard in front of Gabrielle and Peter's home. The others have gone inside—Agathe to put Bertrand to sleep, the rest of the family exhausted and unable to bear any more public scrutiny. Therese, Lucien's mother-in-law, wants everyone to eat, even though no one feels the slightest bit hungry. Lucien suspects she just wants the distraction of cooking and serving.

"I'll be right there," Lucien promised Agathe. But he stays in the yard, fighting against a flood of defeatist emotions the only way he knows how—cataloguing and reexamining every bit of evidence he has collected. The missing boys, Olivier's death, the two murdered expats. Are they connected in some way or is that his frustration speaking? It feels like some grand illumination is just beyond his reach. He keeps turning the pieces of the puzzles, hoping they will click into satisfying place.

When the motorcycle appears in the distance, Lucien doesn't pay it much mind at first. But then the bike stops right in front of Lucien. The driver is Crazy B. He looks shocked and nervous when he recognizes Lucien. Lucien realizes there is a small boy sitting in front of the dealer. He's shirtless; his frail ribcage pushes against thin skin. He wears tan shorts. Light-up sneakers. The boy pulls off the helmet obscuring his face. Thomas.

Lucien springs to his feet. He can't form words. He's aware his mouth gapes open even as his arms stretch toward the boy.

Thomas cries, sobs of relief that shake his body as Lucien sweeps him into his arms. His heels kick against Lucien's back, his light-up shoes sparkling with every smack. Crazy B roars away into the night, with an anxious backward glance at Lucien.

And then Gabrielle is there, drawn outside by some kind of primordial maternal sense. Her child is home. He is safe.

The moment Lucien hands Thomas into Gabrielle's arms is truly one of the most gratifying of his life. Gabrielle's entire body trembles. Agathe, standing next to her sister, radiates relief. Thomas's father, Peter, wraps Lucien in a bear hug and his in-laws, Therese and Moses, openly weep. For a long moment, the three women, Therese, Gabrielle, and Agathe, cling together, with Thomas at the center of their protective huddle. Lucien asks himself if there was ever a more beautiful thing.

Lucien knows he needs to talk to his nephew. He also knows Gabrielle is not likely to support this initiative. He enlists Agathe.

"Agathe, I need to ask Thomas questions."

"No! He is exhausted, the poor little thing! Traumatized."

"But, my darling, if he can help find the other boys . . ."

Lucien looks into his wife's beautiful green eyes and for the first time in months lets down the barriers he had so carefully constructed between them. He allows her to see his pain, his anxiety, his sense of purpose, and his fear.

She takes his hands in hers and nods.

When Lucien emerges from Thomas's bedroom a half hour later, he is filled with determination. He knows what he must do next.

Then

"What's your first best memory?"

It was a rainy Saturday morning a week before their wedding. Rob and Ellie braved the downpour to run out to the little place on the corner for coffee and bagels, then tumbled back into bed. Now they lay, limbs entangled, sleepy despite the coffee, savoring the idea that they could do anything they liked for the rest of the day, or better yet, do nothing at all.

"My first best memory?" Rob repeated. The question, posed by Ellie, troubled him. Rob didn't dwell on memories. There weren't that many that were good, for one thing, and keeping himself firmly in the here and now was a big part of how he managed to live with himself. This sharing, the parsing of intimacies and memories and histories, these sheer onion layers of exposure and trust and deeper exposure that Ellie insisted on, these were all new to him. He relished it. It terrified him. How often hope and fear are one and the same.

Even as all this ran through his head at lightning speed, he said, "You go first."

"Okay. My first best memory is of me and my sister."

"I didn't even know you had a sister."

"She died when I was seventeen. Leukemia."

"How old was she?"

"Twenty. Diagnosed at fifteen."

"Jesus."

"It changed everything. It was like there was one life before Mary Ann got sick and another after. But when I want to remember her, I always think about this memory. It's the very first one I have, and I'd rather remember her this way than think about her weak and dying."

"So what's the memory?"

"I was about three or four, I guess, so she was six or seven. It was raining out . . . kind of like today. It felt like it had been raining forever. Mary Ann at least got to go to school, but I had been cooped up in the house and I was going stir-crazy. Mary Ann had just gotten home, and even in the short walk from the school bus stop on the corner she had gotten soaking wet, so Mom took her into our bedroom to get her changed. She had sat me at the kitchen table with a coloring book and a strict command to stay put—but I was sick of sitting still. I was fidgety and restless. Then I saw it. This china plate my mother had. It had been her grandmother's. It had a rooster painted on it and the words 'My love will stop when this rooster crows.' We were never allowed to touch it. She kept it on a little shelf in the kitchen filled with other mementos, a model of the Eiffel Tower my parents had gotten on their honeymoon, a pair of candlesticks from a family trip to Williamsburg. Anyway, I loved that plate. I decided to climb up on a chair and take it down, just to hold it, to look at it. You can guess what happened. I stretched, the chair tipped; the plate fell to the floor and smashed into pieces. Mary Ann came into the room. She saw the broken plate and then my face. I remember being so afraid of what I had done. And ashamed. I thought Mary Ann would yell at me, or go running for my mother. But instead, she told my mother she had broken the plate. I'm still not quite sure why she did—she lied for me."

"That's a funny thing to remember so strongly."

"I knew in that moment that Mary Ann would always have my back. That in the 'us and them' of kids and parents, she was my 'us.' "

Rob realized he couldn't remember a time when he felt he had an "us" in his life. Not before Ellie. "It must have been awful for you when she died."

"This may sound terrible, but in some ways it was a relief too, you know? She had been sick for so long, and her illness just vacuumed up everything in its path. I've never told anyone that before. About hating what her illness did to me, to our family."

"You can tell me anything." He kissed her and she felt that it was almost true.

Now

Rob hears the car before he sees it. Rattling and wheezing into the driveway, the tires spitting up crushed shells. He hears Ellie whisper a question, confused by the sound. Rob doesn't answer. He strides swiftly into the hallway, scooping up the blood-spattered copper pipe as he goes. Its weight and heft feel reassuring in his hand. Ellie trails after him. He glances at her. Her eyes are wide with apprehension.

Rob accidentally kicks a piece of broken tile and it clatters and skips, unnaturally loud.

An old junker, barely held together by rust and spit, shudders to a stop in front of the mansion. A man exits.

Square-jawed and solid, he plants himself in the driveway. He assesses the ruined majesty of Maison Marianne.

Rob exhales. "I knew he would come."

Rob drops the bloody pipe and runs outside. Ellie doesn't move.

The two men hug, but Ellie lingers in the doorway. Rob turns to her. "Matt, this is my wife, Ellie."

Rob is jubilant that Matt has come. It is evident in the lift in his voice, the light in his eyes. Matt's presence lightens Ellie too, or at least provides a welcome distraction from the thorny facts of Rob and their relationship built on lies. And death.

Matt shares his interactions with Lucien Broussard. How he got the detective to take him to Lou's hotel and how while there he'd found the brochure with Ellie's scrawled message. He compliments Ellie on her cleverness in hiding the note in the parrot cage.

After he had parted ways with Broussard, it hadn't taken Matt long to figure out that "Maison Mary Ann" was actually Maison Marianne. The lore of the house was well known to the locals and it had taken Matt only one round of rum punch at a funky thatch-roofed bar to hear the whole story from an old boozehound. A hundred in cash and another round had convinced the old boozer to lend Matt his ancient rust bucket of a car.

Matt's made arrangements, he tells them. He's going to get them off the island. They must get going.

"What about Quinn?" Ellie asks. "He's still alive. We can't just leave him here."

Matt's fingers stroke the scars surrounding his own mutilated mouth. "Let the bastard rot."

A short while later, the junker abandoned just outside town, Matt leads the way through the crowds thronging the streets of Soufrière. Ellie trails behind him. Rob takes up the rear. Rob feels anonymous here. He wants to stay that way.

He keeps his eyes on Ellie's back, the glossy brown hair of a stranger, the swaying hips of his lover, his bride, his wife.

Panic rises in his gut. He is this close to freedom from Quinn and a life with Ellie, but this desire suddenly feels like a crushing burden. Ellie has proven she would risk her own life for him, kill for him. What if he can't escape the life he has lived? What if he will always be the man he is?

Rob is terrified of failing Ellie, terrified of failing himself.

Matt takes an abrupt turn into an alley. He leads them through a lime-green door, the paint blistered, the door sagging on its hinges. Canned goods jam the shelves. Crates of fresh produce are haphazardly piled. A fat tabby cat stretches in a patch of sun. A restaurant storeroom. There is a tantalizing scent from the adjacent kitchen: aromatic spices, piping hot oil.

A man emerges from the steam of the kitchen. Shiny, freshly shaven head. Pierced eyebrow. Calloused hands. Rob steps protectively in front of Ellie.

But Matt greets the stranger warmly and the bald man replies in kind.

Could it be? Rob's eyes search the man's face. He had had a full thatch of hair back in Cleveland, a leaner look. But that voice. Unmistakable.

"P.J.?" Rob asks tentatively.

The bald man claps Rob on the back. "I live here, man, have for years. But then I hear from Matt? I mean, I thought he was dead. I flew back for the fucking funeral!" P.J. points his finger at Matt. "A zombie, back from the dead. And then to hear you were here? But I'm not asking any questions," P.J. continues in a tone that slams that particular door shut. "I don't want to know. I just know you need off the island. I've arranged to borrow a friend's fishing boat."

"So let's go." It is the first time Ellie speaks.

Matt shakes his head. "We can't quite yet. I need to put together some cash. And the police are all over the harbor. We need to wait until nightfall."

These three people have all always come through for Rob. An unfamiliar emotion presses against his chest. Suddenly he recognizes it.

It is a rising tremor of hope.

Then

The rain was still streaming down the window, blurring the world outside.

"Okay. Your turn. Your first best memory. Come on," she coaxed, "it can't be that hard."

Ellie's head nestled on Rob's shoulder. She traced a pattern on his bare chest with her fingertips.

"Oh, all right. Here goes. I was waiting in a restaurant. It was an ordinary night after an ordinary day. I was waiting for someone I didn't know, and ambivalent about being there at all."

"Wait a minute. Back up. How old were you?"

"Sshh. This is my memory, stop interrupting."

"Yes, sir!" Playfully, she gave his nipple a tweak.

"Ouch! A woman came into the restaurant. She had long blond hair and a green coat."

Ellie picked her head off his chest and looked at him.

"Me?"

Rob continued as if she hadn't spoken. "The hostess led her to my table. This woman was gorgeous, sure, but I wasn't really looking to meet someone. It was too complicated. There wasn't room in my life . . ."

"Tell me!"

He kissed her forehead, the tip of her nose, her lips.

"What happened to you, baby?" she pressed softly. She was marrying this man; she had to know. "What happened in your life that hurt you so much?"

He gathered her tighter in his arms. "It doesn't matter. All that matters is that we look forward. I don't want to look back. Falling in love with you is my first best memory."

They made love. They were tender. They were kind. They felt safe. They could dissolve into each other. They just might.

Now

Lucien pushes open Maison Marianne's front door. He has not been here in six years. Not since the murder-suicide that had not only shocked the island but inspired fevered international reporting as well. Of course it had. Think of all the elements: a rich self-made American; his patrician, wellborn wife; a local girl, no more than a teen, really; rumors of voodoo spells and restless ghosts. Lucien doesn't believe in superstition. He believes in facts and evidence. Still, he can see how the house maintains its legend. The floorboards creak ominously under his feet; the very walls seem to weep.

Lucien shakes off the wispy traces of ghost tales that cling to him like cobwebs. He may not believe in ghosts, but he can't deny the heaviness of the fallen grandeur of this ruin, the welter of pain that shrouds it.

But the house appears to be empty of life, human life at any rate, he thinks as a fer-de-lance slithers in front of him. Lucien stays stock-still until the snake, which he knows to be venomous, the deadliest variety on the island, disappears into a crack in the wall. Lucien's exhale as the reptile disappears sounds unnaturally loud in the moist, stagnant air.

If Thomas had been right, if he had been held at Maison Marianne, it seems his captors have since fled. Frustration prickles at Lucien's skin, leaving him irritable. These heinous criminals are almost like ghosts themselves in the way they have eluded him.

Lucien sees the body as he enters the great room. It is a man. Tall and gangly. He is bound to a cheap chaise longue with duct tape. Blood pools from his stomach. He is still. Silent.

Lucien strides to the body and checks the man's pulse, noticing the dancing skeleton tattoo on his cold wrist. The man is dead. Another murder has fouled Lucien's beloved island.

But it is the bloody severed lip—cleanly sliced from the corpse's face and casually tossed to the dank, filthy floor—that brings a roiling wave of nausea into Lucien's throat.

$\mathcal{T}hen$

Ellie had sent the text to the number she had been given, using a burner phone that she discarded immediately. The text was succinct: *Meet me at La Canne in the Grande Sucre Hotel. 2 P.M.* La Canne was the hotel's main bar, half open-air, half covered, exploding with fresh tropical flowers, clean sand and clear water just feet away. Ellie had seen pictures of the man she was to meet. She also had another advantage. He was expecting a man.

When Williamson entered, Ellie was sitting at the curved bar sipping a virgin rum punch. She wanted her wits about her. It was 1:52. She recognized him from the photographs an Internet search of his name had generated—muscular, deeply suntanned, his hair streaky from salt water and sunshine. Much bigger than she. She watched him scan the bar. She couldn't do this. She suddenly knew she couldn't do this. Could she?

Carter settled in at the other end of the bar, satisfied he was early.

He kept his back to the wall and his eyes trained on the entrance. He was so intent on his expectations he scarcely noticed Ellie sliding onto the bar stool next to him. A rush of power flooded through her; for this moment at least she had the upper hand.

She greeted him softly and he glanced at her once, taking in her blond hair, the lime-green bikini under the gauzy white cover-up, the flush in her cheeks. *Attractive, but not my type,* his eyes said.

"I'm waiting for someone."

"Aren't we all?"

The flash of annoyance on his face amused Ellie. The creep actually believed she was flirting with him.

"It's a meeting," he said. "A business meeting. I don't mean to be rude but—"

"Then I'll be sure to tell Quinn you weren't rude."

Her voice stayed light, but Carter flinched as if she had touched him with a burning ember.

"Shit. I'm sorry, you're . . ."

"Not what you were expecting. Are you disappointed?" She purred the question.

"I thought you were going to meet me at the marina."

"Change of plans."

"Look, we can't talk here . . ."

"I have a room."

Ellie slid off her bar stool and knocked back the rest of her virgin rum punch. "Let's go."

She didn't even need to look to be sure he was following her. He was a desperate man and desperate men did what they were told. She held her head high and let her hips sway. Gave him something pretty to look at. She wanted him distracted, off his guard. Rob had been quite clear in his instructions: *You are going to be told to kill someone. You have to do it. Don't recoil in horror, darling, please, I can assure you, your target deserves to die.*

They reached the elevator bank. A door slid open, disgorging a family of four in a flurry of sandals and sand toys and the chemical coconut blast of sunscreen. After they passed, Ellie and Carter entered. She pressed the button for her floor and the door slid closed.

Rob's instructions chorused through her mind. She had memorized them. *You will be given a plan designed to make your target seem like the victim of an accident. But we have a plan of our own.*

The elevator door opened, and Ellie exited. Carter followed her down the hallway as she sauntered to her room. Ellie unlocked the door and gestured him in. She had a bottle of chilled white wine in an ice bucket, uncorked and ready.

In our bathroom, in a prescription bottle labeled Benicar you will find Seconal, Rob had written. *Get your target to ingest it. With alcohol is best; it kicks up the effects and disguises the taste.*

As she closed the door behind her, fear clawed into Ellie's gut. She was going to kill this man. She had to kill this man. How could she? Then she looked at his face and realized he was nervous. Possibly more scared than she was.

Carter spotted the wine bottle. Poured a glass without asking and gulped it down. Refilled his glass.

"Help yourself," Ellie said wryly. She poured herself a glass and pretended to sip it.

"So what happens now? How does Quinn want to handle it?" His voice cracked on Quinn's name. Ellie and Rob weren't the only ones terrified of Quinn. Carter tossed back his second glass of wine.

"He's angry with you, you know." Ellie's tone was soothing, seductive. She settled into the bucket chair, crossing her legs sinuously.

"Shit, I know that! I didn't mean for it to happen, he's got to understand that. I never wanted a kid to die! It was a fucking mistake— the brat just kept fighting me! It wasn't my fault." Carter paced the room, all jittery nervous denial.

A kid had died? And listen to this asshole. Not his fault. "Why don't you tell me what happened."

Carter gave her a sly glance. He seemed to think he had a sympathetic ear. "Look, Pascal and I . . . we were just testing the waters with the kid thing. It was only a sideline. The routes were already all set up to Miami. And the buyers! Coming out of the woodwork! Willing to pay, cash, no questions asked. So we experimented. Proof of concept. Got a few kids sold, made some dough, but once we knew it was a steady business we were for sure going to cut Quinn in. Shit! I shouldn't have said that about Pascal. Quinn doesn't know he was in it too. Can we not mention that? See? I'm not such a bad guy. Don't want to get my compadre into trouble." He looked hopefully at Ellie.

"Very noble."

Carter took her comment at face value. Not the sharpest tool in the shed. She shifted and crossed her legs again, giving him a good look at her naked thighs. He shot her his best version of a winning smile. "The only question now is, how are we gonna fix it?"

She shrugged her shoulders. "I so wish I could help you out. But you know Quinn . . ." She let that dangle in the air between them.

"Mind if I smoke?" he asked nervously. Ellie pointed silently to the discreet "No Smoking" sign. Carter fumbled in his pockets and lit a fat joint anyway. Gulped down wine. Ellie topped off his glass.

Carter sucked on his joint. "The kid was a total accident! Much more in it if they're alive, right?" A giggle spilled from his mouth. "There's no reason we can't go right back to business." He toked hard on the joint, then set it down on the edge of the nightstand. "But I swear, I was going to cut him in. There were only three before this one. I'll make good to Quinn on what we made on those too."

"How much?" Ellie noted dispassionately that the joint was charring the wood.

"What?"

"How much did you make on the other three kids?"

"Fifty K apiece."

"You sold children for fifty thousand dollars?"

"Okay, it was a hundred! So shoot me for trying to bank a little extra cash! A man's got to look out for himself." Carter slugged down more wine. A crafty look came into his eyes. "How 'bout I cut you in for, I don't know, twenty-five K and you tell Quinn it was fifty? Huh? A little side deal, you and me?" He sidled over to her, put an unwelcome hand on her shoulder.

For fuck's sake, he was making killing him too damn desirable. It was practically a public service.

Then his hand went up to his forehead. "Whoa."

"Are you all right?"

"Just need to . . . whoa. Shit." He reeled back on his heels, sat heavily on the bed. "Whoops! You're not . . . I mean . . . it's just that I have to make this right. I'll make it right, I promise . . ."

His eyes fluttered closed, then open. He sagged back onto the coverlet. His arm swung, knocking the wine bottle to the floor. He was staring at her.

The words of Rob's letter reverberated through her mind: *Don't recoil in horror, darling, please, I can assure you, your target deserves to die*. Even more so than she could have imagined. The monster on the bed before her had killed a child, sold others.

She thought about the man she'd married. She remembered a sleepy Sunday morning a few weeks before the wedding. They had woken just before dawn and turned to each other wordlessly. Sleepy limbs and drowsy breath intertwined and then they were fucking, she sat astride him as he gripped her hips and pulled her deeper on him. They'd come together, explosive, and her body had collapsed like unfolding origami on top of his.

They had had their first talk of children that breathless, sexy morning. In the course of the conversation, she realized Rob shared the same tenderly ambivalent dread she held about having kids. Yet she'd had no idea why. Now she realized that while their life experiences were wildly different, the sufferings they had endured had rendered in them many identical wounds and badly healed scars. This, she realized, was why she really loved him. Because she'd found someone who not only shared her pain, but understood it.

Ellie pulled herself back to the present. Carter's eyes had finally closed.

The easiest way for you to kill the target will be a knife to the abdominal aorta.

Ellie retrieved the knife she had secreted in the bottom of her beach bag. Tugged off Carter's clothes. Drew the tip lightly over his stomach, tracing the trajectory she was to follow. A small nick, and he began to bleed. She gagged. Then stumbled away from the bed, sickened and terrified. Stood there panting, her heart pounding in her chest. Then she remembered the innocent children whose lives Carter had destroyed. She thought about Rob, held God-knows-where, relying on her to save his life. She stepped forward, plunged the knife into Carter's stomach. It was surprisingly difficult to penetrate the layers of skin and muscle and fat. She wrenched and heaved, both hands gripping the handle, panting with exertion. Watched the blood as it began to spill. He jerked once or twice and then was still. She spun away, fighting nausea.

She staggered to the balcony doors, stumbling outside to the salt tang and sickly sweet scent of alcohol, sugar, and fruit too long in the sun.

She had done it. She had killed a man. She had done it for the love of another man. And now they were the same, she and Rob. More united than they had been in marriage, they were united in death.

You will be told to dispose of the body so there is no trace of it. Instead leave the body in a place you know it will be found. What I will ask you to do next will seem grisly, but believe me, darling, it is necessary.

Down on the beach, hard-muscled young men tossed a football in the surf. They shouted and laughed and grunted, their sounds wafting up to the room.

The room where Ellie had just crossed a line she could never uncross.

Now

Magic hour. Ellie peeks out the doorway of the storeroom. The sky is painted with deep pinks, dense purples, a coppery umber. Dark clouds cluster and scud along the horizon, a fiery heat at their center.

Ellie is trembling. She wants to get going. She never wants to see St. Lucia again. She glances over at Rob. He is joking with P.J., old buddies. How can he be so relaxed? The events of the last few days overwhelm her. The man she killed, the woman who died protecting her, that little boy, Thomas, fate unknown. She fights against self-loathing. She thinks of Quinn, left injured and bleeding and bound to a chair in that creepy house. Then she remembers. In her haste to escape, she left her beach tote behind. The remains of her cash. Her I.D. The screwdriver. Her shiny new wedding band twisted into a corner.

"Soon?" she demands impatiently, dropping down onto an overturned wooden crate, her hands rubbing her thighs. "Are we going soon?"

"Matt should be back any minute," P.J. reassures. "It's almost dark. We'll go then."

Ellie presses her fingers over her eyes. She can't sit still any longer. Abruptly she rises from her seat.

"Where are you going?" There's an edge in Rob's voice she pretends not to hear.

"Water." Ellie slips through the kitchen and into the service area of the restaurant. "That's okay, right?" She doesn't wait for a reply.

Ellie slides onto a rickety stool in front of the curved bar. The restaurant is casual. Cheerfully mismatched chairs and paint-splashed wooden tables. The work of local photographers on the wall: richly colored landscapes and two black-and-whites of a solemn, graceful young girl with cornrows. It's before the dinner hour; only a few sunburned early-bird diners tuck happily into barbecue.

The bartender, British and red-faced, is deep in conversation with three adorable Dutch backpackers, telling tales with great gravity. The girls are rapt, hanging on his every lie.

". . . built by an American businessman as a vacation home," the Brit tells them. "But while he was coming down to oversee the construction, he took up with a local girl. He became obsessed with her."

The bartender whispers the next bit. "She was a voodoo priestess, she was. That's how she snared him. But when her spells ran dry and the man returned to his wife, Marianne killed them both and then herself. And now *this*." He shakes his head.

Ellie didn't think anything could surprise her anymore. But this story—so different from the one Crazy B had told her, in which Marianne had been an innocent victim. It hits her hard: Truth is elusive when viewed through the prism of multiple perspectives.

"What can I get you?" the bartender asks, sliding a cardboard coaster in front of her.

"Are you talking about Maison Marianne?"

"Bad for the whole island, that," he answers. "But no point in denying it. It'll be in the papers tomorrow."

"What are you talking about?" The question catches in Ellie's throat. She knows what he's going to say.

"Police found another dead bloke up there this afternoon," he confides. "American, I hear. Murdered. Stabbed in the gut."

"Stabbed?"

He nods and slides a frosty bottle of local beer toward her. "On the house. Strange times."

Strange indeed. The charming restaurant tilts on its axis. White noise explodes in Ellie's head. Dead. Quinn couldn't be dead. He was alive when they left him. Stabbed. How?

Rob. He was the last one to leave Maison Marianne. He killed Quinn. He killed Quinn before they left.

But why?

Did he think killing Quinn was the only way to free them from someone so powerful and depraved? The logic of this resounds with her. But that she understands Rob's point of view terrifies her. She is not a killer.

But wait. She is.

She glances toward the open door of the restaurant, at the dusk-tinged streets beyond. She could walk right out. But go where? Do what? Ellie's very last dreams of a life with Rob spill away with swift, sad finality, sand through an hourglass. The truth slams her. She doesn't know her husband. Not at all. She never did. And she can't trust him. She feels stripped bare. Scraped hollow.

The floodgates of doubt open. Isn't it just weirdly convenient, this P.J. guy happening to be in St. Lucia? Why exactly is Walsh risking his own neck for them, anyway? Has Rob really told her everything? Suspicions scream through her brain, cacophonous, jumbled, ugly.

She feels the grip of the bartender's hand on her arm.

"You all right there? You looked like you might slide right off."
He gives her a toothy grin.

"I'm fine, thank you." Ellie plants her feet firmly on the floor. She
needs to sift to the truth. Needs her inchoate suspicions either proven
or denied.

But now she knows one thing for certain in a world where nothing is certain: She needs to disappear. When and how will depend on
what she learns.

Then

Her hand gripped the knife tightly. His powerful hand closed over hers. Together they plunged the blade deep through white icing and lavender fondant flowers. The photographer snapped a photo. Ellie looked up at the flash. Saw her mother just behind the photographer; she was crying, dabbing at her eyes with a lace handkerchief. Ellie and Rob sliced a piece of cake. Fed bites to each other. They had agreed in advance to handle this tradition with decorum, no messy smashing of cake into faces. Ritual dispensed with, caterers swept in to cut the cake and serve it to the guests.

Ellie felt an unexpected, piercing sadness. Their wonderful wedding was almost over. All those months of planning and excitement, details and decisions, and soon it would all be in the past. A memory that would shift to solidify around the pictures taken, as the "real" of it drifted into the ether. She reminded herself to remember every little facet she could of this, the most important day of her life.

She found her mother and put an arm around Michelle's shoulder. Michelle blew her nose and smiled through her tears. Swayed on
her high heels. It was then that Ellie realized her mother was drunk.

"It was a lovely wedding," Michelle slurred.

"It's not over yet," Ellie replied. "We have the band until two."

"I know. I just—I just can't help but think about Mary Ann
today."

"She's here somewhere, Mom."

"She shouldn't have died." Michelle wept openly. "It should be
her wedding. She always was my favorite daughter."

The remark was offhand, as if it was something Michelle was
used to saying, something Ellie should be used to hearing. Ellie
gasped, a harsh intake of painful breath. She reeled away from her
mother. She felt dizzy.

Air. *Yes,* she thought, *I need air. And a moment with Rob. My
husband. My love. Where is he?*

Now

P.J. leads them through the bustling harbor. Quickly, but not so fast as to draw attention. Fishermen pull in their final catches, day boat rentals return to dock, snack shops and snorkel shacks fold for the night just as the bars and restaurants come to life. Along with the scent of rum, snatches of conversation drift in the humid air. Chatter about flights off the island—vacationers trying urgently to change their plans, book hotels in Aruba or Barbados. Journalists debating the latest details, spinning foolish headlines: *The St. Lucia Sadist; Holiday in Hell*.

Darkness closes like a fist as fear-laced talk buzzes the dock. There is a madman on the loose on this island. The police are out in full force. It will take years for tourism to recover; how will St. Lucia survive?

Slipping past two fishermen sharing a smoke, a hushed, frightful fragment balances in the air: ". . . another dead guy. Stabbed, just like up at the hotel. And his lip hacked off."

Rob's head jerks back. His foot stops mid-stride. But he recovers smartly. He glances at Ellie. Her face has gone pale. She heard it too.

P.J. and Matt have stopped a few yards down, by a battered fishing boat, *Devocean,* painted on the side in a faded, flowery script. Matt hands a barrel-chested stranger a wad of cash. The stranger tucks the money into the pocket of his shorts. Gives Matt a half salute and murmurs, "Later, Pascal," as he is swallowed up by the night.

Matt boards. P.J. follows. Rob reaches a hand to Ellie. She hesitates.

"Ellie, we've got to go." Rob seizes her hand, crushes it in his, surprised at how cold her skin feels in the moist tropical heat. She follows him aboard the boat with jerky steps and eyes that avoid his.

The motor rumbles to life. P.J. guides the vessel away from the harbor and out to sea. Dense gray and black clouds coat the night sky. The ocean is roiling, slate gray, unforgiving. Matt and P.J. stay above deck. Rob leads Ellie to the cramped cabin below.

The cabin stinks of fish guts and diesel fuel. Bleach and tar. A top note of salt spray, a low note of decay. Rob feels queasy.

"Why did you slice off his lip?"

Rob startles at her vehemence. "Ellie, no . . . I didn't."

"Why did you kill Quinn?"

"I didn't."

"I saw you! Just now on the dock! Your reaction! Quinn's *dead*. I bet you thought we'd be long gone before they found him, right? That you'd never have to tell me?"

"Ellie, I swear I didn't kill him."

"So who was it, then? P.J.? Or your friend Matt? Don't you think it's convenient? That your old friend P.J. just happens to live in St. Lucia? That Matt found him so easily?"

"Why are you saying these things?" Rob's throat tightens. His tone turns acid. "I'd call it lucky, given that we're heading out to sea on the boat he found for us." Why is she questioning everything? Why won't she just let things *go*?

"Yeah, and how did he find it? He *knew* the man we got the boat from. How?"

"What you heard was just street gossip. We don't even know if Quinn is really dead. And now you accuse Matt? After he put himself in danger by coming down here to help us?"

"Is there no end to the lies you are going to tell me?" she demands brazenly.

"I swear to you I didn't kill Quinn. None of us did. You have to trust me!"

"Is that what I have to do? Trust *you*?" A hollow laugh escapes Ellie. Her face reddens with anger. "Someone sliced Quinn's lip off. So who was it, Rob? That was *your* message, yours and Matt's!"

"Stop it! I won't listen to this! Just drop it! Let it go!"

Desolate uncertainty shrieks in Rob's head. But he is sure of one thing. He had believed Ellie was the light. His way out. His salvation. Now he knows there is no escape. He is shackled to violence and murder for the rest of his days. Heat radiates throughout his body. His hands tighten into fists. The aggression rising within him is terrifyingly familiar. "Where did you go every Tuesday?"

"What?" Ellie is startled.

"Did you think I didn't notice? I followed you. Who's in that hospice, Ellie? What else are *you* hiding from *me*?"

His seeking eyes find a fish-gutting knife lying atop a dirty rag. He reaches for the blade.

Ellie shrinks back and away from him. The terror in her eyes thrills him in his darkest center.

Then

Ellie felt simultaneously solemn and giddy as Rob lifted her veil. Her mother beamed a smile from the first row. Her father stood next to Rob. How kind Dad was, standing in for Rob's cousin. Ellie's eyes darted around the ballroom.

Marcy Clark, clad in black, sat with other friends from work. Ellie was glad Marcy had found it in her heart to come. Marcy had taken Ethan's death rock hard, disconsolate. She saw Ellie looking at her and gave the first genuine smile Ellie had seen since Ethan's murder. Then a thumbs-up. The bride turned her attention back to her groom. God, how she loved him.

"Do you, Ellie, take Rob to be your lawfully wedded husband?"

Ellie's heart swelled. This was the moment she had been waiting for. "I do."

"You may kiss the bride."

Their eyes met and then their lips. For a moment there was no one else in the ballroom. It was only the two of them.

The bride and groom turned to face their laughing, clapping guests. There were a couple of good-natured hoots. They had done it. They were married.

Now

Ellie ascends from belowdeck, panting and flushed. The last ruddy trace of sunset flirts with the horizon. On the receding shoreline, dark waves lick wet sand. Looming cliffs explode with vines heavy with flowers, their rich colors muted, their sinewy shapes mysterious. They're within a mile of the shore, but she feels unmoored in time and space.

Before them, open ocean. Above, a navy carpet of coruscating stars scudded with thick, angry clouds. The wind whips as the first plump, warm raindrops fall. P.J. pilots the boat in a steady course.

Matt offers her a bottle of water from a cooler by his feet. "Have you been running?" he asks with a flicker of a smile.

Ellie accepts the bottle and chugs down the cold liquid. Wipes her mouth, leaving a red smear on her jawbone.

"Not running." Her voice is flat. "I've just killed Rob."

She shrugs. "I didn't have a choice. He came at me. He didn't like what I had worked out. P.J., you're Pascal, aren't you? Isn't that what the man on the dock called you? You're Carter Williamson's partner."

Matt stares at her with hungry, feral interest.

"And you," Ellie persists. "What's your real story, Matthew Walsh, good friend, good Samaritan?"

She gazes up at him from under her lashes. "Did you kill Quinn?" she croons. "Simple revenge for what he did to you? Or something more complicated?"

"You are really quite something, aren't you?" Matt's face heats with desire. He's close enough to kiss her. "I see why Rob fell for you." He traces a finger through the blood on her cheek. She doesn't flinch. Her gaze locks on him. She's not the same woman she was an hour ago.

"The question is, what to do with you now?" Matt drawls as he strokes her lips with his blood-tipped finger.

Eyes glittering with admiring curiosity, Ellie trails a languid hand across his chest. "Tell me everything. Tell me about Quinn."

"Quinn was my protégé, just as Rob was his. I trained Quinn. Ran him. Loved him, really. Until he betrayed me and tried to take over. So you do see why I had to kill him."

"And P.J.?"

"In my employ since the good old days." Matt smiles at her with no warmth. "It has always been me. Always. And that will continue. Pascal and I will be entirely new people by the time we leave Caracas."

Matt's hands tangle in Ellie's hair. "But you will join your poor dead husband at the bottom of the sea before we ever get there."

Matt's fingers stroke her neck. His hands encircle her throat.

"JUMP!" she hears and whirls toward the sound.

Rob has crested the stairs from belowdeck. The fish knife gleams in his hand. "Ellie, dammit, *jump*!"

She tears away from Matt's grasp. She hesitates. Then, without warning, she turns and topples into the inky depths of the ocean. Has she fallen? Or did she leap?

The water closes over her. Her head clouds with viscous underwater silence. She thrusts her head up, gasping, just when her lungs will burst. Sound floods in; she feels rather than sees Rob and Matt locked and grappling. Feels rather than sees as they tumble overboard and disappear beneath the waves.

As Ellie fights the pull of the tide, struggling to stay above water, her last moments with Rob belowdeck replay in her head.

"You are my first best memory. Even if you believe nothing else about me, believe that."

Next

Lucien doesn't much like to dwell on what happened next.

He had always prided himself on being a good man, an honest cop. But what now became necessary called those qualities into question.

Matt Walsh's corpse washed up along the black volcanic sands of Anse Chastanet beach, discovered by a honeymooning couple taking a sunset horseback ride. Walsh's cause of death was determined to be drowning, although the body was torn and battered. From the coral reefs, or something else? The coroner couldn't say for sure.

Then an exhausted and desperate Ellie and Rob showed up at Lucien's home one morning at dawn. Lucien ushered them away from the house where his pregnant wife and child still slept, but agreed to listen. Ellie's persistent inquiries about Thomas's safety, and her relief upon hearing he was back in his mother's arms, rang true. As for the rest of Rob and Ellie's story, including a wild tale of their escape from certain death at the hands of Matt Walsh; their lonely, frantic swims to shore; finding each other at a prearranged spot in Soufrière and hiding in plain sight until Ellie convinced Rob they should appeal to Lucien—well, Lucien didn't know what to believe. Or what he wanted to believe.

Because then there were the statements and explanations, the half-truths and outright inventions devised to get Rob Beauman and Eleanor Larrabee off the island, all of which still sit with Lucien uncomfortably.

People had died. Murders remained unsolved on his island. Three little boys are still missing.

But she saved his nephew's life. And for that, didn't he owe them?

Nearly twelve thousand miles away from St. Lucia, the sun has a different glint, the breeze a different sort of lilt. The sand is white and soft as powder, the sea an emerald prism. Bali. The island of enchanted honeymoon dreams.

A woman sits on the beach with her toes burrowed deep into the sand; her fingers rake through repetitively, absently. She stares at the shining waves as if they will bring her an answer.

Stains below her blue eyes hint at her exhaustion. Her bright golden roots transition into a glossy brown. She lifts her gaze from the water to watch a striped parasail hovering distantly against the brilliant blue sky. The beach is otherwise empty, but even if it were filled with picnicking families and entwined lovers, there is something about this woman. She seems spectacularly, singularly *alone*.

In the distance, a man trudges through the sand. Sun glints off his mirrored shades. He strides directly to the woman and touches her shoulder. She flinches.

The man snatches his hand away. He sinks down next to her, folding his legs underneath him. They don't speak. The stillness of the beach is broken only by the occasional call of a bird, the rhythm of the waves.

The woman's eyes flick toward the man. Her fingers rake the sand again. There is so much to be said, so many secrets to divulge, so many apologies to be tendered. The gulf between them is as wide as the ocean itself.

Only the most fragile tendrils of trust and love connect them. Will that be enough? We don't know.

Nor do they.

"Well," she finally murmurs. "Our first fight."

"Look at it this way: It'll be hard to top."

"I really thought you were going to kill me back on the boat."

"Myself or Matt," Rob says, shaking his head. "But never you, my love."

He reaches for her hand, stilling her digging fingers. His larger hand encircles hers; he feels her quickening pulse flutter on the soft underside of her wrist.

So our story has come full circle, from one tropical paradise to another. The sun shines, flowers bloom, waves lap dreamily against the shore.

Two ravaged people will do their best to heal.

But make no mistake; this is not the end. More will be revealed. It always is.

Acknowledgments

It is my pleasure to thank my parents, Edward and Jean Sadowsky, who have given me unconditional support even during the wildest turns and twists of my unconventional career. Also thanks to my wonderful and inspiring children, Raphaela and Xander Kleiman (you are and will always be my best creations), and to my stepchildren, Arielle and Daniel Hakman, as well as my bonus daughter, Analia Rey, and my boyfriend-in-law, Darius Margalith. All of you enrich my life. And provide material. I also thank my brothers, Jonathan and Richard Sadowsky; my sisters-in-law, Laura Steinberg and Mary Clancy; and their respective children, Ivan, Julia, Eric, and Katherine, simply for being.

I am deeply appreciative of the feedback from my early readers: Sean Smith, Janet Cooke, Michelle Raimo Kouyate, Carolyn Manetti, Robin Sax, Laina Cohn, Alexandra Seros, and Hannah Phenicie. All of you gave me excellent feedback and affirming love. I also thank my excellent agents, Joel Gotler and Emma Sweeney, and my attorney, Marcy Morris, all of whom rock. I must acknowledge William Meredith (1919–2007), my creative writing professor at Connecticut College, a man who was influential in shaping my confidence as a writer. And thanks to Suzanne Sadowsky, Heather Richardson, Deb Aquila, Betsy Stahl, Brenda Goodman, Shandiz Zandi, Kathy Boluch, Linda Bower, Debbie Huffman, Lisa Kislak, Matthew Mizel, Lenore Kletter, Debbie Liebling, Sukee Chew, Thom Bishops, Judy Bloom, Jeff Stanzler, Mike Ott, Kingsley Smith, Eva Vives, Peter Sollett, Yanni Kyriazis, Robin Swicord, Wendy Leitman, and Ruth Vitale for being my friends and cheering squad.

My respect and affection for my extraordinary editor, Kate Miciak, is unparalleled. Her input has made me a better writer in every way.

I am also grateful to the whole Ballantine team, particularly Libby McGuire, Kim Hovey, Denise Cronin and her entire crew, Dana Blanchette, Loren Noveck, Julia Maguire, and Caroline Teagle (for the beautiful and evocative cover design).

Special thanks must go to my husband, Gary Hakman, with whom I am exploring the pleasures and perils of intimacy (but who also tells me that after reading the novel he sleeps with one eye open).

ABOUT THE AUTHOR

Nina Sadowsky has written numerous original screenplays and adaptations for such companies as The Walt Disney Company, Working Title Films, and Lifetime Television. She was president of Meg Ryan's Prufrock Pictures for more than five years. She was the executive producer of the hit film *The Wedding Planner* and has produced and developed numerous other films. Sadowsky is currently an adjunct professor at USC's School of Cinematic Arts, teaching both writing and producing. This is her first novel.

ninarsadowsky.com
@sadowsky_nina

ABOUT THE TYPE

This book was set in Sabon, a typeface designed by the well-known German typographer Jan Tschichold (1902–74). Sabon's design is based upon the original letter forms of sixteenth-century French type designer Claude Garamond and was created specifically to be used for three sources: foundry type for hand composition, Linotype, and Monotype. Tschichold named his typeface for the famous Frankfurt typefounder Jacques Sabon (c. 1520–80).